THE
Painter

THE
Painter

DEIRDRE QUIERY

Urbane
PUBLICATIONS

urbanepublications.com

First published in Great Britain in 2019 by Urbane Publications Ltd
Unit E3 The Premier Centre Abbey Park Romsey SO51 9DG
Copyright © Deirdre Quiery, 2019

A CIP catalogue record for this book is available from the British Library.

ISBN 978-1-912666-35-5
MOBI 978-1-912666-36-2

Design and Typeset by Julie Martin
Cover by The Invisible Man

Printed and bound by 4edge UK

Urbane
PUBLICATIONS

urbanepublications.com

For Martin, my husband – a marvel of a man who makes me laugh in the crises of life.

PROLOGUE

"The Painter Augustin Silvero born in Palma, Mallorca on 1st January 1967, was named by his mother, Monica, after Saint Augustine of Hippo. The Painter's Confessions, like those of Saint Augustine, tell of a descent into Hell to allow Transformation to be possible. His journal, simply titled 'The Painter' explores this descent and his transformation.

It is a journal which moves between tenses, flows from past to future, leaving the reader on a moving raft in the river of life which has no ending even when reaching the sea. This flow of life, punctuated by moments of stillness is what we know as the genius of the art of Augustin, 'The Painter'."

(Art Critic, Collector and Philosopher – Miguel del Salmorejo – Palma de Mallorca – 2018)

"Late have I loved you, O Beauty ever ancient, ever new, late have I loved you! You were within me, but I was outside, and it was there that I searched for you. In my unloveliness, I plunged into the lovely things which you created. You were with me, but I was not with you. Created things kept me from you; yet if they had not been in you, they would not have been at all. You called, you shouted, and you broke through my deafness. You flashed, you shone, and you dispelled my blindness. You breathed your fragrance on me; I drew in breath and

now I pant for you. I have tasted you, now I hunger and thirst for more. You touched me, and I burned for your peace."

(From The Confessions of Augustine of Hippo 354 – 430)

Wednesday 4th October 2017

The rain falls gently on the ground – a kiss pressing itself into the earth. Ishmael stares at me from the fountain. Did I really kill him? His eyes filled with horror from the last breath that he took. I want to close his eyelids, but I can't bring my hands to touch him again. Did I hold him under the water of the fountain, or had he slipped beneath my fingers? I don't remember.

It is strange that you can love someone in such a way that it turns to hate. I suppose that means that it is never love. Hate is something passionate and consuming. Why is it that we also say that about love?

Why did I have to kill Ishmael to know what love is? There's the paradox if only I could understand it. I don't think I loved anyone before meeting him and yet in the act of murder I knew that I loved Ishmael.

Why am I writing a journal? Why do I not instead paint viscerally as Picasso did in his response to the bombing of Guernica? It would be possible for me to paint my anguish, despair and disgust at myself.

I have a reason for writing this journal. I want every line to be carefully explained, every splash of colour to be placed within the correct context. I desire for you to know each person as they were interpreted by me. I write the journal in a sequence of steps leading somewhere – like every true journey does – one step after another as I remembered them. I will go back in my mind and attempt to recover every moment which for me was a part of the jigsaw journey of my life with Ishmael.

I have never tried so hard with my paintings to be so honest, so true. I ask nothing from you, other than when you have finished reading it – the journal – then you must burn my paintings. Burn anything that I have worked on including my words in this journal – erase them.

They are worth nothing. What I would paint today, if I chose to do so, would be filled with freedom coming with a priceless tag. This journal is a journey into the freedom of my soul.

1

PABLO PICASSO

"Every child is an artist. The problem is how to remain an artist once he grows up."

Tuesday 6th October 2015

I remember Ishmael walking up the driveway to my house. It was before the rain. There was a crunching of his shoes against the gravel. He didn't wear sandals but polished shoes that shone, reflecting the mountains around. His trousers were smooth. That's what I remember. Smooth – glistening, perfectly ironed. He wore a blue, flowery open-necked shirt and a rucksack on his back which didn't match his clothes but then nothing matched with Ishmael. He was one of those folks who made you think that by his very being, he was not joined up. There was something missing in the glue that held him together. There was a mystery about him waiting to be known or put together.

He sweated as he strode up the driveway. His cheeks slightly flushed; sweat dropping onto his shirt and under his armpits, pools of moistness spreading down to his waist. He smiled at me as he combed hair away from his face with his fingers. I shook his hand. It was clammy but not unpleasant. I squeezed it and imagined drops of sweat falling and watering the dry earth. He leaned forward, kissed me on the cheek and slapped me on the back like an old friend.

He had been recommended to me as a gardener by a friend; José del Pardo in La Coruña who exhibited my art in his gallery. He claimed that in one year, Ishmael had transformed his garden, creating an orchard with orange and lemon trees, planting pomegranates and kiwis. Galicia with La Coruña as its capital is called 'The Ireland of Spain'. Orange and lemon trees were not common. Ishmael could make anything grow, anywhere.

For José del Pardo, he created a labyrinth tiled with blue and white mosaics and opened up a view to the sea where he placed oak benches so visitors could watch the sun set over the Atlantic. José only had praise for Ishmael's work. What puzzled him was Ishmael's background. Where did he come from? Why had he come to Spain? He certainly looked Spanish with curly black hair falling onto the collar of his shirt, dark brown eyes and a swarthy, lined skin which conveyed a maturity beyond his thirty years of age. José mentioned that Ishmael had lived previously in Malmo, Sweden but when I checked, there were no references for his work there and internet searches revealed nothing of his past or present.

I don't know why I looked at Ishmael's shoes first and then his trousers and rucksack. I did eventually get to his face. He looked at me as if he knew me – as if he was coming home. He had a handsome rugged look. A straight nose, piercing blue eyes, lips curved into a smile, hair parted on the left and curling with snake-like twists. He drew me in. I knew that he was special. I never thought for a minute with the scent of jasmine hanging in the air, that I would be the one to kill him. I did kill him. I know before that I said that I wasn't sure, but I know I did it.

I'm also sure that he had tried to escape that fate from others. He had a look of someone who knew that he would be hunted to death. Why did he walk up my driveway and ask to be the gardener? It was a lie from the start. He had other plans in visiting me. He should never have told that lie. He should have told me who sent him and why he was there. That lie about wanting to be my gardener created the end for him. It wasn't me. He did it to himself. We all have to take the consequences of our actions.

Within an hour of arriving, I felt obliged to give him a cup of tea. Gabriela my housekeeper had gone to Palma to buy food for Ishmael's arrival. She had already made his bed up with fresh linen and lit a log fire in the inglenook fireplace in the sitting room. Although the autumn sun still burnt the body, inside the house it was cold.

I had never made a cup of tea for anyone in my life. I liked the innocence of this new tea ritual with him and the sound of a kettle boiling for the next cup. As he sipped at the Rooibos tea, I felt embarrassed that I had no biscuits to offer him and no cake. I apologised, explaining that the pantry would be full of delicious Mallorcan treats when Gabriela returned. He shook his head quickly from side to side. "Don't be silly. This is perfect. I am more interested in the fact that your house is called Can Animes – which I know to mean a house of courage, soul or spirit. There's nothing that's a coincidence in life. This house is made for you. You will learn how to become a courageous spirit here. You need go no further. This world is here for you in this house."

That was the first time that I felt annoyed by him. I responded gruffly. "You do not know me. How do you know that I am not courageous? I may be more courageous than you."

He sat the teacup gently on the table beside the inglenook fireplace. He looked at me, his eyes smoulder-ing brown like the logs on the fire. "We do not know one another. I am sure that will change over our time together. If you are a courageous man – you will be only the second courageous person I have met in my life. I apologise. I should have said that I am hoping to gain greater courage from my stay here. I am sure you have to make your own learning journey."

That last comment irritated me. I found it downright passive-aggressive. There was an implication – little hidden – that I needed to change. I managed to maintain silence as I poured another cup of tea for us both.

He looked around the sitting room. "I like the fact that you have not put in central heating or air conditioning."

I replied with what I heard as a hint of arrogance in my voice: "I refuse to put air conditioning into the house. I want to experience what life really is instead of pressing buttons and controlling life with a perfect temperature around me."

"Why do you want a perfect garden? Why not leave the plant life wild, feverishly unfolding its beauty aligned with Nature rather than controlled by man?"

I didn't want to answer that question because I suspected that he knew the answer. It was a valid question for a gardener to pursue but one that Pep would not have asked me. Pep knew his place.

Before Ishmael arrived, I had a gardener called Pep Conejo. Conejo means rabbit and he was affectionately called Conejo because the local people from Soller joked that he came from a family who bred like Conejos. He had seventeen brothers and sisters. Pep's character was strong but his body fragile. In spite of all the physical effort he put into pruning the orange and lemon trees, growing tomatoes and taking care of the fig trees, which I would have thought would have built muscles on his chest and arms – it didn't. With his shirt open to the waist, it revealed a scraggly body with a long scar in the centre of his chest from an earlier heart operation.

One day when I was away at an art exhibition, he climbed an olive tree to trim the branches. He fell from the tree on top of his own knife and managed to accidently chop off four of the fingers from his right hand. I knew nothing about it until I returned from Madrid. By then he had collected his four fingers, placed them into a plastic bag and with the bag inside his trouser pocket, he drove to the Health Centre in Soller.

Doctor Carlos was shocked that Pep waited in a queue to be seen with a bloody bandaged hand. He placed Pep's fingers with tweezers into an iced bag, telling him to go urgently to the hospital of Son Espaces in Palma. An ambulance had been called but Pep insisted on driving himself to Palma with his bandaged hand on the steering wheel and the bag of fingers in his trouser pocket. Once there, the doctors stitched the fingers back on, shaking their heads and sighing without hope that the fingers would heal. They did. He was asked in Son Espaces to return for work to be carried out to rehabilitate his hand – to force those turkey claw-like shaped fingers straight. He refused. Instead, each day, he placed a towel on an outside table, covered his hand on top with a second towel, and hammered his fingers. When he visited the hospital for a check-up a few months later the doctors were amazed that his hand was straight and the fingers working perfectly.

That was Pep Conejo whom I admired in a certain way as he was so different from the world within which I circulated. I liked to share brunch with him and listen to his stories. Normally they were about a new dispute with his brother, or the fact that his son and daughter-in-law didn't care about him and were waiting for Pep and his wife to die to inherit the parents' property. I listened carefully over bread with olive oil and cheese and a bottle of red wine. It was easy to get distracted and instead of listening I found myself watching the spaces in his gums where numerous teeth had fallen out. In the last year, he only had two teeth in the middle of his upper gum. I thought that God had a sense of humour transforming him rapidly with each passing year to resemble a Conejo. I watched the way he ran across the olive grove with his long thin legs and a bob in his step as he jumped over rocks embedded as sculptures in the grass.

When Ishmael arrived, I felt that I no longer needed Pep Conejo as a gardener. That might have been a mistake as it would have been amusing to observe how they interacted with one another. From the first day of Ishmael's arrival, I was infatuated by him and didn't want Pep Conejo smiling at me or getting in the way of me making an impression on Ishmael – or even worse watching him laugh with Ishmael. God forbid that Ishmael would enjoy Pep's company. I wanted to keep as much of Ishmael for myself as I could. I didn't know that at the time. It was only on reflection that the hidden meaning of my relationship with Ishmael became clear.

The way I treated Pep Conejo shows you how callous I am capable of being with someone who worked so hard for me and whom I rewarded poorly. Whereas with Ishmael, I showered him with money and presents, including a dark blue Boggi suit with a waistcoat which looked stunning on him.

I let Pep Conejo collect oranges that fell from the orange trees as they sat gathering heavy dew in the December early mornings. I offered him hard kiwis which hadn't ripened, and which frankly would take months to do so – if indeed they ever did. I acted on the tip I was given about pricking the top of the kiwis with a needle which aimed to hasten the ripening process, but it never worked for me or for Pep Conejo. I handed my kiwis over to him as if in an act of generosity. They sat in a plastic bag in his sitting room until even he gave up on them ever ripening and threw them on a compost heap of leaves. I gave him permission to collect lemons rotting on the ground – with a white mould that looked as if they had been frozen for a dessert – as a payment to him rather than provide him a salary whilst I on occasion sat alone drinking champagne and ate strawberries for breakfast.

In summer he shared with his friends his gathered over ripe tomatoes. Oranges, kiwis, lemons and tomatoes became a friendship currency in Soller. I didn't care that everyone talked about my meanness. As the Painter, I knew that I was better than all of them – even if they didn't know it. I then believed that I had to place boundaries around people. I suppose it was a little bit like an Indian caste system. I was on the path to discover Atman – my true self – a transcendent Braham and to do this, it was necessary to circulate with care the 'Untouchables'.

How ironic that it was I who became an 'Untouchable', or at least deserved to be called one. I became an expert at hiding my dark side when I needed to. There was never a greater need than to hide what I did to Ishmael. After murdering Ishmael my life was never the same. I crossed a threshold in the same way you do when you leave the safety of your mother's womb and face the world. I did my best to keep my secret from the world until now. I did not want to see my face on national television, photos of me and my art in the press and to see my reputation as the Painter destroyed forever.

From that first cup of tea together, Ishmael was someone I wanted to touch. I was drawn to his body like a magnet. When the sun set early that evening, it plunged not behind the mountains but into his oiled hair. I wanted to hold his hair; to hold the sun shining within its darkness and allow it to burn my hands.

I heard the sound of my BMW in the driveway. I had lent it to Gabriela as she had quite a lot of food to buy for Ishmael's arrival. Once a month, I allowed her to drive to Palma in my BMW rather than be forced to shop in Soller on her motorbike.

Ishmael jumped to his feet. "Is that her?"

I nodded. "There's no need to get excited. She's only brought the shopping."

He sounded pleased to see her – as if he knew her. He ran to the front door, reaching out a hand either to shake her hand or to help her carry the shopping indoors. She handed him two shopping bags and then two more. She looked at him the way you might inspect an alien life form – letting her eyes roll over his body from his head to his shoes and then scanning across his shoulders and down his arms. She talked to him in an unusually meek soft-spoken apologetic voice. "We were expecting you. Sorry I'm a little late there was an accident outside Palma."

He placed all four shopping bags on the ground and opened his arms wide to embrace and kiss her. "I am Ishmael Domini, pleased to meet you."

He carried two plastic bags in either hand, walking indoors. I felt obliged to copy his act of friendship and held my hands out for more bags from Gabriela. She handed me six bags.

Ishmael smiled at her. "Let me to take another couple of bags. They are heavy."

She shook her head at him. I looked at her before walking to the front door. She didn't look as if she had washed her hair. It was greasy and dull. She wore a pair of heavy black jeans and a lumberjack red and white checked shirt which made her look manly. Her feet looked weighed down with black leather Dr Marten's, thickly laced up; although the lace of the right boot had become loose and trailed along the ground. I thought that she could trip on it but if she couldn't work that out for herself, why should I tell her? She was an adult. I followed Ishmael into the house.

He asked: "Where do you like to store your food?"

I explained. He turned around, looked past me and warned Gabriela: "Be careful. Your lace is undone. It's so easy to have a nasty fall. Do you know I had an aunt who tripped in the kitchen while making a cup of tea, hit her head against the tiled floor and died?" He gave a chuckle after he said that which I thought inappropriate. He explained: "Life is so uncertain. We might as well enjoy it and not take what it throws at us too seriously."

With food safely stored and the Serrano ham hanging from a hook in the cooler part of the kitchen far from the wood burning stove, Gabriela served us in the sitting room – a glass of chilled champagne, almonds, black olives and sobrasada with unsalted bread – before returning to the kitchen to cook lunch.

I took my opportunity. "Well Ishmael – tell me a little about yourself. I have received excellent references for your work and attitude from José del Pardo. Congratulations. Where else have you worked? Where are you from originally? Talk to me."

Ishmael pressed a teaspoonful of soft bloody sobrasada – a Mallorcan minced pork with paprika delicacy – onto a small piece of unsalted bread and, before putting it into his mouth, said: "You have the references from José. I have been a bit of gypsy in my life. I am afraid I cannot put you in touch with anyone else with whom I have worked for a considerable amount of time and completed a significant project which would warrant a reference. Is that a problem for you?"

I stuttered as I lifted an olive from the dish: "Of course it is not a problem."

There was a silence between us. Ishmael got up to place a log on the fire. Then he walked to a bookcase and began to flick through local walking books. "Which of these walks would you recommend?"

I eagerly began to talk about my love for climbing the Barranc if it was not too hot, too cold or too windy. I told him of the marvellous views from the top of L'Ofre mountain. On a good day, you could see the entire island. As I extolled the beauty of the Barranc and L'Ofre, Gabriela called us for lunch. As I pulled a chair up to the oak table, resting a cotton napkin on my lap, I realised that Ishmael had not revealed where he was born, nor had he mentioned anything about his life in Malmo.

As we sat at the kitchen table, I explained: "I have a dining room, but I prefer to eat here in the informality of the kitchen. Is that alright for you?"

Ishmael clinked his glass against mine. "It is perfect."

He looked at Gabriela who was pulling on her coat after opening a bottle of wine for us and placing it beside me to serve. Ishmael pushed his chair back. It screeched across the tiles as he rose to his feet. "Surely you will have something to eat with us?"

She laughed. "You are very kind. No thank you. I will be going home now – as always."

She glanced at me in a way that made me think that she felt that I was ungrateful for her efforts and for the way that I treated her as a maid rather than a friend. But she was my housekeeper. In 2015 we didn't talk about maids, but she was one. I know that for sure because my mother Monica had been a maid to Doctor Alfonso in the 1960s right through to the 1990s. It dawned on me that Ishmael was merely a gardener. He replaced Pep Conejo. I never had dinner with Pep Conejo – only that mid-morning brunch I mentioned before which I doubted I would repeat after the arrival of Ishmael. Gabriela needed to understand that Ishmael was different. He was a guest in my home. Pep Conejo had his own home and family. He didn't need to eat with me. His wife and rather unpleasant son and daughter-in-law awaited him at the end of a day's work. It was not my fault that he ended up in a house of loveless people.

I soon noticed a difference in Gabriela. Before Ishmael arrived, I enjoyed Gabriela's anonymity. She faded into the white walls. There was a spaciousness around her that allowed me to breathe. I think it was the absence of make-up and hair falling onto her shoulders like waves embracing the rocks in the Port of Soller, that gave her a natural existence which I didn't have to pay too much attention to. Within a week of Ishmael's arrival, she was like an exotic flower, pushing herself against me to smell her scent. It was as if Ishmael had begun to nurture and prune her into a person who could blossom. I wasn't sure how I felt about that.

2

PABLO PICASSO

"The purpose of art is washing the dust of daily life off our souls."

Tuesday 20th October 2015

During the following two weeks, I discovered that Ishmael indeed knew that I was a famous painter, visited by the rich and wealthy. I told him that they liked to ask me questions about the inspiration for my art. I thought he would be impressed by the successful people who thought that my art had value. Ishmael was not interested in that at all. From an early observation of him, I thought that he wanted to learn how to bury himself into the earth and to reach for the stars at the same time. He was one of the few people I knew who was 'embodied' or incarnate.

He told me, when I shared with him how I thought he was different from everyone else that I knew, that he thought that many of the people he had met were 'split' people – split within themselves – from mind, body and soul, from one another, separate from life and death and split from what you might say is an acceptable self and an unacceptable self. That last split he found interesting.

He asked me: "Do they not know that they can be seen

through? Nobody believes that an acceptable self is real – no matter how well it is dressed up. It is not credible that you see yourself as acceptable based on your fame, fortune and creativity. When you know who you really are, you know who everyone else is too. You can't be fooled anymore by anyone because you are not fooling yourself."

If anyone else had said that to me, it would have angered me. With Ishmael I found myself nodding with him in agreement even if I didn't understand what he meant. It wasn't lost on me that I was one of the 'split' people.

Maybe it was because Ishmael was a gardener that he found it easier to be embodied rather than to be split. He had his feet in the earth – not on the earth. The earth I remembered is called 'hummus' and the word humiliation means to fall to the earth. I need humiliation to become embodied – an earthed human being. I wondered what had humiliated Ishmael to the extent that he had become a real person. What happened to him to make him so vibrant and alive? Every time I attempted to ask those questions in different ways, he skilfully side-stepped giving me an answer. He did it in such a way that I didn't feel that it was right to press him further. I thought it a better strategy to give him more time, to build our relationship; and when he was ready, he would tell me willingly. He would allow me eventually to know as much about him as I needed to understand.

Instead, we shared thoughts about the development of the garden. The garden before Ishmael's arrival embarrassed and annoyed me. Pep Conejo did his best but it wasn't good enough. There were orange trees but not an orangery. There was a pathetic fountain with water spouting from a Cupid's penis. Visitors pointed at it and laughed. It was vulgar. It spoilt the impact which I wanted to make for my guests which was for a garden to be an expression of beauty – like a carpet of rose flowers scattered on the earth taking them somewhere mysterious.

Within a short time of Ishmael's arrival, he drew up detailed plans for how he could create a garden which included a labyrinth beside a swimming pool, a proper orangery, a series of fourteen Moorish-influenced fountains and a patio close to the where we could have parties for invited guests to the Studio.

The labyrinth had a complex design with high Cupressus Leylandii hedges intermingled with the occasional Red Robin shrub for colour. When completed, he led me inside to the centre and then ran away laughing. I was lost in there for over an hour. It was only the sound of his calling to me which guided me safely to the entrance. He embraced me as I emerged confused and irritated by his cheeriness. He kissed me on the cheek. Although it is a common gesture to be kissed on the cheek in Mallorca, when I returned his kiss, it felt to me that we were two Judases destined to betray one another.

He questioned me about the labyrinth. "Do you like it? It was originally designed by Daedalus for King Minos of Crete to hold the Minotaur – a monster half-bull, half-human. Trapped within the labyrinth the Minotaur was eventually killed by the hero Theseus."

I looked at his triumphant and what I fleetingly interpreted as a sadistic grin. I knew that he thought of himself as a Daedalus and a Theseus. I was the Minotaur. Imagine that I would ask for a labyrinth to be created to make my death at the hands of Ishmael inevitable. The half-human person I knew myself to be could potentially be destroyed by his genius. That didn't happen.

Nevertheless, I was absorbed with Ishmael – in the way I cannot stop myself watching an engrossing film unfold and develop an unhealthy passion for the key protagonist no matter how good or evil they are. They grip me. I surrender willingly or unwillingly to their power.

3

PABLO PICASSO

"Painting is just another way of keeping a diary."

Ishmael and I fell into a comfortable routine together. On a Saturday, he had the habit of ringing me from the pay phone in the market. He would tell me if he had discovered a new flower or cactus for the garden at the flower stall in the Plaza. He would also forage for food for lunch. "Do you want me to buy fish for lunch? There is fresh swordfish with new potatoes or fresh salmon."

Saturday and Sunday were Gabriela's free days. Ishmael and I cooked together.

On Saturdays, Ishmael was the key chef. I sat at the kitchen table, talking about my paintings or how work was progressing within the garden. Garlic sizzled; onions splashed into hot virgin olive oil. He timed the swordfish in the oven to perfection – even in the best restaurants I often found swordfish tough and inedible. Ishmael's swordfish was juicy and placed on top of a bed of creamy herbed mashed potatoes.

It was a simpler way of living than I had been used to before his arrival. The sun shone through the kitchen door and the smoke from the pepper sauce swirled around him as if he was buried within a cloud. The sun at times broke through the smoke clearly and shone on his face as he turned to talk with me. I found myself holding my breath in anticipation of what he would say. His face glowed. Our conversations were a mixture of spontaneity and a deepening knowing of one another.

I breathed out deeply and on those Saturdays, I touched a peace I had known before I became the Painter. I remember that peace when I was seven, before I met Gregoriano. With Ishmael, it wasn't at first as deep or as lasting, but I was deeply contented to know that I could still find it – even if without the same intensity. I hoped that with Ishmael the peace would begin to flow, to expand like the sea around us.

On Sundays it was my turn to cook. Often, I made a suggestion that instead of cooking in the kitchen we go to the Port of Soller and eat in a restaurant. We sat outside in the sun on the Repic side of the Port listening to waves breaking on the sand and ducks quacking to one another as they splashed in the Torrente where it rushed to embrace the Mediterranean.

One Sunday we decided to lunch in a boutique Italian restaurant with atmospheric golden lights. We listened to the sounds of the world and were quiet. As we ate pasta with a sage and butter sauce, I was overcome with an urge to talk with Ishmael about Gregoriano. I started with a question: "Who has made the biggest impact on your life?"

He sipped on his glass of wine and shifted in his seat. I knew immediately that he didn't want to answer. "There have only been a few people." He raised his right hand. "There have been less than the fingers on this hand."

I laughed. I was familiar with his games of avoidance. "Well I only can think of two significant people – a man called Gregoriano and my mother Monica. If I tell you about both of them, will you trust me enough to tell me about two of yours?"

He nodded. "Yes, but I will not tell you today – another day. I know you like to talk and no doubt it will be getting cold with the restaurant closing before you are finished."

I ignored his sarcasm by transferring the last ravioli from my plate to his which was empty. "You need this more than me. OK, I will first tell you about Gregoriano. I would appreciate hearing what you make of him. I am clueless."

He played with the ravioli on his plate, swishing it around in the remaining butter and sage sauce. He tried flattery with me, which he didn't do often. "You have a way of getting my attention."

I began, knowing that he was right, that I talked too much. He feigned interest. "Gregoriano. That's an unusual name here. Where is he from?"

I shook my head. "That is the problem. I don't know where he is from, where he is now or what he wants from me. I Googled the meaning of his name and discovered that in Latin it means 'vigilantus' or 'watchful'. That made me shiver as that is what he does – he watches me."

"I'm sure a person of your fame and fortune must be used to being watched. You're on a public stage when you talk about your art or hold an exhibition. People will want to know who you really are."

"I know that the public want to know who I am, but you know that I keep myself to myself. I need solitude to paint – so what people know about me is limited. They know what they read in the press or what I choose to reveal in building my brand as 'The Painter'. Gregoriano watches me in a way that only one other person does – my mother Monica."

Ishmael ordered a second bottle of red wine. "I might as well make myself comfortable. I see you have a need to get something off your chest. Begin."

I didn't really want to talk about Gregoriano, yet something made me – some emotion deep within me which wanted to release itself through words. I started: "I was ten when I first met Gregoriano. I climbed the Barranc on my own as I used to do and still do. He was then thirty years old. The age you are now. Then he had a bushy black beard that is all the fashion these days, but it was unusual in those days. His eyebrows almost joined the beard and his hair was curly – even curlier than yours. He sat on a grey stone wall looking at me as I approached him. I breathed deeply. I thought I should run past him as there was something about him that scared me."

Ishmael interrupted. "What scared you?"

I sighed. "I don't know. The peace he radiated sitting on that stone wall, jolted me. It felt paradoxically like a lightning bolt, burning my body with a previously unknown knowledge and an anaesthetic at the same time. Does that sound insane?"

He rested his chin in both of his hands with his elbows on the table. "So far, no. Continue. Nothing much has happened."

I smiled at him. "Maybe nothing much has happened so far, but I have only just started. Wait until I have finished. When I was younger, I smiled at myself in the mirror, knowing that I had a gift which nobody else could give to the world. I knew that I was different. I felt full of endless and infinite promise."

Ishmael laughed again. "It's called being young, delusional and egoistical. At that age it is perfectly normal to believe that you are the centre of the world."

I waved at the waiter to order a dessert. I asked Ishmael grumpily, "Exactly, when did you grow out of that feeling of being the centre of the world?"

Ishmael, looking at the dessert menu, replied, "When I saw it for what was."

The waiter arrived with a notebook. "How can I help you?"

I looked at Ishmael. He pointed at the menu. "The chocolate coulant, thank you."

I glanced for a second time at the menu, but it was a blur. "I'll have the same."

I was irritated that asking for dessert had interrupted my story. I also found Ishmael's comments slightly offensive, if not patronising. Was he hinting that I acted as if I were the centre of the Universe? I wished that I hadn't started this disclosure about Gregoriano. I snapped at him: "I'm going to move through this as quickly as I can. OK?"

"Of course. Take your time. We are in no rush. The chocolate coulant takes at least fifteen minutes to cook."

I continued, slightly out of breath. "Gregoriano clicked his wooden walking stick three times on the ground as I levelled with him. I noticed that he wore sandals, although it was winter. He slapped his chest with his right fist. He rose to his feet like a wave on the sea approaching land. "You have arrived at the right moment."

My heart beat in a feverish way. I asked him, "Who are you?"

He answered, "I am Gregoriano. You have nothing to be afraid about."

I looked at Ishmael to gauge his reaction. He seemed re-engaged with me. He looked into my eyes in silence. I continued, gesticulating with circular movements of my arms for emphasis.

"Yet how could I trust him? I knew that I had every

reason to be afraid of him. He was a stranger. I was a fly caught in a web waiting for him to spin a cocoon around me. What surprised me was that I didn't struggle to get free. Instead, I listened to him say, 'Follow me'.

"I climbed the mountain behind him. He lifted his wooden stick and pointed to the right where there was an overgrown path. I had to be careful not to bump my head against the branches of the olive and carob trees whose entangled branches created a tunnel through which we stumbled. He pointed a second time with his stick to the left. There we walked along a crazy paved path which wound a wavy way towards a small Castle.

"There were three turrets on the Castle, circular walls with stained glass windows projecting out from rooms inside. The tiles on the roof were shaped like curling giant leaves of lemon verbena and were green rather than the typical red terracotta tiles of Soller. Persianas on the arched windows were blue, held open against the orange stone walls with yellow starfish shaped tentacles. As we neared the Castle, I could see that the arched front door was open.

"Gregoriano turned and invited me forward. 'It's more comfortable inside'.

"I followed him through a patio filled with unusual plants – purple and cream snail shaped flowers which had dropped a few leaves onto the patio tiles. Turquoise and orange branches rooted in circular holes cut in the tiles, burst from the earth with fine tentacles at their tips shooting into the air like fireworks. Beyond the patio there was a darker room, lit by a mellow glow emanating from a lamp shaped like a twisted tree trunk with orange, pink and turquoise foliage. I heard a crackling sound to my left within a circle of stone on the floor, heaped with wood – the flames breathing into the room as if from a dragon's mouth.

"Two chairs were positioned beside the fire. The walls were covered with seven gigantic paintings – all of which from where I stood seemed to be painted with blocks of black oil. They contained no shapes – no dashes of red, yellow or blue which I liked to use when I painted. I looked at the painting closest to me. I could see that within the apparent darkness of the painting it wasn't only black, but it contained the outline of a headless man. The blackness around him was not static as I had thought at first glance but moving as if space itself was moving around him – creating him."

I stopped talking in an attempt to get Ishmael's attention. He had placed a hand over his mouth as if to stifle a yawn. Knowing I had seen that, he sat upright in his chair, straightened his back and pretended to be alert.

I continued: "Gregoriano pulled back one of the chairs shaped like a throne with a curved back and legs like a lion. He instructed me, 'Please sit. This will not take long'.

"My feet didn't touch the smooth stone tiles below.

I swung my legs backwards and forwards in a nervous way as I felt queasy and unsure of what was going to happen. I then felt a sense of drowsiness flood over me and I made myself sit up upright on the chair."

I stopped again as the waiter approached with the two piping hot coulants. I raised my voice, shouting at Ishmael, who had again slumped back in his chair with his eyes closed. "Did you hear me say that I made myself sit up? Would you sit up and not be so rude."

Ishmael's eyes fluttered open. He corrected his posture as the coulant was placed before him. He smirked at me. "Have you been talking for fifteen minutes? I can't believe it. Time has flown by." Ishmael thanked the waiter, picked up a small teaspoon to eat and leaned towards me. "Please continue. I was listening I assure you. I concentrate better with my eyes closed. Eat your coulant as it is best hot."

I took a spoonful of the rich sponge. The thought crossed my mind to throw that coulant with its oozing hot sauce at Ishmael's face. Ishmael watched me pause before placing the spoonful of sponge in my mouth. I think he was reading my mind. Then he polished off his coulant rather too quickly for my liking. He pointed at my plate. "Go on. Go on. I've seen you eat and talk before now."

I talked with my mouth full knowing that it would disgust Ishmael. "Gregoriano laughed. He poked at the fire and then searched in his pocket for a folded piece of paper which he handed to me. That was it."

I pushed my plate away from me, leaving half the coulant uneaten. Ishmael reached for the plate. "This is delightful – you are insane not to finish it. Back to your story – there must be more. What was written on the piece of paper?"

He now sounded interested. I knew what to do. It was my turn to lie back on the chair and stare at the ceiling.

"I can't remember. I was only ten. I read what was written on the paper. He then grabbed the page from my hands, saying, 'I don't think you can do it'.

"I felt a flicker of anger within me. Who was he to tell me what I could or could not do? I wanted to shout at him, of course I can do it. He didn't look at me, as he threw the paper on the fire. 'One day you will understand what these words mean'.

"I wanted to dash towards the fire, retrieve the paper before it twisted into a fine black leaf. As I jumped from the throne, Gregoriano pushed the paper with his poker into the depths of the smouldering embers. He said, 'You can go now. I will be watching you, whether you see me or not'.

"I ran out of the Castle, trying to remember the way we had come and headed in the direction of Barranc with the words from the three statements circling in my head. Gregoriano has appeared at least once every year since that first meeting. The second time I saw him, he

stood at the back of the room in a Press Conference for
an exhibition in Milan. I was eleven. He shook his head at
me. The following year he attended a Press Conference
in New York. He gave me a cold penetrating stare. A
feeling of a sickening shame twisted together with a
feeling of pride in my stomach. He confused me. I mean
he confuses me as he continues to stalk me. I do not
know whether he likes me, hates me or what he thinks
about me. He is around. I know that I don't always see
him, but he makes sure that I am aware that he is there
at least once a year."

I sat up in my chair and watched Ishmael sip on an
espresso. He shook his head. "That is some story. You
have a good memory for details."

I quickly drank the espresso he had ordered for me.
"What do you think is going on with Gregoriano? Who is
he? What does he want from me?"

Ishmael clasped his hands together on the white
cotton table. He pressed his fingers tightly into the back
of his hands. White pressure points formed on his hands.
His lips straightened into a horizontal line. He asked,
"What was written on the page he handed you?"

I looked out towards the sea, breathing deeply. "It
was a long time ago. I was only ten. I don't remember. It
isn't important. I am more interested in what you think
is going on in Gregoriano's head. That is why I told you
the story."

Ishmael reached a hand towards me and rested it on top of mine.

"It is impossible for you to have forgotten the words on that page. What did he write for you? That will answer your question as to what is going on in his head. He wants you to do whatever was written on that page. You mentioned that there were three items? Can you remember one of them? That might trigger the memory of the remaining two."

I replied, "Yes. There were three statements. I will try to remember them accurately if you think they are so important."

Ishmael watched the waiter bring change from the paid bill. He looked in his wallet and left a hefty tip. "I don't believe that you don't remember them. How can you remember so many details and not remember what was most important? You don't want to tell me. Why?"

My lower lip quivered as I asked, "Why don't you tell me without asking about those three statements what you think is going on with Gregoriano?"

"He seems to have the potential of being an interesting and perhaps a wise man. Who knows? When you remember what was on that page – it might be obvious whether that is true or not. If he is neither interesting nor wise, you might want to consider contacting the Guardia Civil. You are a famous and wealthy artist. That means you may attract people who want to stalk and prey upon you. I would inform either the local Police or the Guardia

Civil of your concerns. Gregoriano may want to rob you, kidnap you or be merely obsessed by you. He may also want to protect you and act in your best interests. How can I say? You refuse, for some reason, to tell the whole story."

We walked home to Can Animes in silence, listening to the seagulls screaming overhead. Three wild mountain goats scrambled along the cliff edges of the mountain on our left with four small black kids, following in a line behind. How I wished I had someone to help me discern how to confidently walk this edge of life which felt dangerous since Ishmael's arrival. It also frightened me what he said about Gregoriano. I was no wiser as to whether Gregoriano wished me harm or wished me well.

Before arriving at the front door, Ishmael broke the silence. "When did you last see Gregoriano?"

I was taken aback by that question but of course it was an obvious question to ask. I hesitated before replying which I know he would have noticed. "I had a long meeting with him a week before you arrived. We had lunch together."

Ishmael threw his hands into the air. "What are you saying? You must have asked him why he is watching you. That was your opportunity."

I turned the key in the lock. "I did ask him. He is like you – he didn't answer my questions. I am no wiser about his motivation. He seems, again like you, to be skilled at getting me to reveal my past but sharing nothing about himself. I also threatened him with the police."

We walked along the hallway towards the sitting room. Ishmael caught me by the arm. "Why didn't you tell me this earlier?"

"I don't need to tell you everything."

I realised that for the first time since Ishmael's arrival, I wasn't sure what to do that evening. I was frustrated by emptying my soul to Ishmael and receiving so little back from him. I felt constrained for the first time by his presence. If he had not been here, I would have gone to the Studio and painted. I found that the best way to exorcise these low moods which fell upon me from time to time. I wondered how he felt about spending time with me. Maybe he was now bored by me. I asked, "Would you like to have a rest? I can paint. I have four paintings to work on for the Reina Sophia exhibition. I know I don't have to complete them until later next year, but I work best when I go slowly with them."

Ishmael put a hand on my shoulder. "Today is Sunday. You are right, it is a day of rest, but I don't want to be banished to my room like a naughty child. I don't think you should paint today. Paint tomorrow. Why don't I light the fire, you pour us both an absinthe? We sit on the sofa and you tell me about your mother Monica."

"I thought you had enough today of my reminiscing about the past."

"You asked for examples of people who made an

impact on my life – who were significant. You shared something of the impact of Gregoriano on you. I am sure there is more to reveal about him. However, why not change direction and talk about your mother. I would like to hear about her. Also, about your father – is he alive?"

I shook my head and couldn't stop a tear rolling down my cheek. Ishmael saw it.

"I'm sorry. Were you close to him?"

I shook my head. "No. Not at all – quite the opposite."

As I hung my jacket on the coat rack, I heard a soft thump on the sitting room window. I rushed to see what had happened. A blackbird had flown into the glass window and lay on the ground. There was a trail of blood on the pathway oozing from his beak. I shouted at Ishmael, "It's dead!"

I headed for the kitchen door, swung it open and ran towards the shiny black feathers. One wing moved into the air as I approached and then remained still. Ishmael was beside me. He said in a soft voice, "Poor thing. It didn't know that was going to happen when it flew from its nest this morning. I guess none of knows what the day will bring. We are all bruised by bumping into certain people in life – not necessarily windows."

We buried the blackbird under a fig tree and placed a stone on top of the red soil. I felt a soft lava flow move around my heart which surprised me. I recognised it as a movement within me which might have been compassion. It was not something I had experienced often in my life.

It seemed as if my interior world was changing, melting in a mysterious way. It was as if there were levels within me – depths – which I did not know how to access but I was getting a glimpse of their existence.

How might I describe it? Imagine that I have my hands tightly closed together – the fingers interlocked with such energy that it would be difficult for anyone to pull my hands apart. Then, I look at them and notice that there is movement which reveals a small gap between the fingers. I can see through them – not much – a little, but they are moving slowly apart – separating – one hand from the other. I am not making it happen. It's happening of its own accord. For most of my life from the age of ten, I have lived with those fingers firmly closed, with no awareness of a world existing beneath the surface.

Ishmael and I returned to the house. I asked him, "Do you think it is a bad omen – the bird flying into the window?"

He shook his head. "I'm not superstitious."

I walked through the kitchen door. "I've heard that it can be a message of a death that will happen."

Ishmael closed the door behind us. He smiled at me. "Well that is hardly a premonition. People are dying every minute."

I am relieved to have returned to this safe relationship with him, where I know that I can be myself, say anything to him and not be judged. I feel grateful for his presence and that he has chosen not to leave.

"Let's go to the sitting room. I could do with that drink. Could you light the fire? I'm cold."

I couldn't stop myself shivering. I found a jumper, lying on the sofa and pulled it on. I poured two glasses of absinthe.

Ishmael had the fire roaring in no time. We sat side by side on the sofa. He asked, "Your mother – where do you want to begin?"

I knew I wouldn't be able to stop myself crying. I continued to shake but this time not from the cold, tears rolled down my face. I wiped them away with the sleeve of my jumper. I sobbed. "I want to go back ... back to before I was Augustin – 'The Painter'. What were my first memories? I remember love and fear. My mother Monica was and continues to be a loving mother. She was there for me from the day I was born. I felt the smile from her lips fall upon my face as a tickle of gossamer. I felt safe, warm, held within an outside womb.

"Is it possible Ishmael that I remember the moment of the separation of my consciousness from hers? I think I do remember it. What age could I have been? Maybe eighteen months old. Before that I swam within her eyes, splashing within the pool of her gaze. Her gaze was my gaze. I was love seeing love. I felt overflowing with undifferentiated peace and joy. Life had meaning. The world wasn't a frightening place to live in."

Ishmael sipped on his absinthe and whispered, "I

think it is more than possible for you to remember that. I'm sure it's true that you do."

I took a deep breath. I felt strangely calm. Words spilled, unfiltered, from my lips. "One day she gave me a bottle of milk as she always did, but on this occasion, I felt the world crumbling apart. It broke into a new form of being. That plastic teat which I greedily sucked on became the instrument which shattered everything into fragments. I knew fear. I was a fragment separate from my mother and dividing at a frenetic speed from everything else. If the umbilical cord had been cut at my birth, I then knew what it meant to be cut off from everything. I knew what it meant to be separate – to be isolated.

"My mother Monica helped in those early years show me what love was, to sow seeds of peace within me and allowed me to understand how to live with isolation and separation. It was natural for her. It was a part of being human. She thought that God had placed the desire for happiness in every human being but deliberately did not allow us instinctively to know how to find it. That was what growing up was meant to be for a human being. We were meant to embark on a journey or an adventure and find out what will make us profoundly happy."

Ishmael refilled my glass. He asked, "What do you think made her look at the world in that way? It's not that common. She sounds remarkable."

"Yes, she was and is remarkable. But she had her work

cut out with me. She didn't get through to me at a deep level. I listened to what she said but her words or way of being didn't change me. They stayed on the surface. She sacrificed a lot to give me the best education possible. I was sent to an international school in Palma and then University in Barcelona. I studied philosophy, theology and art. I don't think I received the education which I needed. I was too successful at University which followed on the heels of my art success as a child. I needed to suffer more to learn like mother what it means to grow up. I needed people not to praise me but to humble me. It would have been good if I had learned like the dead not to become angry when insulted or puffed up when praised.

"My mother, on the other hand was what some might call an 'uneducated' woman. She left school at fourteen and went to work cleaning houses – not for the wealthy foreigners who are now here – but for a Mallorquin, Doctor Alfonso. It wasn't long before her cleaning expanded into cooking and caring for Alfonso's children. She wore a navy-blue dress with a white apron. In those days you could buy a uniform in a shop. Everyone who had a maid ensured they wore a similar uniform. The wealthy like to have a symbol for the world to confirm superiority. I think that those navy-blue uniforms with white aprons were not much different from the orange uniforms worn today by prisoners at Guantánamo Bay.

I have always had a hatred of uniforms and what they symbolise – control, authority and separation."

I stopped for a minute to check if Ishmael wanted me to continue. He had his eyes closed, resting his head against the back of the sofa, continuing to hold the glass of absinthe in his left hand. I don't know how I knew, but I knew that he was listening. He was different from the way he had been in the Italian restaurant. His face was softer.

I continued: "When Doctor Alfonso was dying, Cristina, his wife, called for my mother to be with him. Cristina could not bear his dying. My mother had no fear of death. She told Cristina that God had two hands and we had to accept the embrace from both. The left hand gives life, nourishes with a softness of touch and the right hand takes everything away. They come from the same Being. If we want to have a life of pleasure and success, then we have to pay the price for this by becoming nothing again. The right hand makes that happen. It makes us nothing. When Cristina heard those words, she ran from the bedroom and sitting on the bottom step of the stairs, sobbed, holding her head in her hands.

My mother, sitting beside the Doctor's bed, took his hand. He opened his eyes, sat up in the bed, looked at my mother with great tenderness, dropped his head back onto the pillow with a thump that mother said could have broken the frame of the bed and died. Mother took care of the practicalities of closing his eyes, brushing his hair back off his head, closing his lips which had fallen open, placing a bandage around his head to make sure that the mouth would not open again, before slipping downstairs to notify Cristina of his death. She told me that story when I was seven years old. I remember thinking how brave she was in the way she could deal with death – brave and practical. She didn't try to control either the Doctor or his wife Cristina. She did what needed to be done.

"She then did what she needed to do for me. Throughout my life, my mother could see the good in me. She knew that I was dissipating my life and talent, but she told me that for God anything was possible. She believed that I could change. She never complained about me. Maybe she should have. As I said, I was someone who needed to be disciplined before I could learn. I needed to be told that I was selfish."

I looked again at Ishmael. He opened his eyes as if he knew that I was looking at him. He sat up on the sofa and with one gulp drank the remainder of the absinthe. He asked me a question which no-one had asked me before: "Your mother sounds like a woman of great faith. What about you?"

"Well, I have been influenced by my theological studies which included exploring the writings of Thomas Aquinas, Saint Theresa of Avila and Saint John of the Cross. I have even sporadically practiced meditation but that was only because so many wealthy, famous and successful people meditate. I had a selfish motivation.

So, in answer to your question, if I was asked to honestly say if I believe in God, I would say, 'I don't know', and I would also say, 'If I have a God. It is I. I am undoubtedly the most selfish and untruthful person I have ever met'."

Ishmael placed his empty glass on the table between us. He chuckled. I so loved the way he chuckled – it was a gentle, soft guttural purring. What surprised me was that Gregoriano laughed in the same way. If I closed my eyes and only listened to the chuckle, I don't think I would be able to tell if it came from Gregoriano or Ishmael. Ishmael picked up the problem with me saying that I am untruthful in a way that made me laugh. It was a great gift that he had – to be able to take your weaknesses and not make you feel bad about them – to feel accepted with all those vulnerabilities, weaknesses and to place a spotlight on what was unique and good about you.

"Maybe that's a lie. How can I know if anything you have told me is true? I need to think about everything you have said about Gregoriano and your mother and imagine what I would discover that was true about them – if everything you have told me since I arrived was a lie."

I filled his glass a third time. "We have a saying here that a person can look 'as ugly as sin'. I have looked at myself in the mirror over the years and I have seen changes in the way I look. I am not talking about physically ageing – beauty does not disintegrate as you get older. In fact I see in my mother that it can be enhanced as she transmits a glowing, transcendent 'otherness'. In myself I see twistedness, a hardening of the face, a cruelty which is tangible. All a result of dissipating the artistic talent with which I had been endowed and squandering a fortune instead of providing for my mother. I have lived a life of debauchery and of lies. I get away now with lies about my painting. I tell a story about what they mean, and art critics and collectors believe it. They pay a fortune for lies. I seek out people who are vulnerable, weak minded and easily influenced. There is only one art critic who has seen through the deterioration of my art and talks about it – Miguel del Salmorejo. He is the only art critic I respect. I attempt to learn from his comments, but it is impossible. I have to change before my art will change. I know what is wrong with what I am painting but I am helpless in correcting it. It is like knowing how to speak a language but not being able to allow words to emerge in a way that they can be heard. It is devastating."

Ishmael responded as he threw another log on the fire. "The relationship between a painter, his painting and his psyche must be complex. Ghandi said 'Be the change you want to be in the world'. Why don't you be the person you want to be and maybe the art will improve of its own accord?"

I walked to the window in the sitting room and looked at the mountains which were turning tangerine in the light of the setting sun. The sky was clear – a blue light which would gradually lose its colour and descend into a blackness which also disguised the infinite space hidden from my ordinary awareness. I reminded myself that the setting sun was only one of a hundred billion of stars in the Milky Way which is one of at least hundreds of billions of galaxies in the Universe. There was no way I could imagine what that meant with my rational mind, other than know that my life was a flicker of dust, appearing and disappearing in a nanosecond. I gave it such significance. I worried and fretted while space expanded into infinite mystery. I walked back to the fire, warmed my hands and answered Ishmael. "I don't know who I want to be. I am paralysed. I am a fraud. I am an angry, jealous, envious, devious man who doesn't know how to be any different."

During the week Ishmael continued his work of restoring abandoned orange trees and began work on the orangery. With help from others, bulldozers and cranes, he re-planted orange trees into spirals which gave the appearance of oranges being planets and the leafy green dark space within which each orange shone, deep space. Lemon trees were planted to welcome visitors as they turned off the road from Soller, with a fragrant perfume as they drove or walked along the driveway towards the Studio. Fig trees stayed in their original location behind the swimming pool and were transformed by placing mosaic topped tables and olive wood chairs below each tree to allow visitors to relax and contemplate a garden loved into being by the gardener.

That is how Ishmael saw himself – as a custodian of Nature – a steward carrying out duties to help the trees, flowers and stones live in community and harmony together.

In addition to the garden with its orangery and labyrinth, Ishmael designed and built fourteen water fountains inspired by the Moors who created the Alhambra in Granada. The first fountain he situated outside the front door. He removed Pep Conejo's Cupid fountain and created a new statue of Cupid standing within the fountain holding a bow and directing an arrow at the front door. He insisted that Cupid aim an arrow with a sharp golden point rather than the arrow with a point of lead.

I knew the importance of the golden tip to the arrow – anyone struck by the golden tip would be filled with uncontrollable desire. However, he insisted that Cupid would also have the arrow with the lead tip lying in water, implying that he could use it when necessary. Anyone wounded by the lead tipped arrow would be filled with aversion and a desire to flee.

"Which would you prefer Master – an arrow that strikes you with uncontrollable desire or one where you are pierced and flooded with aversion? The only desire you have is to flee?"

I laughed at the nonsense of the question and answered, "Desire will always turn into aversion. It's only a matter of time. Desire is not love – is it?"

I didn't know what made me say that. After all, I had never loved. Being with Ishmael encouraged thoughts to appear in my mind from a space I didn't recognise.

As he turned the statute of Cupid to point its golden arrow again at the front door, I saw that his face was sweating in spite of the cold water lapping around his knees and an icy breeze stroking his body. He scrambled from the fountain and kissed me on the cheek. The sweat from his face transferred to mine like a damp sponge. I felt a shudder of revulsion and fascination move through me. I wanted to wipe that sweat away but didn't want him to see me do that. I waited until he walked towards the front door and rubbed my left cheek with the cuff of my jumper, until I was certain that it was dry.

That should have been a warning for me that I was filled with both desire and aversion for Ishmael. There was something about the physicality of his body which entranced me – that rounded pert bottom easily seen as he wore tight jogging trousers when working in the garden and the t-shirt, showing off the sleekness of his torso and the toned muscles of his arms. He wore the same clothes in summer as in winter, in summer only changing the jogging trousers for shorts. It was as if his body was impervious to conditions around him.

I was entranced and repulsed by his sweatiness – a dripping saltiness which exuded from every pore of his body with the minimum exertion on his part. The fact that he didn't care that he rubbed his oozing salty face over mine, filled me with a simmering anger as I felt an inexplicable wave of personal insignificance and powerlessness over him. His spontaneity and warmth exaggerated the awareness dawning within me – I was doing nothing to make this relationship grow, it was all down to Ishmael. I'm not saying that he manipulated me, but rather that he treated me in the same way he treated everyone. He was the same person wherever he was with whomever he met. He would make any relationship grow. I was not special.

4

PABLO PICASSO

"Everything you can imagine is real."

As the Painter I have a sense of creating and also of destroying. When I paint over a canvas, I know that another day I can create something even more sublime. My private self-made world fades and I become conscious that what seems to be impossible is always possible. This means I have to destroy. I learned that both movements of giving life and taking it away in my paintings lay within my hands – not God's.

After Ishmael swung the Cupid towards the front door, he asked permission to create a statue to Persephone whom he suggested should be positioned with her back to the front door, holding a grain of wheat, staring at the fountain.

"Why do you want to place Persephone, the Queen of the Underworld, married to Hades, the God of the Underworld, so close to the house, or even in the garden? Are you not going to confuse visitors with the positivity of the symbolism of Cupid's love and the close presence of Persephone from the deathly Underworld?"

Ishmael bent down and with one hand grasped a

bunch of daisies and with the other he meticulously removed a creeping weed from the soil. "First of all you have to remember that Cupid is often thought to be the chubby child of the love goddess Venus and the war God Mars – so he is not a symbol of a simple child of love. He is a child of conflict between love and war.

"Persephone is the personification of vegetation which shoots into the world in spring, withdrawing in winter. She is a fertility symbol. She represents the cyclical nature of life and death. With gentleness she tells us our true nature – that we are never separate from life and death. It is who we are and what all things are, moment by moment. She tells us that there is no difference between the daisy which we love and the weed which we hate. We create that difference. Persephone welcomes all life as it is without judgement and with mutual respect."

I looked at him wondering, what kind of a gardener have I hired? Before I could stop myself, I glibly said, "Thank goodness we sorted that one out. I'm sure the visitors will understand it perfectly."

In Ishmael's response I heard a love and fascination for the garden. I was beginning to see how little love I was capable of either giving or receiving as a result of my lack of attention. Ishmael's attention to the creation of the garden – which included an intensity of symbolism, structure, and layout – were indicators of a vibrant lively interest and love of life. He worked totally in the present moment with no distractions caused by worrying about the past or anticipating the future. I envied him this deeper place of being moment by moment.

I felt myself constantly worried and in a state of anxiety even though I pretended to myself that I didn't care what the art critics and others thought. The truth was I did. It would be more accurate to say that my body worried with turbulent waves of concern, but my mind couldn't work out exactly what made my body feel so unpleasant. It was a battle between my mind telling me that everything was fine – I was wealthy, successful, had a world stage presence and received great reviews for my art, apart from those I mentioned before by Miguel del Salmorejo. My body didn't believe these superficial messages. At a cellular level my body shouted at me for attention. I ignored it. I knew it held a deeper truth and if I banished those thoughts it would tell me what I had to do. I knew that I could listen to it but I was bored with people like Gregoriano and my mother Monica telling me what to do – not with words but with their bodies talking to mine.

You will have heard me say that I thought of the garden as Ishmael's garden rather than mine as I had invested no love in it. I watched the subtlety of what he did. Weeds were not uprooted and burnt but replanted to bloom into a wild English country garden.

There were a few plants he placed in a herb garden, beside the labyrinth. I recognised the thyme, rosemary, mint and basil but there were others he refused to name.

I think they included the ones which he and Gabriela later used to drug me. I remember seeing them both stroke those plants as if they were kittens. Ishmael held them up to his nose burying his head into their furry petals. I watched him knowing that he was doing something important. He gave himself away not by great acts but in the small movements he made.

I tried to make sense of why he insisted that I drink absinthe every evening after supper. He laughed as he topped up my glass with the vibrant green liquid which, to be honest, I did not like. But we drank it together and fell into an easy relationship. Now I wonder if that absinthe was his way of controlling my body. If he kept my body subdued maybe I would never find out the truth about who he was or why he had been sent to me as a Gardener.

In those days (BM – Before Murder) we would sit on the sofa together. I placed an arm around his shoulder. It is hard to describe what that contact meant to me. I know these behaviours are easily distorted today with political correctness issues and #metoo accusations. An arm resting on his shoulder gave me a sense of deep friendship and connection. It was a deeper love than brotherly love. Neither was it a touch of lovers. I didn't understand it. The nearest I can get to it, is that it reminded me of the term 'agape' – which I learnt about in my theology class. It is the Greco-Christian word referring to the highest love. Cupid represented erotic love which I understood and had experienced in my life. With Ishmael the experience was more like what I imagine the love that God might have for man and man for God, as hinted at as far back as Homer.

In the first year, we stared together at the paintings I was working on. I moved from the Studio to paint in comfort, when inspiration allowed me to do so, beside the burning log fire in the sitting room. Other larger installations and paintings, I continued to develop in the Studio. I increasingly found crackling logs, flickering flames and the presence of Ishmael, propelling me to be more courageous in splashing lime green and orange together on the canvas. Out of the corner of my eye, I noticed that he watched me as intently as I did with him when I observed what he did in the garden. He rarely commented on what I was painting. Instead, he asked questions. "What made you choose that colour? What options did you consider? What do you want to express? What emotion do you think you are provoking in the observer?"

Sometimes I ignored him and continued painting. Other times, I would try to explain but it was challenging as I realised that I did not paint from my thinking mind. The colours and form came from somewhere deeper in my body. I wondered if it was possible that the new inspiration also came in a telepathic way from Ishmael. My paintings were changing, becoming more positive, lighter and childlike. They were improving – even Miguel del Salmorejo commented that I seemed to be returning to a time of former greatness. He bought one of the paintings I had planned to exhibit in the Reina Sophia exhibition. He promised that he would lend it back to me to be displayed for three months.

On occasion, after dinner and before going home, Gabriela leant against the door frame with a worried look on her face watching me paint. I thought at first that she was suspicious of Ishmael's intentions. She was right to be concerned – not about Ishmael but about me.

5

PABLO PICASSO

"Painting is a blind man's profession. He paints not what he sees, but what he feels, what he tells himself about what he has seen."

Thursday 17th March 2016

Within six months Ishmael miraculously finished his garden, with the fourteen fountains, the orangery, herb garden, swimming pool, labyrinth and patio. We planned a party to celebrate his success. I invited fifty people and the five gardeners and labourers who had assisted Ishmael in this humongous effort. Ishmael asked, "Can we invite Pep Conejo? He did a lot of groundwork which I built on. It would be good to thank him and let him see how it has changed."

I felt my face flush with embarrassment. I had sacked Pep Conejo when I committed to hiring Ishmael to create the garden. Ishmael asked to include Pep in the five assistants who would work with him. I refused. I was afraid that Pep might attempt to sabotage Ishmael's success. Ishmael did not know the local suppliers – Pep did. He could convince suppliers to be out of the ordered materials. Or, he could light a fire after a day's work and burn the labyrinth to the ground and make it look like an accident. Additional ideas about how Pep could harm the project flashed endlessly into my mind.

If I said 'yes' to Pep Conejo attending the party, it would be embarrassing to meet him again and maybe downright dangerous. What might he say or do in front of the guests? My instinct was to say 'no' – that I didn't find it appropriate for him to attend. I heard myself say instead, "Yes. If you think that is a good idea."

Ishmael slapped me on the back. "Good decision."

In the six months that Ishmael had been working on the garden, we lived like hermits, in the same house, in separate cells, rarely going outside to socialise and meet with others. He did not ask permission for free time to allow him to escape from solitary confinement, to go to Palma or tour the island in my BMW. He replied, "My work is here. My life is here."

I was worried, that with the garden being completed, he might look for another project elsewhere – perhaps on the peninsula again. I decided to ask him directly as he trimmed the tall Cupressus Leyandii and Red Robin hedge which formed the walls of the labyrinth.

"What are your plans now that you have completed ..." – I coughed – "... not only completed but excelled in the creation of my dream garden?"

I was holding a stepladder steady for him as he shaved the leaves from the top of the hedge with an electric hedge trimmer. The labyrinth walls were three metres in height, the trees placed close together to form a dense wall which no-one would physically be able to penetrate or to see through. The ladder slightly shook as he leaned forward. I remembered Pep Conejo's fingers and positioned my feet further apart on the ground to steady myself and gripped the steel sides of the ladder with both hands.

He turned the trimmer off and looked down at me. "I was going to ask you the same question – what are your plans for me?"

I shouted up at him: "Why do you always answer a question with a question? Can you not give me a simple answer? I asked you first."

I realised how childish I sounded. It wasn't exactly a way of talking to him which would encourage him to want to stay as my gardener. I lowered my voice and decided to be semi-honest. "Sorry, I'm a little nervous about how the inauguration of the garden will go next week. I would like you to stay as my gardener for as long as you want – with an open-ended contract. This garden has only just begun. It will need a lot of maintenance to keep it looking as good as it does now. I only ask that you give me sufficient notice to find someone to replace you."

Ishmael descended the ladder and with his feet firmly on the ground threw his arms around me. "That is exactly what I wanted to hear. I agree – there is still a lot we can do to make the garden even more dramatic. Perhaps we can build in themes from your paintings. I thought of creating a rose garden with each rose having the name of one of your paintings. You can create new provocative sculptures to challenge thinking in the way you excel. I have reached my sculpture limit with the fountains, Cupid and Persephone."

My heart beat quickly. This was more than I could have hoped for. I blurted out, "I could teach you how to create the sculptures. We could do them together."

He moved the ladder a little further along the hedge. "That would be a new stage in my life. I would like that. You wouldn't get jealous would you, if my sculptures were more highly respected and valued than yours?" He bent over, held his stomach as he laughed looking at the ground. Catching his breath, he looked at me and wiped laughter tears from his eyes. "That would be a real test for you and your battle with jealousy."

Thursday 24th March 2016

For the organisation of the 'fiesta' I contacted Doris and Chris from a German catering company which I had used on several occasions. I totally trusted them to do an excellent job in impressing the guests. Gabriela would help to supervise the kitchen, showing them where everything they needed was stored and later assist in serving wine.

Guests were due to arrive at seven o'clock in the evening. Doris and Chris approached the house in their van at midday. A fleet of cars followed them with three assistant chefs, two waiters and two waitresses.

The five chefs commanded the kitchen and began to organise who was prepping and cooking what. Gabriela showed them the kitchen equipment. The waiters and waitresses were in casual clothes for now and began unfolding ten large tables from the van, covering them with white cotton tablecloths, silver cutlery, Lafiore flute glasses for champagne and goblets for wine. The tables were finished with vases of roses and scented vanilla candles.

At four o'clock the waitresses changed into pink lace dresses with a satin belt and a pink rose in their hair to match those on the tables. The waiters wore black trousers, white shirts and pink braces with a rose motif.

I wore a black tuxedo with a white shirt and black bow tie. The tuxedo had been hanging in the wardrobe for nine months. It smelt a little damp. I sprayed it profusely with Gucci aftershave.

I walked to the buffet table to see what was on the menu which I had left entirely in Doris and Chris's control. I gave brief instructions about how I wanted the cake to look on its table of significance.

There were canapés of caviar, tapas of chorizo, Spanish omelette, sea bass, a Mallorcan trampó, a salad filled with tuna, potato, tomatoes and iceberg lettuce, a Mallorcan version of pizza which is called a 'coco' – with a topping of roasted red peppers and an extensive range of local cheeses. Then to hint at my global reach with my art there were dishes from three countries I had exhibited in recently and would be returning to. There was a Japanese corner with a variety of a sushi, an Italian corner with antipasto, pasta salads, focaccia bread, an Indian corner with samosas, fish pakoras, peshwari nan bread, tarka dal, vegetable jalfrezi and madras chicken.

The cake I commissioned on its separate table was a towering iced cake structure with fourteen layers, one to represent each fountain. I wanted guests to take a slice home and had created individual cake boxes with dates on them for the upcoming exhibitions.

I hired an Argentinean duo that played Spanish guitar and sang Tango songs from the 1930s as guests arrived, including 'El Día que Me Quieras' (The Day that you Might Love Me) from Carlos Gardelas and 'Gracias a la Vida' (Thanks to Life) from Mercedes Sosa. They brought with them two Argentinean tango dancers who glided around the patio beside the swimming pool.

I lit a cigar watching the guests marvel at the Orangery and herb garden. They approached the labyrinth. In the last few days Ishmael had placed a fountain on either side of the entrance, water under high pressure shot high into the air, descending through a series of dishes which changed colour. I heard them laughing as they reached the centre. Although the party was primarily to celebrate the gardens, I wanted to show them the Studio and the works of art which I had prepared for Tokyo and

Madrid. As I puffed and blew aromatic cigar smoke into the air, I wished that I hadn't bought Ishmael that Boggi suit. He looked too good in it, with the waistcoat tight against his slim chest, a white Boss shirt which he had bought himself and the shiny black shoes he wore the day he arrived.

Guests emerged with gasps of delight from the labyrinth. It was annoying to see how long it took them to walk a few steps along the path to the patio beside the swimming pool. I gave a signal to Sergio the main singer to increase the volume of the music and whispered to Andreu the dancer to dance towards the guests, attract their attention and encourage them to move towards me. I was beginning to feel a bit of a fool standing all alone beside the cake tower but didn't want to look too desperate to disentangle them from Ishmael. I know that jealously is easily detected.

However, guests continued to buzz around Ishmael asking questions about unimportant topics like where he bought the pansies and the lobelia in the hanging baskets and how he planned to keep the orangery irrigated in the heat of summer. It was so obvious how all of that would happen. Yes, it is true oranges need water, but they only had to look at the black tubing along the tilled soil with holes in it and water trickling from the holes. What did they think it was – another work of art on the ground?

It was as if I was invisible when the garden with its fountains and sculptures was only meant to be a red carpet as I mentioned before – a scattering of roses, leading to what was really to be celebrated; my art and sculptures.

Eventually guests found table plans, scanned them for their names, found seats with name tags and then queued up to shake my hand before going to the buffet. It felt as if I was at a funeral rather than a party, receiving condolences for the death of a loved one. However, the atmosphere changed as they talked around the buffet table, pointing out favourite dishes and gasping from time to time in surprise.

Gabriela, who had been helping in the kitchen, appeared, now wearing a pink lace dress with a rose in her hair which was piled high on top of her head with a few ringlets falling onto her shoulders. She looked radiant. Before joining the waiters and waitresses, she waved at Ishmael who was helping himself at the buffet table, ran towards him, and kissed him on both cheeks. I heard her say in a loud voice: "Congratulations. What a success for you."

Ishmael held her head with both hands, looking into her eyes, and then tucking one of ringlets behind her ear, he whispered something into her ear which I couldn't hear. He looked around the patio and approached my table smiling.

Ishmael sat on my right and Pep Conejo on my left. I ignored Ishmael for at least fifteen minutes, persevering with a conversation with Pep Conejo which started with: "What do you think of it Pep? Do you like it?"

To which he replied, "He's a good man. I like him."

I knew from that reply that I was in for a hard time. I passed him bread and olives and felt my lips moving into a false smile as he told me about new developments with his son and daughter-in-law. I nodded sympathetically – I hope.

The singing continued and the tango dancers in long lingering movements, swept around the tables. The levels of laughter and conversation swelled. I looked around at the tables, breathing in my success with pride and cursing under my breath that I hadn't been successful in showing off my art in the Studio. I blamed Ishmael for his thoughtlessness.

Friday 25th March 2016

The evening after the party, Gabriela threw, with uncustomary aggression, a bowl of rice with vegetable broth, onto the table in front of Ishmael. The green liquid splashed artistically onto the cotton tablecloth. She slid a bowl towards me giving me a smile which I imagined came from years of intimacy together. I wondered if jealousy was in the air. Gabriela was jealous of what she thought was my deepening friendship with Ishmael. Or so I believed.

I was confused however, by her kissing Ishmael the night before. Which behaviour was the true one – the kiss or this sulkiness which I now witnessed? Maybe something had happened later in the evening with Ishmael which had offended her. I watched them dance together when the tango dancers left and the disc jockey, Tomeo, took over the music. They seemed to be enjoying one another's company – although Ishmael kept looking over at the table where I was sitting. I sat alone drinking a cognac. I hope that he felt guilty, not only about taking so much time with the guests in the garden, but also about leaving me alone at the first party we hosted together.

As Gabriela mopped the soup slops from the tablecloth, I noticed that she was wearing well applied makeup with fashionable heavy eyeliner, long false eye lashes and purple lips. Her hair was again piled on top of her head. As she cleaned the spill, long ringlets on either side of her face fell like a waterfall, brushing against Ishmael's hand.

There were mixed messages with her behaviour, but I thought that there was a gentleness in her eyes when she looked at me and disgust when she looked at Ishmael. I had never thought about it before but maybe she had hopes that there was a chance that I would fall in love with her and that my friendship with Ishmael was getting in the way of deepening her relationship with me. It happened quite frequently in my circle of wealthy friends that their cleaner or housekeeper had designs on their wallets and bank accounts. Over dinner, we would talk about these 'atontados' – the infatuated wealthy men, who lost the power of reason and discernment when absorbed with a pretty face serving them dinner or vacuuming the floor. The power of reason and discernment wasn't the only thing that they lost. One friend lost ten million pounds within five years due to the insatiable desire of his ex-cleaner – who was now his wife – for designer clothes, yachts, and jewellery.

Reflecting now on what I know to be true, I realise that I was suffering from lies of perception. I saw in Gabriela what I wanted to see – not what was real. That capacity for distortion of the world helped improve my art. It made the paintings almost mystical. As a Painter I understood the importance of being able to lose my mind to connect with what lay beyond thinking.

I created alternative worlds with my painting. These certainly added to my success. However, the distortion of reality didn't improve my relationships with others. I realised that with people I needed to touch depths of truth within their being. I felt that was happening with Ishmael. There was a blurring of boundaries of where I ended and he began. It felt real because it was constantly changing like life itself. It was flowing and endlessly surprising me.

I decided to try a different approach with Gabriela – to take an interest in her. Maybe that would defuse any sense she may have felt of not being appropriately acknowledged and valued by me. I gushed at her: "Gabriela, I don't know if Ishmael mentioned to you but we both thought you looked absolutely stunning last night. The pink dress really looked wonderful on you. It made me think that it is some time since you have had an increase in salary. How would you feel if I gave you a monthly increase of ten per cent of your salary which you can consider as a dress allowance? It will allow you to choose dresses of your choice for special occasions like yesterday. You will stand out from other waitresses as a hostess rather than waitress. How does that sound?"

She poured me a glass of white Chablis, setting the bottle beside me. Placing her hands on her hips, she said, "Have you got a fever or something? Ask me that again tomorrow and I might believe it. I'm off now. Enjoy your evening."

She pulled her coat from the coat rack and didn't wait to put it on in the house – even though it was cold outside. A few minutes later, I heard her bike crank into life and rumble down the driveway. Ishmael helped himself to a glass of wine as I opened the kitchen door and listened. In the distance I heard Gabriela's bike fall silent as she stopped to allow traffic pass by. When there was a space, I knew that she would start the motor again. I heard her bike splutter into life and knew that she had swerved onto the main road in the direction of the Port of Soller.

So, our lives continued with the same routine over the next eighteen months. Ishmael continued to improve the garden as promised and we began to make sculptures together. He had an idea that we choose a fragment from my favourite paintings and select an image which we could work on as a sculpture.

His creativity and discernment of what would work best as a sculpture frankly amazed me. We made sculptures which represented the clouds of Mallorca, the sea, the mountains, the goats, old men sitting in the Plaza and a sculpture of a herb tree buried within a huge bottle to acknowledge the importance of 'hierbas' from Mallorca.

These sculptures were strategically placed around the garden and within the labyrinth. He designed a game – 'Find the Sculpture' – in which visitors could complete, ticking off how many sculptures they found, taking a photo of them on their Smart phones to ensure they were not cheating. These were checked by Gabriela and each month a prize of a mini sculpture, which we also made together, was awarded to the winner.

6

PABLO PICASSO

"The artist is a receptacle for emotions that come from all over the place; from the sky, from the earth, from a scrap of paper, from a passing shape, from a spider's web."

Wednesday 20th September 2017

One day, as the second anniversary of Ishmael's arrival approached, I found Gabriela talking with him in the herb garden. She had plaited her hair and tied it with a pink ribbon. She wore black tights, a red tunic and boots which came over her knees. She pointed at the unnamed herbs and Ishmael pulled leaves from one beside him and he talked to her in a low voice. I couldn't hear what they said to one another. I could see a look of surprise and interest in Gabriela's face. She bent over, gathered flowers from other herbs and a few leaves from the one which Ishmael had rubbed between his fingers.

I continued to paint each evening beside the log fire. Ishmael and I had an early supper around eight o'clock. We followed a routine where Gabriela brought me a cup of camomile tea before she left. I noticed that she did not bring tea for Ishmael but topped up his glass of absinthe.

She then left to go home. Ishmael took away my half-empty cup of camomile tea sitting on its china saucer and topped me up instead with a glass of absinthe.

I felt increasingly a sense of exhaustion and anxiety in my body. I wondered if Gabriela with Ishmael were poisoning me. Although I dismissed these ideas as fleeting moments of paranoia – as there was no rationale to justify these thoughts. Yet there was a hint of doubt about how much I could trust them both that seeded in my soul.

Wednesday 27th September 2017

A week before I murdered Ishmael, I kissed him on the cheek. It was the day before he told me about his childhood. It's always an intimate moment when anyone reveals the depths of their past – except when they are making up a lie about it – which happens more often than we would care to believe. He looked at me as he drew me to his chest saying, "Of course I love you – who wouldn't? You are loveable."

I felt distraught. I didn't want to be loved in that way – not with a total, absolute, unconditional and sexless love. It was too much for me. With it, I felt myself bursting into a universe that was infinite and I didn't want to go there. I wanted to feel safe within my tiny body – not to explode into an immensity of being. I wanted to exist within a small point in time which contained me.

Although I felt distressed, I heard myself say, "I am

glad to have you here with me. My life is changing for the better. I have never been happier. I have no-one to leave my money to apart from my mother. I have, of course, created a will and at the moment she is the sole named beneficiary. I would like to include you. My mother is seventy-five. Under natural circumstances I should outlive her. You are twenty years younger than me. You should outlive me. It would make me proud to think that someone like you would keep the garden evolving and have the financial freedom to continue with your sculptures."

He shook his head. "That is unnecessary. In fact – I would feel uncomfortable if you do that. What about Gabriela? She has taken care of you for many more years than I have been here."

"That will be up to you. If you choose to bequeath a portion to Gabriela – that will be your choice at the time."

He placed his hands over his ears. "I don't want to hear you talk like this. You are young. You don't need to think of your death. It's morbid."

The next day we walked into Soller, down the path flanked with lemon trees, arriving on time for the eleven o'clock appointment with the notary. The will was amended. I gave a copy to Ishmael. "Don't lose it."

Wednesday 4th October 2017

One evening after a light supper of vegetarian dim sum and sushi with wasabi sauce, washed down with a glass of Rioja, Ishmael unexpectedly received from Gabriela a cup of camomile tea rather than a glass of absinthe. I noticed for the first time a conspiratorial look between them. She handed him two cups of camomile tea. He sniffed at both cups and handed me the cup in his right hand. I noticed his cheeks were red below the deepening shadowed bags under his eyes. I shivered as he passed the cup of tea to me. Why did Gabriela not directly pass the cup to me? Why did she need Ishmael as an intermediary? I began to wonder if Gabriela was in love with Ishmael and not infatuated with me as I had previously smugly considered being true.

During the last eighteen months I couldn't work out if their relationship was platonic and Ishmael was merely being charming and kind as he was with everyone. I had never seen him demonstrate unpleasant behaviour – whereas I continued to be volatile from time to time; but felt that I was improving.

Even though I did not want a relationship with Gabriela other than to have her as my housekeeper I felt a stinging anger move around my heart observing that puzzling exchange between the two of them.

There is an intimacy in having a housekeeper. They know you. They see the kind of dirt you make around you – the crusted tomato sauce burnt black inside the oven, the half-drunk bottles of gin and whiskey and a dishevelled bed. There are some things I would never allow Gabriela to do – to pick up my dirty linen in all of its forms and place it into the washing machine. I made sure the clothes had finished their cycle. She only had to pin them on the washing line and iron them when they dried. I heard Gabriela folding the ironing in the kitchen. That particular evening, I felt uncomfortable sipping on the camomile tea with Ishmael's eyes fixed on mine. "When Gabriela leaves, we can have our nightcap of absinthe. We don't need to pretend to be so good. We can be ourselves."

I didn't want to drink that vile drink. Nevertheless, when the front door closed, I could not resist Ishmael pulling a chair closer to me and filling two glasses. That particular evening, he did not sit beside me on the sofa, but stayed in a chair close to the painting I was working on. He looked at the painting rather than at me – even when I reached a hand towards the bottle of absinthe hoping to touch his hand. I was in danger of making a fool of myself.

He turned towards me. "Sorry, how rude of me, I should have placed it on the table closer to you." He leaned forward and touched the painting. "Do you think this is one of your best?"

"It's not something I'm proud of – so I would say no."

"What's wrong with it?"

"I would like it to have more form. The colours are fine, but the painting overall has lost meaning through a lack of form."

We talked a little more and I fell asleep. I don't know

for how long. I wakened. Between slits of half-opened and half-closed eyes, I watched Ishmael correcting my painting. It was subtle what he was doing – a stroke here, a dot in another place. Did he think that I would not notice what he had done? My head swirled with absinthe or was it also with something else? Perhaps a flower plucked from the herb garden by Gabriela and Ishmael, disguised within my camomile tea.

The outside world began to blur and move. I looked at the ceiling. It appeared to be covered with insects swarming towards the light hanging from the middle of the ceiling. I knew they were not real. I blinked several times, but they didn't disappear. I looked at Ishmael again. He was standing at the canvas, holding a paintbrush in his hand. He took a few steps backwards to enhance his perspective. He moved forward again, dipped his brush into Titan blue oil and with three smooth strokes allowed the contour of a woman's body to emerge from the gold, turquoise and cerise oils.

Ishmael was destroying my art – my reputation. How did he dare to do that after the warmth of my friendship towards him? He had used my home like a hotel and now he was betraying me. I stared at the canvas. I knew that he had improved the painting. That had to be delusional thinking. It was another side effect of the drugs they had given me. How could a gardener with no formal artistic training paint better than I? It was impossible. I felt a surge of hatred towards him. I couldn't stop myself doing what happened next. I felt myself possessed, out of control. I had turned into a killing machine. If anything moved, I had the desire and the will to kill it – to stop it in its tracks.

I struggled to my feet and took Ishmael by surprise by grapping him by the neck of his shirt. He dropped the paintbrush onto the ground, broke free from my hold and ran towards the hallway leading to the front door. I found myself laughing out loud at this act of cowardice. Why didn't he face me and fight? I ran after him. I could see him clearly in the centre of my vision but the peripheral vision around him was hazy. I knew exactly what I had to do. I caught up with him by the fountain.

He shouted at me. "I'm only helping you. I want your exhibitions to be a success. You said that you weren't happy with the painting. It was meant to be a surprise. It was a present for you. Then I planned to tell you about the two people who were most significant in my life and you would understand how I knew how to improve your painting."

I didn't listen. I lunged at him. He didn't move. I don't think he believed what was happening. He was paralysed, frozen to the ground. It was easy then. I squeezed his neck with both hands. He broke free, staggered backwards and hit his head on the Cupid statue.

Lying on the grass, Ishmael placed a hand to his head. He stared at it. "Oh my God – it is covered in blood. You've hurt me. I need to get to a hospital."

He shouted at me in a voice which I heard to be truly filled with fear. Whatever was inside me made me laugh hysterically out aloud. I enjoyed hearing the terror in his voice and his staring eyes, pleading for me to regain my sanity.

"What are you doing? Are you insane? You are going to kill me." He attempted to catch my arm and scramble to his feet. I then had my chance. I heard a noise. I glanced to my right. Was there someone there, hiding behind the olive tree or to the left in the labyrinth?

I ignored it when the olive tree began to morph and twist in my vision. It had to be the drugs again. There was no-one there. I had to act fast. I looked at Ishmael. He crawled onto the grass beside the fountain. There was a fuzzy moment before I easily lifted him from the ground. I had developed superhuman strength. I laughed again as I thought that they hadn't considered it might be an unexpected side effect from the drugs.

I pushed him into the fountain and held his head under the water with my left hand. His arms flapped wildly. I only needed a minute or maybe two or three. There was a spluttering sound and bubbles rose to the surface from the bottom of the fountain. I searched in the water below the line of bubbles with my right hand and found what I thought was his mouth. I placed my hand over it, allowing another minute for the pressure from my hand to do its work. When there was no movement, no bubbles, or thrashing about, I knew it was over.

The fountain began to spin around in my head. I fell backwards onto the gravel.

I remember seeing stars circling above me. I don't know how long I lay there. At some point I struggled to my feet, peered into the fountain. Ishmael was in the fountain and not moving. I pushed my fingers into his neck to check if there was a pulse. There was nothing. His neck felt hard and grainy like an olive tree. He was dead.

Another memory is returning to me now. When Ishmael fell into the fountain, I pushed him under the water with such force that the golden tipped arrow fell from Cupid's bow and stabbed me on the hand. I threw it to one side, vaguely remembering pressing Ishmael's shoulders into the side of the lead tipped arrow which lay at the bottom of the fountain. I recovered the golden tipped arrow and replaced it in Cupid's bow. I looked at my left hand and there was a small hole the size of a one-euro coin. For a moment, I thought that it looked like one of the wounds of Christ, where a nail had been hammered into this hand. I looked at my right hand to see if there was another hole but of course there wasn't. I fumbled in the sculpture to retrieve the lead tipped arrow. As I grasped it, I was aware of how sacrilegious that thought was of making any connection to what I had done and thinking of Christ. Cold water lapped around my calves. I took the lead tipped arrow and plunged it into my right hand. I wanted to punish myself. I scrambled from the fountain with the arrow in my hand. I ran towards the labyrinth and hid it within the Leylandii by the entrance. I twined leaves from the Red Robin shrub around the arrow and pushed it deeper into the wall of the labyrinth. No-one would find it.

I returned to the fountain, swung my legs over the edge once more. With difficulty I twisted the Cupid statue around so that the golden tipped arrow pointed at the spot where I intended hiding Ishmael's body.

I knew I had to work quickly. The body had to be hidden before sunrise – before Gabriela returned and anyone found out what happened.

I needed to focus. I dragged his body from the fountain and placed it within a casing which would hold him upright in the garden. My head was not spinning. I was clear about what I had to do. I didn't feel the nausea that made me vomit minutes after I killed him. His murder wasn't a planned act. A good lawyer could perhaps have helped me to walk free. What I did afterwards was premeditated. What worried me was that I didn't recognise him. Maybe the drugs that I suspected Gabriela and Ishmael gave me were responsible for that.

I worked on the sculpture like a blind man. The moon was my guide. I did not want to see what my hands were doing. That was not so unusual. I often painted like that. When the sculpture was finished, I smelt the herbs planted by Ishmael in the tubs beside me. I tasted salt on my lips. I bit my lips so hard that I they tasted not only of salt but of blood. I knew as I rooted the sculpture into the ground that it would be an acclaimed work of art – perhaps the best sculpture of my life.

After I had secured the sculpture in the garden, near the front door, I kept an eye on the moon as I rushed towards the Studio. I unlocked the heavy oak door, heard it scratch against the tiles. I uncovered the four paintings which I had completed for the exhibition in the Reina Sophia. They rested on canvases, ready to be dispatched within the next few days. Miguel del Salmorejo's painting had already been sent. In the dark with the help of moonlight shining through the Studio windows, I saw how Ishmael had changed them. It felt like a game and a welcome distraction to identify which lines and colours he had added. I moved close to each painting, frowning in an effort to concentrate. His work was subtle. He had improved the paintings. To do that, I knew that he to be a painter with a talent greater than mine.

I locked the door behind me and walked back to the house, taking the path past the swimming pool on my right before reaching the labyrinth where I turned left towards the house, without looking at the sculpture outside the front door. It was open – ajar in exactly the same position as when I ran after Ishmael seething with anger. For a moment, looking inside, I thought that I saw a shape resembling that of Gabriela sitting on the sofa. My heart fluttered in what I knew was an unhealthy way. As I approached the sofa, it was easy to see that the shape was formed by a bundle of cushions which I had piled one on top of the other, having a siesta after lunch.

I lay on the sofa, burying my head into the cushions and tried to remember the sequence of the evening's events. An additional concern came to my mind which seemed to be emerging from its groggy state. I wondered about Gabriela. She served dinner and left. She couldn't have seen what happened. She had gone. Although, a doubt arose in my head because I didn't do what I always compulsively did. I didn't go to the kitchen door and open it to make sure that I heard her motorbike stall as it did before she joined the main road to the Port of Soller. Each evening I wanted to know that she had definitely gone. It gave me a sense of freedom. Then I waited until I heard her bike start up again and drive quickly away pursued no doubt by an Alfa Romeo or a Lamborghini, with a driver most likely heading for supper in the five-star Jumeirah Hotel in the Port of Soller.

Tonight, I had changed my routine. I didn't listen for her motorbike. I was too busy lurching in a frenzy after Ishmael. I didn't plan to murder Ishmael, but I was filled with rage that he thought he had the right to alter my painting. I didn't know where or how that feeling of intense, reckless madness entered my mind. It happened as quickly as flicking a match on rough ground and seeing it burst into sparkling energy or as quickly as my thumb clicking on a lighter and twisting the top of it to ensure that the flame soared high into the sky. It was in this state of incensed being that I pursued him. I had only experienced that level of insane anger once before in my life and that too ended disastrously.

Although I did not hear Gabriela's motorbike start up again to join the road to the Port of Soller, it was only paranoia to think that she didn't drive home as she always did. If she had a reason to return, when my fury abated and the murder had been done, I would have heard the motorbike spluttering around the bends and crunch onto the gravel path as it always did in the morning – in the same way that Ishmael's feet burrowed their way into the stones with every step he took the day he arrived. I would have heard her as I buried Cupid's lead tipped arrow in the wall of the labyrinth. I remembered the heavy silence that night that covered me like a cloak. It would have been interrupted by the sound of her bike.

I lay back on the cushions, convinced that I had been drugged. How else could I have been so out of control? I wondered why Gabriela had conspired with Ishmael to drug me. She might have thought that I was unstoppable unless she intervened.

What did she want to stop? It could have been the development of my relationship with Ishmael. Or, more realistically, it could have been due to her perception of the spiralling envy, anger and jealousy which she perceived. I know my envy, jealousy and anger were not limited to Ishmael interfering with my painting. They had a wider reach. I could not stop seething at the way visitors to my Studio applauded him, circled around him, refused to walk swiftly to the Studio to see what I had created. What happened at the party eighteen months ago repeated itself regularly. She might also have wanted Ishmael in addition to the acclaim as the garden, to be recognised by the world as a better Painter than me. She had watched us together. She heard the questions which Ishmael asked about my painting. He was trying to learn from me, to steal the secrets of my genius. I was a fool to answer any of his questions. It would not surprise me if Gabriela had sat in a chair in the Studio when I was taking a siesta and watched Ishmael add those finishing touches to my paintings.

I turned my head to the left and bit at the cushion – the way I imagine that a prisoner on Death Row bites on a piece of cloth they place in his mouth before the lethal electric shock is administered. I can't work it out. I am blaming Gabriela and Ishmael for what happened. How insane. I am the one who committed the murder – everything else that I am imagining is coming from a fragmented head that wants to see the world in a distorted way and believe it to be real.

I bit a second time at the cushion and shook my head violently; I am surprised that I didn't lose my teeth. I tell myself that Ishmael is taken care of. His life will continue in other ways. He will be admired. I am sure of that. I only have to look at his garden tomorrow to know that. The plants he nurtured will continue to flower, seed and reproduce. They will be brought into being again and again. In the circulating seasons Ishmael's hands will operate invisibly.

Tonight, when I murdered Ishmael, there was a full moon. Hours after his murder, I walked to the kitchen door and looked at the moon. The moon saw what had happened. It was the only witness. As I stared at it, I had a sense that Ishmael's consciousness had jettisoned itself to the moon the moment that he took his last breath. Every time I looked at a full moon, Ishmael would be watching me.

I needed to get some sleep. I climbed the stairs, removed my shoes and got into bed with my clothes on. It took a while, but I did manage to fall asleep. I awakened a few hours later with the noise of the gates opening which triggered lights flooding the garden, flickering onto the oleander trees. I know that because I wriggled from the bed like a worm and peered through the window seeing the pinkness and whiteness of oleander flowers. I trembled. My hands shaking the way I witnessed my father's hands shake on the day he died.

I didn't know whether someone had entered the olive grove after I murdered Ishmael or whether they had been there all the time and were now leaving. However, the gates could only be opened with a remote control. The only people who had access to a remote control were my mother Monica, Gabriela, Ishmael and Pep Conejo.

I listened for the sound of her motorbike. Only the hoot from an owl broke the silence.

It was enough to send the trembling from my hands into my body as a wave. I felt nauseous. I wanted to vomit again, but my stomach was empty as I hadn't eaten since the dinner I shared with Ishmael. Something wanted to cast itself out from my body. The way the violent demon-possessed men whom Jesus met requested to be cast into the bodies of pigs.

I didn't want to go downstairs and into the garden to see if there was anyone there. I was afraid. Instead, I opened the window in the bedroom, pushed my head outside and squinted into the floodlit garden to see who might have entered it or perhaps have left. I felt demons twist and howl within me. There was no-one to set me free. I did not deserve to be set free.

Thursday 5th October 2017

Gabriela arrived to cook and clean the next day. She asked where Ishmael was. I told her that he had gone away for a while. I didn't know for how long. She didn't have her hair in a bun – instead it looked unwashed and dishevelled, falling onto her shoulders in a rather fuzzy way rather than wavy. I noticed for the first time that it was flecked with grey. She wasn't wearing make-up that day. I couldn't bear to see her like that. It wasn't that she had returned to the Gabriela of before but rather she had rapidly aged and disintegrated for some unknown reason. I asked her to take a few weeks holiday as I had nothing much planned other than to paint for my exhibitions in Madrid and Tokyo.

How had she allowed herself to look so abandoned? It was as if that she knew that Ishmael was dead and that she couldn't be bothered to make herself look beautiful anymore. And I had not forgotten that I had my suspicions that she worked with Ishmael to drug me.

Gabriela was talking to me while I was caught in these thoughts. We were in the kitchen where the night before she served dinner. Her words fell easily like raindrops on my head, making no sense, a vibration shaking a world into twilight. I sat at the oak table and scratched its surface of unpolished wood with my fingernails. Ishmael will be hiding now in the moon which has disappeared. I imagine that he is sleeping and will see me again later this evening.

Instead sunlight dropped onto the kitchen red tiled floor. There was a shadow from a plane tree shimmering across the floor. I concentrated on the dancing light and shadow. I sniffed at the air like a retriever who scents a prey close by. There was a roasted smell coming from a bag which I thought contained freshly baked croissants. Gabriela sat beside me at the table, opened the bag and offered me a pain au raisin rather than a croissant. I was shocked at how my body flooded with pleasure at the pain au raisin which I much preferred to a croissant. What addictions to pleasure was I capable of? She pressed the button on the Nespresso machine to make coffee. It gurgled. The burnt coffee bean smell wafted towards me and again horrifies me with its scented beauty of early mornings and nothingness. I attempt to make sense of her words. I listen, concentrating fiercely on what she is saying.

"When should I come back? Where is Ishmael? I need to see him."

She thumps the cup of coffee in front of me. She doesn't place it as she normally does on a saucer. I hear it rumble on the table – quivering as if it might tumble and spill. I hold it still with my hands – cradling it without looking at her. I have quickly got used to doing that – not looking at anyone – dead or alive.

I skirted around her questions pushing money into an outstretched hand. She could read my mind but not perfectly, I hoped.

"I'll give you a ring and let you know when to come back. As for Ishmael, I don't know where he is. Maybe he has returned home."

She looked at the money, glanced away and asked, "Home? Where is home for Ishmael? I thought it was here."

I raised my hands into the air. "That's for him to decide – not for me."

She counted the notes in her hand. "That's too much. That means it's at least two months before you want me to return."

I shook my head. "It's OK. Take it. If I need more time alone – I will still pay you. I'll call you if there is any news from Ishmael or if you need to come back."

I watched the space over her upper lip turn completely white – like a white moustache. "You said 'if' I need to come back; are you telling me there is the possibility that you do not want me here? If not, why not? What have I done to you that you would dismiss me?"

I was shocked at her directness and also what I considered to be her impertinence. Who did she think she was talking to? I felt a familiar flame of anger burn in my stomach. This level of disrespect made me think that I should grab the money back from her, immediately dismiss her and change the locks on the door so that I could be sure I would never see her again.

She continued in a gentler tone of voice, ignoring her last question to me. I also chose to ignore it. That moment of empty space between us allowed her to ask a completely different question. "How do we know that Ishmael doesn't need help? He's a fragile, sensitive person. We need to find him. Perhaps he has had some kind of mental breakdown. That can happen to people can't it?"

That convinced me that for reasons as yet unknown to me that she had a deep and intimate relationship with Ishmael. What would she know about Ishmael's mental state of health unless they had cosied up together on the sofa and chatted when I was not around? I had thought of her as dangerous and now I was convinced that they both betrayed me. She was not only dangerous but treacherous. They had a secret life, one that was deliberately hidden from me. That is the only way that they could have deepened their relationship. There had to be a betrayal of some kind from them both.

I hadn't thought before that a lie could both be beautiful and hold an essence of truth. In the past I saw the world as black and white – even though I, as the Painter, use vibrant colours. Since Ishmael's murder hours ago, the world is clear and not clear. The blackness and whiteness of the world – or I should say of my mind – are only a canvas for splashes of colour I flick onto life like Jackson Pollock.

I looked fearlessly into Gabriela's eyes. I saw a beauty in the depths of their murky darkness. There was also a smell from her which had a perfume of wisdom. She hated me but she would stay with me as my housekeeper as long as I wanted her. So, there were lies already seeded between us. Within a lie there is a lingering cowardice. Cowardice is never beautiful to me, no matter how well it is driven from an inner truth. Cowardice disgusts me. I replied.

"I don't think that Ishmael is insane or in need of our help. He will return."

She pushed the money into a small purse which bulged as she attempted to zip it. She looked at me with a twisted mouth, which I interpreted as evidence of a deep-seated hatred for me as she turned her head away looking at the door. "We will see." She walked briskly towards the kitchen door and, before leaving, turned around and asked, "When did you make that sculpture? It wasn't here yesterday."

I walked towards her. The thought came into my head that I might need to kill her. She seemed to imply that there was something suspicious about the sculpture. I dismissed that thought. Had I not done enough damage in murdering Ishmael? I had to learn not to act out every thought that came into my head.

I opened the door for her to leave. "Ishmael and I had been working on it for quite some time in the Studio. It was finished a week ago. It was Ishmael's idea that we assemble it in the garden last night. Maybe he wanted to see how it looked before he went away for a while."

She turned on her heel, walked through the door, stopped, grabbed the door handle and slammed the door behind her. She didn't jump onto her motorbike immediately. Instead, she walked towards the front door where she would find Persephone, the sculpture and the fountain. I walked into the sitting room and looked out of the window. She walked quickly to the fountain and stared at the water. What was she doing?

She walked back to the house and knocked on the front door. I ran to open it.

"Yes? What's the matter?"

She pointed at the fountain. "Where is the second arrow – the lead tipped one?"

She didn't come into the house. I stood in the doorway. "That's observant of you. You know Ishmael has been constantly improving the garden. He didn't like the energetic vibe coming from the lead tipped arrow. He asked if he could think about how he could turn it into another sculpture. He must have taken it away with him. I can't wait to see what he will do. You know that he is gifted with creative ideas. I think he will want to turn it into a sculpture of a snail which he will place in the labyrinth."

She gave me a cold stare. She didn't believe me. I had to think about what that meant for both of us.

7

PABLO PICASSO

"If only we could pull out our brain and use only our eyes."

Friday 6th October 2017

After Gabriela left, I felt that I needed to walk, to place my feet on the ground and know myself rooted in the earth. Although it was warm and sunny, I imagined that the weather would change but maybe that was only guilt freezing around my heart. I wrapped a navy-blue scarf around my neck over the top of my white shirt. I knew that it looked odd – everyone I passed wore sandals and shorts.

I hurried along the Calle de la Luna, heading towards Barranc. It's a climb towards L'Ofre and Lake Cuber which I knew well. There is something about mountains. They are sacred places. They do their best to take you into the Universe. They give you space to think. I wanted to think about Ishmael. When I think about him – it is almost as if he is not dead. Although I planned to think about Ishmael, my thoughts turned, as they normally did, to thoughts about me. I had been given so much in life – health, talent, a beautiful island to live on, a world to explore and a mother who only wanted me to see the errors of my ways to allow me to live the life that I was born to live.

I am not in a good place; my talent is not real but rather is a deceit. I will have no friends when the murder of Ishmael is known in the world. Life is stripping me bare. Not life – I have done it to myself.

It is two years since Ishmael arrived here. Those two years seem like one long summer. Spring, autumn and winter never seemed to be born during those two years. There was only summer with its parching heat, occasional storms and possibilities. I have always loved summer. Other seasons seemed to be either a preparation for or a saying goodbye to summer. Summer was vibrant, passionate, filled with fiestas, music and life.

In climbing the Barranc the day after his murder, I was reminded of Ishmael's love for the uncultivated creativity of Nature.

In the Torrent to my left yellow flowers burst open surrounded by bamboo shoots with feathery purple tops choked in a multitude of foliage. Is Nature taunting me with life which will not be extinguished? Life will continue without Ishmael. I listened to the news before I left the house as if I expected to hear about Ishmael's murder. No there were only bizarre reports of a pregnant woman who had been murdered in a submarine by a wealthy oligarch who denied his guilt. I was aware that my reaction to the story was one of revulsion – especially of the disclosure that after he killed her, he cut off her head and threw it into the sea. I imagined that, in a desperate attempt to escape her fate, she would have run around the confined quarters of the submarine which drifted in the depths of an inky black sea, before he caught up with her, held her by the arms and murdered her. It reminded me of Ishmael's desperate attempts to escape from me. In burying him in a sculpture, I am no better than that oligarch. The disgust I have for him is no different from the disgust I have for myself.

I looked at L'Ofre, that distant triangular mountain that I have climbed more than a hundred times in my life. Today there are dark rain clouds collapsing over its summit. They are falling as clouds of rain rather than drops, thumping on the top of L'Ofre as if to waken it up and make it move. I smelled rosemary and thyme which reminded me of Ishmael's herb garden. I imagined him bending over with a pair of scissors, cutting thyme and rosemary for a Saturday lunch of lamb, slow roasted in the oven. Everything beautiful reminds me of Ishmael.

Today, I crossed the first bridge on the way up Barranc. The rocks were a stormy grey and smooth. There was no water in the canyon. The rain had cleared, and the sky opened its heart to the emptiness of the Universe. The air temperature is benign. I walked quickly as if I had somewhere to go.

There was nowhere to go. I wanted to get out of the valley – to leave the garden and the sculpture within which I have entombed Ishmael. I walked past the Plaza de Jean Dausset who won the Nobel Prize for something to do with cells, genetics and immunology. There is something to do with our genetics that fascinates me and also what happens in our bodies unconsciously; what drives us to do what we do, do we even know?

I was told by mother that my great grandfather Josep – a painter and writer – died in World War I. As Spain was neutral during the war, he joined the French Foreign Legion – the 3rd Battalion of the 1st Marching Regiment of Africa. He submitted regular columns to 'Iberia' the magazine designed to recruit support for the Foreign Legion in Spain. Before he died on 25th April 1915 in the landing at Kum Kale, he succeeded in persuading 2,000 Spaniards to join the Foreign Legion.

In spite of my Great Grandfather's courage, which I admired in giving his life for a cause he believed in, I don't want to know who my ancestors are. I don't want to feel them creeping within my body like woodworm, poking their little heads out to see the world through my eyes. I know that they are within me and they will make themselves known to me whether I like it or not, but I will not pay attention to them. They say that human beings need attention. If babies don't receive it, they will die even if they are given ample nutrition. I can control the influence of my ancestors on me by ignoring them.

My feet trampled the earth in a statement of being here. I looked to my right. The valley overflowing with violet iridescent trumpets settling into heart shaped blue leaves like butterflies. The mountains to my right stretching above the valley were in shadow. The olive terraces below were bathed in sunshine. Some of the olive trees were scraggly like an unkempt haircut. Others glistened as if coated in silver, but it was only the residue of this morning's rain. A plane tree quivered to my left. The sun had lost the intensity of summer fierceness.

My head buzzed with disjointed words and half sentences. I can't imagine what my life will be now without Ishmael. A part of me wants to pretend that I had never met him. I want to stop thinking about him. Another part of me yearns for him – to be with him.

Memories of my childish reaction of jealousy and anger with him fade, replaced with a heavy greyness in my head an aching desire in my body for the phone to ring to hear him say, as he had said once before, that I am loveable.

If he talked to me in a gentle voice, laughing at me – that would be enough. I didn't need to hear the words 'I forgive you'. They were unnecessary. I didn't believe either that I needed to make an apology for what I had done. I knew that Ishmael's love was so great, so vast that even in death; he knew the depths of my remorse. Can there be forgiveness for me without an apology? Most people would say 'no', but I am not so sure.

In climbing Barranc, I attempted to escape into birdsong. There were two or maybe three birds chittering away to one another – or maybe they were singing to themselves. I sat on a low wall and heard the tramp of hikers approaching, their sticks clicking against the cobbled path. I looked at the cracks between the rocks on which I sat where baby cacti burst through the fissures of the mottled, blotched stone to my left. I wondered not about Ishmael but about the cacti. Why were they here at all if no-one saw them? That brought me back to Ishmael. Even if I had taken his life, had I not given him life for a short while total attention? Was that not love? In the last two years no-one as far as I knew had contacted him. He refused to have a mobile phone. No-one rang him on the fixed line.

Last night as I couldn't sleep, I lay in bed with the window open. I watched the mountains in the distance – dark black knife edges against an indigo sky.

Friday 6th October 2017

Three days after the death of Ishmael. I went into his bedroom and opened the drawers where his clothes were stacked in neat little bundles whereas I threw my clothes which were not ironed into a drawer and then slammed it shut to hide them.

Ishmael ironed his underpants and socks. He colour-coded them with pinks on the bottom, then blues and finally whites. He had socks to match the colour of his shirts. I removed a pair of his underpants. They looked new. Maybe he had never worn them – Gant – multi-

coloured with trees like an Amazon jungle. He didn't
seem to know where to place them within his stack of
coloured underpants with their mixed orange, green and
blue designs. He folded them delicately on top of his socks.
There was something about their pristine condition that
made me hold them against my face and cry into them.
They contained the stainless purity of Ishmael's soul.

Then I went into the garden and made a circular
bench to fit around the sculpture. I hammered the wood
into place. I couldn't bring myself to think of the state of
Ishmael's body inside. It must be disintegrating like the
fresh figs I had placed in a bowl and had forgotten about
a few days after Ishmael's 'disappearance'. That's how I
liked to reframe it now. He's disappeared. If anyone asks
me, I will tell them that I don't know why or where he
has gone. That's partly true – where has he gone? His
spirit I mean. The body is in that sculpture, suppurating.

Everywhere in the garden, I see abundance – figs,
olives, carob pods toasted black lie on the ground, some
trampled into the soil. They will not be eaten; many will
not even be seen. There is a mystery in life seeding itself
into the earth, promising some future growth.

In comparison, what value do my paintings have?
They stimulate a moment of interest and then pass into
the hands of art collectors whose intention is to make
money from my efforts without any appreciation of the
source of inspiration from which they have emerged.
Why should I criticise these collectors for something I

am guilty of myself? I have lost contact with the source
of my inspiration.

I sat on the bench beside Ishmael's sculpture and
wondered if mother could bear the knowledge of what I
have done. I think so, because she told me several times
that not to forgive another person is only a form of power
over them – a way to manipulate shame, diminish and
control them. She said that I had to learn that every
step in life was a step towards powerlessness. I wished
I had understood what she meant by that before I killed
Ishmael. I knew that she would most likely quote a
Desert Father from the fourth century at me – someone
she liked – perhaps St Macarius the Elder who she told
me before had said, 'If, wishing to correct another, you
are moved to anger; you gratify your own passion'.

I am used to listening to her wisdom and the wisdom
of others, but it has never changed me. How I have
tortured my mother in her life. She prays every Saturday
at Mass in the Church in La Huerta with Father Mariano,
that I will be converted, that I will see the destruction I
am making of my life and change direction.

There is a knock at the door. I must go. It is the
postman. I wave at him after he hands me a letter which
I see is from Gregoriano. The postmark indicates that
the letter was posted in Sweden on the 2nd October –
two days before I murdered Ishmael. Why would he not
have sent me an email? Maybe he thought that I wouldn't
open it and knew I couldn't resist reading a letter. Before

reading it, I want to remember the last three times I saw Gregoriano. Maybe I can see patterns in his behaviour which will help me understand who he is and what he wants from me. I met him the week before Ishmael arrived in October 2015. The second time was a week before the party to celebrate the inauguration of the new garden in March 2016 and the third in June of this year, four months before Ishmael's death.

8

PABLO PICASSO

"They ought to put out the eyes of painters as they do goldfinches in order that they can sing better."

A week before Ishmael arrived on the island, I was invited to sail in a wooden yacht from the Port of Soller and have lunch in Deia on the West Coast of the island. Deia is a place frequented in the past by Princess Diana and other dignitaries. Andrew Lloyd Weber and Bob Geldof live nearby as does Claudia Schiffer. Catherine Zeta-Jones and Michael Douglas have a house near Valldemossa. All of these famous people have my paintings hanging on their walls.

I had to meet the owners of the yacht, Alfonso and Victoria, in the Port of Soller. I accepted the invitation to lunch mainly because I hoped to tempt them to buy some of my older unsold paintings which were taking up space in the Studio. I wanted to explore with them which paintings would work for them and where they might hang them. I also needed to get a hint of the price range they might be prepared to commit to.

It was the end of summer. In preparation for what I thought would be a successful lunch in which I would make at least one sale, I arrived with a bottle of Hendrick's gin and Fever Tree Indian tonic water.

I knew the rule of removing shoes before walking up the passerelles. With bare feet, I walked slowly up the slight incline towards the yacht, keeping my eyes fixed on the wood panelling of the passerelles.

I wouldn't say that I cared about Alfonso and Victoria. I don't think I even liked them that much. But sometimes it is better having friends you don't like than having no friends at all. What I see in Alfonso is a cube-shaped man who looks like an ex-rugby player who struggles to keep himself fit, an effort which has turned him into a dice shaped, solid, compressed human being who would be happy to spend his life rolling on a casino table.

Victoria has a head of hair that defies belief. Long, wavy, copper coloured, and in an expensive salon in Palma. She does yoga, meditates and gives the impression that she has vibrated to the highest levels of consciousness. Maybe she has, and if that is what higher consciousness looks like, I don't want to go there. She looked at me in the way you would look at a pitiful flea-invested animal hardened by fights with feral cats. In her presence, I feel myself to be a tainted man in the presence of perfection.

I took my eyes off the passerelles as I neared the yacht. I looked around for signs of Alfonso and Victoria and was surprised to see Gregoriano emerge reaching a hand towards me. He wore a white linen shirt with green cotton shorts. He had removed his socks and shoes.

His feet were bare, with well pedicured toenails. I felt annoyed to see him standing so confidently in front of me.

My voice went up a notch in pitch. "What are you doing here?"

"I'm here for lunch like you. Let me help you."

I felt that I was nailed to the wooden gangway. I held onto the steel handlebars guiding me on board. "Who invited you?"

He dropped an arm to his side with a small sigh. "Alfonso, of course, who, as you know, owns this yacht with his delightful wife Victoria."

I pushed past him and stomped inside to hand my bottle of gin over to my hosts. Gregoriano followed me. He grabbed two glasses, bulbous in shape with a long-handled, twisted spoon in each of them.

"Ice?"

I nodded.

He poured gin from high above allowing it to cascade along the handle of the spoon and splash onto the ice. "Tonic?"

"A little – to cover the ice and no more. Where are Alfonso and Victoria?" I heard my voice gruff and unfriendly.

"Unfortunately Alfonso and Victoria cannot make it – better plans have come up for them. You know the way it is on the island in their circle of friends. There can be last minute changes when a better offer comes along.

They have kindly offered us the yacht. I can sail it for us to Deia."

"I can sail a yacht as well you know." I threw myself onto a wooden backed chair. "I'm not a fool who needs to be mollycoddled." Then I changed the subject. "You've shaved your beard off? Why? You've had that beard for forty years."

Gregoriano laughed, ignored my comment about his beard and pointed at the steering wheel. "No, you're not a fool but you are an angry, proud man. It's all yours. You take the yacht out. I will rest. I've been busy." He sipped a small amount of gin, placed the glass on a table beside the sofa and threw himself on top of feathery cushions. "What would you like to talk about?"

"I'd like to talk about why you are messing with my life. Are you some kind of control freak who likes spying on people and telling them how to live their lives? I should report you to the police and get a restriction order."

Gregoriano sat up on the sofa, stirred his gin and tonic and smiled at me. "I see that your temper hasn't improved. As for the police, I am sure there will be an engagement with them for you at some point in your life." He took another sip of gin. "You haven't gone very far on your journey since the first time we met. I might even say that you've regressed but then life is a spiral rather than a linear staircase. You're simply taking a rather long diversion backwards and downwards. You might want to talk about why that is happening. We have all day."

I thumped the table making the gin glasses wobble and the silver spoon tinkle against the edge of the glass. I was convinced that Gregoriano orchestrated the non-appearance of the yacht owners because he was hatching a plan of sorts. He wanted to extract something from me. I jumped to my feet. "I will take the wheel." I marched outside and gripped the steering wheel. The yacht eased onto waves, out of the Port of Soller where I swung to the left.

Inside Gregoriano swiftly fell asleep on the sofa. I looked in through the window to see him curled up like a cat and heard his soft snoring which could have been mistaken for purring. For a moment he seemed childlike. His hands were clasped together as if in prayer, his eyes closed, his mouth a little open from which emerged a purring, silence, purring again.

I guided the boat gently through the waves in order not to waken him. It would be easier to survive the day together if he slept. He wakened as I steered into Deia cove. Without speaking we dropped anchor and climbed down the passerelles to the beach to lunch in the restaurant. Gregoriano walked ahead of me skipping up the stone steps which led indoors. Inside we found a table near a window so that we could gaze into the turquoise swirling waves. The restaurant was only half-full of wealthy looking families – no doubt passengers from the yachts bobbing in the bay. I recognised a famous film star at one table and a pop star at another. They stared at us as if trying to decide whether we were interesting or not. A man at a table near the door pointed at me and then turned to whisper to his partner. He recognised me as the Painter.

I smiled at Gregoriano for the first time that day and leaned forward and whispered. "That man over there recognised me."

"Did he indeed? Marvellous. Do you recognise him?"

"No. I don't think so."

"What a shame."

He didn't explain what he meant by that. I thought perhaps the man might be interested in buying one of my paintings, especially as I had lost the opportunity today with Alfonso and Victoria.

"Should I introduce myself?"

"I don't think you would like to do that. He is unemployed. The owners here do charity work for the Red Cross. Once a month, they invite a dozen homeless people to a free lunch. Generous of them don't you think?"

Gregoriano ordered a Spanish omelette with salad and a bottle of sparkling water. I ordered the same. I wanted this lunch to be over as soon as possible.

When the runny omelette arrived, Gregoriano leaned towards me. "It's going to get worse for you – you know that?"

I shook my head. "I don't know what you are talking about. Life is good."

Gregoriano paid for lunch. I didn't thank him for it. I wondered how he earned his money and where did he live? Did he still live in the Castle which I couldn't find no matter how hard I searched the paths leading off the Barranc. How did he know what the Red Cross were doing in Deia?

We walked down the steps and I noticed that in the short time we had eaten lunch, the cove had emptied of yachts. There were a few people swimming and others trying to remove sand from between their toes. I thought 'what a waste of a life'. They were going to walk in that sand again. Then they would remove the sand again and again. Sisyphus came to mind, condemned to rolling a ball up the hill only for it to run down again.

I had to walk onto the yacht up the passerelles once again following Gregoriano. This time I had an anxiety attack. I hyperventilated, sweated and gasped at the air. Gregoriano looked at me from on board and returned down the passerelles to the pier. The fact that he reached a hand toward me, made me feel more panicky. I couldn't touch his hand. By now there were at least twelve people watching from the restaurant. I found myself laughing loudly as if to say to them that nothing was wrong with me. I wanted to convey that I was mentally sound and would be on board the yacht within minutes. I didn't want to get onto the yacht because I knew with Gregoriano's presence in a confined space, I would be forced to learn something or to say something.

Gregoriano manoevered behind me. He embraced me, holding me tight around the waist, saying, "Move forward, one centimetre at a time. Look up. Don't look at the water."

I edged anxiously forward. He continued to hold me around the waist from behind. I laughed aloud again to appease the increased number of people watching, not only from the restaurant but those swimming in the water and sitting on the sand.

With so many eyes on me and Gregoriano's arms around me inching me forward, I successfully made it on board.

Gregoriano took the steering wheel. I sat inside for a few minutes and then made my way towards him. There was something I had to tell him, but first a question: "You said that my life was going to get worse. What do you mean by that?"

The yacht rolled from side to side as a storm approached within a wall of black clouds rolling towards us from the West. Thunder crackled overhead. A lightning bolt hit the mast. The yacht shuddered. There was another bright flash and thunder.

"Something drastic needs to happen in your life for you to understand what you need to change."

"Drastic?"

Gregoriano steered the yacht to the right. "Yes.

Drastic. But that is not what you wanted to say to me is it?" Looking out to sea, he whispered, "I know why and how you did it."

"Did what?"

"You murdered your father, Paco."

I sat down on the wooden seat to his left. For a few minutes, I couldn't talk. I could hardly breathe. I looked at him. He stared straight ahead at the horizon.

"How do you know?" I held onto a metal handrail behind me with both hands. Gregoriano continued steering, turning the wheel vigorously left as the yacht leaned forty degrees to the right.

Gregoriano replied without answering my question. "You were fifteen at the time."

I nodded. "I will never forget that day."

"That's good. Don't forget it. Learn from it at the deepest level of your being and move on."

"You see my father was a difficult man to live with."

I stopped to catch a breath. Gregoriano responded, "And you're not?"

I didn't know where this conversation was going. "My mother is a saint."

Gregoriano shouted at me above the next crash of thunder. "And you're not?"

Gregoriano looked into the dark grey, bulbous storm clouds. I closed my eyes. I released one hand from the handrail and pushed my fist into my mouth. I briefly bit at my knuckles.

I said, "You see he was bad to her. I had to watch what he did and to listen to him. He enjoyed what he was doing. He was a painter like me, but he did not have a heart." I knew what Gregoriano would say next.

He did say it. "And you have a heart?"

"I have a bigger heart than my father. He was a Cubist. There were no wavy lines in what he did or how he lived. It was easy for him to use a knife to cut through a heart. I couldn't bear to see my mother suffer any more. One day, I heard him argue with mother in the kitchen. She did not reply in anger. The fact that she did not defend herself made me all the more enraged. I hid behind the sofa in the living room. When he entered the room, I took my chance. I hit him over the head with a chiselled stone from the garden – with one of his sculptures with sharp edges which he had created. He didn't see me. I watched blood trickle onto the tiled floor. It was thick and purple. I thought that blood would be red. It was syrupy and glistening. I thought it would have been watery. His body twitched once or twice before ..."

Gregoriano stared again into the clouds before asking, "I can imagine. What happened next?"

"My mother called the Doctor and convinced him that there had been an accident in the garden – a branch had fallen from a tree in a storm and had hit him on the head. The Doctor didn't question her. She was known for her kindness of heart and brutal honesty. She was considered totally trustworthy. Of course, we both knew that it wasn't true."

Gregoriano steered into choppy waves. "Do you continue to think that she is a saint, in spite of her telling lies?"

"Yes, I do. Saint Gregory the Great refused to pardon one of his monks on his deathbed for confessing to stealing a few coins. That doesn't seem to be the work of a saint and he is considered one of the greatest saints in the Church – hence the word 'Great'. What do you make of that?"

"Saints aren't always perfect. Nobody is. What makes them different is that it is their intention to put God first in their lives. We never know another person's intention. They rarely know it themselves."

9

PABLO PICASSO

"When I die, it will be a shipwreck, and as when a huge ship sinks, many people all around will be sucked down with it."

After our day together on the yacht, Gregoriano appeared at an exhibition which I held in Palma following Ishmael's arrival and before we had the party to celebrate the inauguration of the garden. He asked me how everything was going. I told him that I had a new Gardener. He seemed interested. I was glad to find a neutral topic to talk about with him.

He asked, "What is he called?"

"Ishmael."

"Where is he from?"

"I don't know. I heard about him and his work from a good friend in La Coruña. He worked there for a while before accepting the offer to be my gardener."

"What do you think of him as a person?"

I blushed. Ishmael had been living in Can Animes for about six months, but it felt as if I had always known him. I didn't want to say those words as for some reason I was embarrassed.

I looked around for a glass of champagne for us both before saying, "There's a lot to learn about him. He doesn't say much about himself. He is a good worker and an unbelievably talented gardener. The garden is a breath-taking pure work of genius. We are going to celebrate its success soon."

Gregoriano sipped on his champagne and then let out that chuckle which I found annoying in him and amusing in Ishmael. He threw his head back and closed his eyes. While they were closed, I noticed that he was dressed much more smartly than normal. He had a white shirt and a blue tie with pink flowers, black linen trousers and well-polished black leather shoes with exaggeratedly pointy toes. I wondered how a man of seventy years of age had dark black hair. It didn't look dyed. He had one of those straight partings on the left, with a long fringe and shaved short at the sides.

After he had stopped laughing, he said, "He sounds as if he will be good for you. Congratulations."

I was becoming bored and restless with the 'I have an opinion about what is going on in your life' attitude from him. I decided to be direct. "How will he be good for me?"

Gregoriano placed the unfinished glass of champagne on a silver tray on the table. "Remember the three pieces of advice you received when we met in the Castle. You haven't acted upon them. Maybe he will help you to fulfil them."

He was talking about that piece of paper again –
the one he gave me when I was ten. I thought, 'this is
ridiculous. Why doesn't he talk openly about what it
means and why he gave it to me? That would be more
helpful rather than talking to me in riddles. It felt as if he
enjoyed torturing me'.

He left the art exhibition, as he always did, without
me understanding who he was and why he was there. Yet
with each passing meeting with him, I had an increasing
sense that he genuinely cared for me. What was puzzling
was why did he care for me? Why would a stranger care
what happened to me over a forty year period? How did
a stranger know so much about me?

10

PABLO PICASSO

"Every act of creation is first an act of destruction."

Tuesday 6th June 2017

The last time I saw Gregoriano was four months ago. He didn't see me.

I had decided to climb up the valley from Soller. Not up Barranc but instead took a path initially towards Fornalutx and before leaving Soller, turned left to climb towards a restaurant and the viewing point of the Mirador de Ses Barques. Ishmael was working on the rose garden which was in perfect bloom. He sourced a company who allowed him to name his roses after my paintings. Together we chose twenty paintings and four matching rose colours – Apricot Sunburst, Blush Pink, Ivory White and Classic Red. We named five paintings under each colour. Today he wanted to tie the names to the roses, dead head them, water them and train a selection of roses along a wooden garden arch pergola which formed the entrance to the rose garden at the centre of the orangery.

I was glad to escape from the Studio after a week of intense painting preparing for the exhibition in the Reina

Sophia. Ishmael and I planned to attend the inauguration together. He seemed enthusiastic about seeing my paintings in one of Madrid's most prestigious art galleries and about seeing other works of contemporary art. We also planned to visit to El Escorial, Toledo and Segovia.

I climbed steadily upwards, past the pomegranate and walnut trees. Walnuts from last year lay on the ground, black shells like soaked carbon balls crunching under my feet. Green oranges sparkled in the bright sun; chard on my left like leafy umbrellas pushed its way through the earth damp from a recent fall of rain.

Half way up the mountain I reached a small Chapel, beside a former convent for Augustinian nuns. The steep climb to the Chapel was well worth the effort as the Chapel reminded me of Gregoriano's Castle which I had been unable to find since the age of ten. The chapel roof was made of curved terracotta tiles, leaf-shaped like those in Gregoriano's Castle. It must have been the same architect who designed both buildings. Even though I am not a religious believer, I liked to stop by the Chapel on my walks to the Mirador, sit in the rocky garden and look down on the town of Soller.

I opened the wooden gate and made my way towards the chapel. As I neared it, I heard voices coming from inside. I recognised them both. One was of my mother, Monica and the second was that of Gregoriano. I breathed rapidly, aware of a sharp pain in my chest. I had to hear what they were saying without being seen. I clambered onto a thick flat rectangular stone. Through the stone latticed window, I saw to the right that the front door, locked on previous occasions, today was open. I scanned inside. There was a statue to the Virgin Mary near the altar table, beside her a flickering candle in a red holder, wooden pews and shifting my gaze, I saw Gregoriano and mother sitting together, looking intently into one another's eyes. Mother was talking.

I took a deep breath, unable to believe what I was seeing. Yet the mystery of how Gregoriano knew about the murder of my father Paco had been solved. I strained to listen and heard my mother say, "I'm worried about him. I have a premonition that something terrible is going to happen to him. Can you not do something?"

Gregoriano leaned forward on the bench as if he didn't want me to hear what he was saying. "I have already done something. I am doing something. You know that. I promised you that I would take care of you both."

Mother shook her head. "You do not know him as well as I do. He acts from dark places."

Gregoriano took my mother's hand and held it for what seemed a long time before saying, "I think we are making progress. I've told you what I've planned for next steps. He will be forced to change." Gregoriano leaned forward and whispered, "It is organised. It will work. Believe me."

11

PABLO PICASSO

"I am always doing that which I cannot do, in order that I may learn how to do it."

It was time for me to read the letter from Gregoriano posted in Sweden. I decided to read it in Ishmael's room in the West Wing. I rummaged for white linen sheets to make the bed. I hadn't been sleeping well. I wanted to lie in bed, find out what Gregoriano wanted to tell me and then, if at all possible, fall asleep.

I held the letter with a shortness of breath provoked merely by looking at the envelope. Ever since his meeting with mother in the Chapel, I had wondered what Gregoriano planned for me. I didn't see evidence of anything different happening. I hadn't the courage to tell Ishmael about the last two encounters with Gregoriano. I knew that he would be horrified that I had let two more opportunities go by without getting to the truth of who Gregoriano was and what he wanted from me.

Before opening the envelope, I lit a small log fire in Inglenook fireplace in the bedroom. I say bedroom but it was more like a monk's cell reminiscent of those found in

La Cartuja in Valldemossa where Chopin stayed in 1838 with George Sand for three months and wrote Preludes.

There was an oak door into the suite, which led into an area with a sofa and the fireplace, an en suite bathroom and a bedroom with French patio doors leading out into the patio with views of the swimming pool ahead and the mountains to the left. The sun shimmered on the turquoise water of the pool. Logs on the fire spat and hissed. I pulled back the sheets and crawled into bed. With my head sunk deep into the pillow, I opened the envelope and pulled out three handwritten pages, each with an embossed red cross at the top. The letter was dated Monday 2nd October 2017.

Dear Augustin,

It has been a while since we talked. I hope when you reflect on our relationship that you are able to intuit that I care for you. I know that our relationship is not a "normal" one but that does not mean to say that it not deep, authentic and meaningful. When I say "meaningful", I think we find meaning in the work we do and by doing something significant. We also find meaning in loving and caring for another person.

It may surprise you to know that I think your work is significant. You are a talented Painter. However, over the years I have seen that what you do does not have the authenticity and inspiration of your earlier days. It is as if you are making fake copies of your own art. You are an Emperor who has no clothes and no-one will tell you.

You do not seem to love or care for anyone but yourself. You are selfish and immature. I am sure that is upsetting to hear. You may feel that I have no right to interfere in your life. There is a reason why I am giving you this feedback. I hope you will one day understand that it is for your good and it is to fulfil a promise from the grave which connects our lives.

You are a creative person, applauded by the world. Your creativity cannot survive and thrive unless you are prepared to face your dark side. We all possess a capacity for destruction, decay and death within us, essential for the flourishing of creativity. By facing your dark side – you will know yourself deeply. In doing this work, paradoxically your bright side will shine in the world with greater intensity.

I offer you a new opportunity to love another person and to know yourself. It will take courage. It will enliven and invigorate the gift you have been given as a Painter and allow your work to fulfil its promise. However, this opportunity will contain a shock for you. I also know and care for Ishmael. There are reasons why Ishmael and I have not talked to you about the nature of our friendship. It does not seem appropriate to disclose these in a letter. I assure you, you will be told the whole story. It will make sense – not only about Ishmael's past but also about mine.

I invite you to come to Malmo, Sweden to meet

with Ishmael's flatmate Sophia and her son Oñé. Their relationship is complicated, as you may imagine, or Ishmael would have already mentioned her to you. Recently, Sophia has been diagnosed with cancer. She will need to undergo chemotherapy and radiotherapy. It should take no longer than six months. Sophia and I have talked and she has agreed that it would be a good idea for you to bring Oñé to Mallorca during this six month period. He will benefit from your company and you will learn from him.

I believe that the first question that you would like to ask is why has Sophia not contacted Ishmael and asked him to collect Oñé? It's a good question. Firstly, Ishmael left Sophia and Oñé under 'unusual' circumstances which you will find out about. Secondly Sophia is not the wife or partner of Ishmael and Oñé is not Ishmael's son. You will discover why he was Sophia's 'flatmate' in due course.

Imagine how different your life will be if you not only find a new meaning in your work, but also learn to deeply love someone other than yourself. Remember the words burning on the page in the Castle?

Oñé will tell you in his own time the circumstances of Ishmael's departure from Malmo. You will find him a talented precocious child. He will remind you of what you were like aged ten.

I will not be here when you arrive. However, Sophia is waiting for you. You will meet in the Turning Torso,

Malmo on Wednesday 11th October at mid-day. She will be downstairs waiting for you with Oñé.

You may wish to tell Ishmael that you are going to Malmo. That is your choice. It may encourage him to tell you the truth about his past and his relationship with Sophia and Oñé. Please come quickly. Sophia needs to ensure that Oñé is in safe hands as soon as possible to allow her to begin her treatment.

My love as always to you.

Gregoriano

12

PABLO PICASSO

"The people who make art their business are mostly imposters."

Sunday 8th October 2017

I packed a bag for Malmo. I wasn't sure which clothes to bring. I do not know why I am doing this. Yet what else is there to do? Ishmael is dead and I have no desire to paint. The letter from Gregoriano surprised me on many levels. There is the fact that Ishmael and Gregoriano knew one another. Neither inferred that was the case. Even when I explicitly talked to Gregoriano about Ishmael and asked for Ishmael's help in understanding what Gregoriano was doing in my life.

Then, there is the surprising revelation within the letter that Gregoriano cares about me. I have read the letter at least a dozen times. What does he mean by he is 'fulfilling a promise from the grave' and that we are 'connected'? The third major surprise and shock was the revelation of Ishmael being a 'flatmate' of Sophia. What does that imply? He never mentioned her once in two years.

I am scared about what to do about Ishmael. I don't

feel yet ready to tell the world about his murder. I will do it, but not now. How will I explain that he is not here? Is it right to bring Oñé to Mallorca to live with me on my own? I could destroy him. I don't know how to take care of myself never mind a ten-year-old child.

With unanswered questions, I arranged for a taxi to take me to the airport next day at eleven o'clock. I walked to the Plaza, ordered a cup of coffee in Café Soller and had a look at the local Sollerics and tourists. Coffee was served with what looked like a cube of breakfast cereal for a biscuit. I saw worn out faces, hips quivering on walking frames, balding heads of women, eyes searching, hoping for connection, blotches spreading across sun crevassed faces. Death was not far away for many.

Occasionally a beautiful woman, sitting to my right held her baby against her breast, swinging her long blonde hair from left to right with a watchful eye to see if anyone noticed. The baby seems to be an extension of who she was. Her lips, swollen red with Botox, were surprisingly enticing. I was shocked that a fleeting sexual desire tempted me four days after murdering Ishmael. However, death is obsessing me and at a second glance, I see that her eyes are dead, disguised by painted blue lids, with shades of purple and yellow.

Life in the Plaza, like the fallen leaves moving on the patio, reminds me that everything is changing. I can't see or feel anything that does not change. My face is changing, developing a subtle double chin. My eyes are no longer clear but bloodshot and blurred. There is a softening in the muscle around my stomach. I see change in all of its multiple forms implying the death of what went before.

At the foot of the steps of the Church walking across the Plaza, I saw a familiar face. It was Pep Conejo. I can't let the results of Ishmael's garden fall into decay. He spotted me waving wildly at him and turned in my direction. "Pep, I am so glad to see you. I've been meaning to talk to you. Please sit down. Let me get you something. Would you like a coffee, a beer, something to eat?"

I embraced him and he pulled away laughing. I think he was in shock. I had never embraced him before.

He sat beside me, looking at his watch. It was midday. "Well, it's nearly time for lunch isn't it?"

He waited for my reaction. I knew that he ate lunch around three o'clock. It didn't matter. He could have whatever he wanted. I raised a hand to catch the waitress's attention.

Elena arrived in her black jeans, t-shirt and apron. She had piercings in her right eyebrow, lower lip and the upper part of her ear. "Hi Agustin. What would you like?"

I turned to Pep. He rubbed his hands together as he ordered. "To start with I'll have spinach croquettes and baby squid. For the main course, salmon with that yellow sauce if you have it, potatoes, carrots, and a glass of red wine. Don't worry about dessert for now. I'll order that later."

For the first time since Ishmael's death, I heard myself laugh. "I'm glad to hear that – we need to put a bit of fat on you to get you through the winter. I'll have the spinach croquettes." I gave a thumbs up to Pep. "I'll join Pep with a glass of red wine. Thank you."

Pep rubbed his mouth with the back of his hand. "You're not having much are you? Are you on a diet?"

I wanted to laugh again, which I thought was a good sign. I have always found that people who were extremely skinny seemed to have weighing scale eyes. He probably knew exactly how many kilos I had around my waist and how many I had put on in two years.

"Well, I am not as active as you Pep. I can't help piling on the kilos with my lifestyle. But there's no fat on a skeleton. We might as well enjoy it while we can."

As soon as I said that, I remembered the sculpture and felt nauseous, unsure that I would be able to eat the croquettes when they arrived. Better to keep talking.

"Pep, I know I haven't treated you well. I'm sorry about that. You are a hard worker. I have no complaints about your work. I took Ishmael on as the gardener because he had specific experience in transforming the garden – to include a labyrinth, swimming pool, fountains, an orangery, a herb garden … You know he had done it before in La Coruña whereas you hadn't."

Pep took a toothpick from the pocket of his shirt and scratched at something stuck between his two front teeth. "You employed five Sollerics to help him. You didn't pick me. How do you think I felt? I could have learnt from Ishmael. It would have been good for me. I don't often get a chance to do anything new around here."

The red wine appeared. We took large gulps of it in synchronisation, setting the glasses on the table in unison.

"I see that you are annoyed with me. I don't blame you. I can make it up to you if you let me."

"How's that then?"

"I've been stupid Pep. Ishmael has up and gone. I don't know where. I'm left with a major problem. I need a gardener. I know you can do it, but do you want to do it? I know we had an arrangement to pay you in kind. You could take as much as you liked from the olive grove – fruit from the trees and olive wood for the fire. I am prepared to change that – you can take what you want, and I will pay you in addition the salary which I paid to Ishmael."

Pep sat back in the chair and stretched his legs out in front of him and looked me straight in the eyes. "What about back payment? I've been underpaid for years."

I smiled at him. "Don't be greedy. You know that it is a generous offer. There will be no back payment."

The tapas arrived. Pep popped a whole croquette into his mouth and swallowed it in one. I had forgotten that he only had two teeth. He mushed the second croquette against his gums for a few seconds before swallowing. Pep continued: "It doesn't surprise me what you say.

Don't get me wrong – I liked him – but I saw him with a couple of people that made me wonder about him. You know it's a small town. Everybody knows everybody. There's nothing goes unnoticed in Soller. If you sneeze someone in the Plaza will be talking about it five minutes later."

I gulped the entire glass of wine. "Who did you see him with?"

"That housekeeper of yours – Gabriela had coffee with him most Saturdays. They sat right here where we are, bold as brass. Not that I want to gossip about them behind their backs – a coffee is only a coffee after all. It's innocent enough. But did you know that they were seeing one another?"

I shook my head.

"That's what I mean. If it was as innocent as it looked, wouldn't he have come back from the Plaza and told you?"

I nodded. What a betrayal by Ishmael. I thought of those phone calls from the pay phone in Soller on a Saturday morning asking me what I wanted him to bring back for lunch and not a word mentioned about seeing Gabriela. Then again, if he wanted to have a relationship with Gabriela – what was wrong with that? He was, as far as I knew, a single man. He certainly didn't deserve to be murdered for having coffee with my housekeeper.

I remembered again how the gates had opened in the early hours of Thursday morning. I studied Pep. He had a remote control. Could it have been him? He had moved onto his salmon with hollandaise sauce and was mashing his potatoes. He didn't appear to be holding anything back from me, so I continued, "You said there was another person?"

Pep wiped his mouth with the cuff of his jacket. The napkin lay on the table beside his plate with the knife on top to stop it blowing off the table. "Yes. There is a strange man who lives somewhere in Soller. He doesn't often come into the Plaza. We normally know everything in Soller – who is selling their house, who's received money in a brown paper bag to complete a house deal, how much did they get, who's robbing whom, who has fallen out with whom, who's having an affair with whom, who's committed suicide and why they did it. Nobody knows the name of this stranger or where he lives. The only word about him is that he is a Doctor and he travels to those war zones you see on the television and treats the injured in the hospitals that have been bombed. If he is doing that then he is a good man – but he's not right in the head. I don't know of anyone in Soller who would jump on a plane and go to likes of Syria or Iraq, rather than stay at home with the family, make paella, have a few beers or a share a bottle or two of Rioja. You would have to be crazy to fly somewhere where the only lunch you'll get will be fired at you from a machine gun."

I took my time over the croquettes to encourage Pep

to keep talking. "You're telling me that you saw Ishmael with this man?"

"I am. Are you ready for your dessert?"

"Wait a minute. Where did you see him?"

"That meeting was a bit more suspicious than when Ishmael met Gabriela. The last time I saw the two of them together, was only last week – Tuesday. They weren't in the Plaza. I was on my moped on my way to Fornalutx. I took the road that goes through Biniaraix. There's a little café there that I sometimes stop by for a 'Pa amb Oli'- they do a great cheese one there with cheese from Mahon, olives and tomato. José, who owns it, is a good friend and every Tuesday we meet to have our 'merienda'. I stood talking with José at the bar and to my right I saw Ishmael with his back to me, talking in a low voice to the Doctor. He didn't see me. They seemed to be engrossed with one another – planning something I would say. Whatever they were talking about, it was serious. José called me into the kitchen at the back to eat with him. I asked Ishmael if the Doctor had been there before and if he lived nearby.

"He told me that they had coffee and talked for an hour or so, several times a year. They didn't pay attention to José. It looked to him that they didn't want anyone to know that they were there. He knew when to leave a client alone. There are not many places to hide in Soller and few local people from Soller would make a special journey to go to José's place in Biniaraix. It's a pity for

him in the winter as he barely makes a living. The spring
and autumn are when he can make enough money to
live on with the tourists climbing the mountains. He
didn't know where the Doctor lives but suspected it was
somewhere up the Barranc. Out of nosiness one day, he
pretended to be cleaning the tables outside and watched
where he went. It was in the direction of the Barranc.
There is only one other possibility that he could have
turned left before climbing Barranc, towards Fornalutx."

I signalled to Elena. "Pep, do you want another red
wine? A dessert?"

Pep scraped at the plate with the back of his fork.
"Yes, another red wine and apple pie with cream."

With the order placed, I leaned forward to Pep. "Pep,
if you see Ishmael around, you will let me know?"

He picked again at his front teeth, nodding yes.

I continued. "What did the Doctor look like?"

"Tall, dark hair, well-dressed. He looked as if he had
money. Well he would if he's a Doctor."

"Was there anything special about the way he looked?"

Pep nodded. "Those green eyes. I haven't seen anyone
with eyes as bright green as his. Though these days you
never know what's real or what's not. People with money
can wear coloured contact lenses."

My hands were sweating. I placed them on my
trousers to dry off so that I wouldn't give Pep a clammy
handshake when we said goodbye.

"Pep – do you accept my offer to start back as my

gardener? I'd want you to keep the garden as it. I don't need you to add to it or change it. I think that might have been why Ishmael left. He had done everything he thought that he needed to do. He told me that he had gypsy blood in him. I imagine that he's moved on to somewhere else. I would like to thank him and say goodbye to him properly if possible. It doesn't feel right to have spent two years with him and not to see him one more time. If you or any of your friends see him, let me know."

Pep wiped his mouth again and smiled at me, showing me those two front tombstone teeth. "You said that I can help myself to what is in the olive grove and have the same salary you gave Ishmael? If that's the case, when do you want me to start?"

"Tomorrow. I'm away for a while. I don't know how long but you know where everything is. You'll know what to do when you see it. You've got a remote control and a key haven't you? I'll pay you two thousand euros a month."

I imagined that Pep's two front teeth wobbled in his mouth when he heard that. You didn't get that kind of money for a job in Mallorca if you had been to University and were Head Teacher of the local Convent school.

I walked slowly home, letting the conversation with Pep Conejo play over and over in my head. I hoped that he would spread the word around Soller that Ishmael had 'disappeared', that I had been left in a bit of a hole and wanted everyone to keep their eyes open for him.

It had to be Gregoriano who met with Ishmael last Tuesday. He must have posted the letter in Sweden, caught a flight back and met Ishmael the next day. I tried to remember Ishmael's movements last Tuesday – the day before I murdered him. He told me that he wanted to buy a bag of fertiliser, a hoe and a bag of peat from Can Bibi, the hardware shop in the Calle de la Luna. I offered to drive him down to Soller.

He shook his head and told me, "You concentrate on your painting. You said that you wanted to make a few changes. I'm happy to walk."

He would have had time to walk up the Calle de la Luna all the way to Biniaraix, meet Gregoriano and call into Can Bibi on the way back.

13

PABLO PICASSO

"Are we to paint what's on the face, what's inside the face, or what is behind it?"

I am in Malmo, Sweden, staying at the Park Inn Hotel. From my hotel window, I see the Oresund Straits and the Oresund Bridge that connects Sweden to Denmark. It feels strange to be in a country I do not know. In Mallorca, the sun in winter warms the bones but when it disappears, it is like Sweden; there is a freezing cold with dampness sinking with a deathlike touch twisting my bones.

Since arriving I have sketched, written in my journal and walked along the seafront. I have not felt bored – rather I have felt safe. If the local police in Mallorca discovered that I had murdered Ishmael, they wouldn't find it easy to locate me here. I could keep running – catch the train back over the bridge to Copenhagen and if necessary find my way to Norway or Finland. It feels liberating to be away from the small island of Mallorca where crimes are more easily solved.

I walked alone along the seafront into a chilling breeze. I am looking for the 'strange place' recommended by the receptionist, where music plays twenty-four hours a day. I discovered a grassy rounded tomb-like mound only a metre from the seafront. I listened to morose, doleful music playing. It is interesting rather than depressing. Who invented this place of singing sirens? For whom are they singing … tempting? There is no-one here. Music played to frozen grass, reaching out to lapping waves, eroding shingle on the beach and to the screeching gulls circling overhead. It helped my mood. I can't be the same person when I am in a totally different culture, meeting people who are so different from those at home.

I sat on the grassy tomb, which is clear from snow but not from ice, looking out to sea, not worrying if my trouser bottoms were soaking in melting ice. The mound reminded me of Megalithic sites I have seen on my travels – passage tombs with large stones used to create chambers under the ground, where the dead were buried. Although I did not see evidence of a stone structure here, I imagined that it existed and that under the grass I was sitting on, were bones of those who walked the earth more than 5,000 years ago. They were the bones of the dead sleeping together, waiting for the winter equinox and for sun to stream along the passage to their resting place and to flood it with light and hope.

That subtle lightness of heart of enjoying being away from Mallorca and experiencing a new culture was short lived. On the way back to the Park Inn, a car drove along the main road beside me. It swung around menacingly with a handbrake turn. I jumped. I was edgy. I feared that there would be a reprisal for Ishmael's death, that I was not as safely hidden in Malmo as I had thought. I could be found at any time, in any place. The man in the car sneered at me as he drove into the distance. Of course, I may have imagined it. He also waved at me with a hand movement which seemed aggressive, but it might have been friendly or apologetic. I knew that I was unstable. I had yet to meet Sophia.

14

PABLO PICASSO

"I don't believe in accidents. There are only encounters in history. There are not accidents."

Wednesday 11th October 2017

Today I will meet Sophia and Oñé. It is one week since Ishmael's murder. I constantly check the time after a breakfast of pickled herrings, tomatoes, lettuce and rye bread. The meeting is planned for midday.

I saw the Turning Torso – the tallest building in the Nordics – twist into the sky from my bedroom window. It won't take more than fifteen minutes to reach there from the hotel. Nevertheless, I check at reception the exact directions to take. I don't want to arrive late.

At eleven forty-five I stumbled along a path by the canal until I reached the Turning Torso. I stared up at it. It was a marvellous construction, twisting into the air like a corkscrew. There was something about the off-centeredness of it, holding it together – I wished that I could do that with my mind.

I looked at my watch. I was eight minutes early, so wouldn't go inside. I stood outside with the smokers and looked up again, this time watching a heavy mist hang over the top of the Torso draping itself around the penthouse like an octopus enveloping its prey. The smokers went indoors, leaving me alone. My head feels full of water as if the canal is emptying itself into me with the immensity of the water touching Malmo and the edges of Sweden – the Oresund Straits, to the west, the Baltic and the North Sea. That intensity of that water holding cargo boats with steely structures heading out into an unknown world, captured for me the Swedish mind. It is a mind of merchandising, heady thinking, emerging from darkness. My thoughts – I cannot catch them – are bobbing on the surface of my mind, floating westwards, beyond reach.

I am fickle. Yesterday I thought that I felt safe and free here in Malmo. Today I miss the mountains of Mallorca in this flat and watery land – mountains pushing out from the sea with strength coming from deep in the earth. I miss pomegranates splitting open with real life – giving seeds; kiwis hanging hidden and unnoticed within emerald leaves, oranges dropping onto a fertile soil with their lemon neighbours, olives crushed by the hands of locals who know how to split them to let salt enter into olive bones. It's an island vital, organic, and promising – a beating heart within soil tilled by solid men of the earth.

In Sweden a December of darkness is approaching. In Mallorca on sunny days, we will have small delicate yellow flowers spreading through winter green. The sea will sparkle and clouds will pour over the mountains trimmed with white fur soaked in sunshine.

I look at my watch. It is midday. I climb the steps and push the revolving door.

I step inside. It is obvious who Sophia is. She has to be the woman sitting with a straight back gazing at me, holding the hand of a young boy who must be Oñé. Sophia smiles softly at me, her hair piled into a dark bun. She has the posture of a ballerina with a sense of strength within her body like that of steel that holds the Turning Torso and roots it into the earth. There is movement within her. I watch her turn and twist to look at me again.

At first sight Oñé seems to be a trembling, troubled child. He holds his mother's hand as if it was a life support. He looks at me with a penetrating stare. He had no fear of me.

Sophia rises to her feet, walking towards a table in the restaurant, gently pulling Oñè behind her, expecting me to follow. I obey. We shake hands. She leans forward and kisses me three times. I bend over to take Oñé's hand. I hold it between my two hands in silence. I act on instinct. I have no training in this world of children.

Sophia breaks the silence. "So, at last we meet, Augustin. May I present to you my son Oñé. Oñé I would like to present to you Gregoriano's and Ishmael's friend, Augustin. It will not be long before we get to know one another. It will be an adventure together. Let's sit down and have something to eat. I will explain."

She waves at the waiter. There is a grace about her movement as she bends over and whispers into Oñé's ear. "Would you mind playing over there for a few minutes?"

Oñé looks at her with a certain disgust – squeezing his forehead into a wrinkled frown. "That's for children. I'm not a child."

She smiles at him and gives him a kiss. "We won't be long. I will order your favourite fish."

He drops his mother's hand and walks slowly to the play area where there are swings, a slide and a small yellow plastic house with several doors giving access to the inside and a wooden ladder leaning against the front wall. Oñe climbs the ladder, sits on the red roof, looking at us like an owl, his eyes wide open, his ears listening.

The waiter arrives. Without asking me what I would like to drink, Sophia asks for two glasses of white wine.

"It's a Spanish wine – I thought you might like it." She moves closer. "I don't want Oñe to hear it again. He knows that I have cancer and need to receive treatment in the hospital for six months which will mean that I cannot take care of him. I have explained to him that Gregoriano suggested that he will enjoy life in Mallorca and learn how to improve his painting. I will visit as often as I can between treatments."

Her eyes water. I wipe her tears away with the back of my hand which I then withdraw seeing her shoulders shudder. I sip the wine. I tell the planned lie.

"Ishmael has disappeared. I don't know if he will

return. How appropriate is it for Oñé to come with me to Mallorca when I do not know when or if Ishmael will return?"

She nods as if she had expected that to be my reply. "Yes, he does that from time to time. Sometimes he can't cope with the slightest stress. He disappears to avoid it. That is a consequence of his Post-Traumatic Stress Disorder. I understood that, being a Nurse and having worked in Iraq during the war and then in Syria. It was more difficult in Iraq and Syria to treat PTSD than to stop the bleeding in a leg which had been severed by a mortar or to comfort a mother blinded by shrapnel."

The waiter returns to refill our glasses. Sophia orders lunch – Vasterbotten cheese pie for starters, fried herring with mashed potatoes, parsley butter and lingon berries. She waves at Oñé to join us. "He will be OK now to listen to us. He knows Ishmael's story."

As Oñé runs towards us, I quickly ask Sophia, "What happened to Ishmael?"

She hasn't time to answer. Oñé pulls his chair up to the table, cuts the Vasterbotten cheese pie in half, pushing one half to the side of the plate and eating the fried herring.

"My mother tells me that you will take me to Mallorca. I will miss school here. What are your plans to make sure that I do not fall behind in my education? I am top of the class here. I do not want to return and discover that is no longer the case. I have to work hard to be the best painter in the world like Ishmael."

Sophia pours Oñé a glass of water and hands him a bread roll with a dish of herb butter. "Let's talk about that a little later. Augustin asked me a question about Ishmael. I need to explain what happened to him. There is a lot to tell."

She laughs at me. "I suppose we were all like that when we were ten."

I interrupt. "Oñé said that Ishmael is a painter. I only knew him as a gardener. Is that true, that he is a great painter?"

She eats a small portion of herring and Vasterbotten cheese pie, slipping it into her mouth delicately as if she could only open her lips a few centimetres and no more.

"Yes, it's true. He is a gardener but that was self-learned under difficult circumstances – creating gardens in the deserts of Syria. His education, training and practice lay in the world of art. What has he told you about his life? I do not want to repeat what you already know."

"He has told me absolutely nothing, other than to describe the work he did in Jose del Pardo's garden in La Coruña. I asked him on several occasions to talk to me about his life before La Coruña. He promised that he would. He never did."

I stop. My breathing speeds up. My heart flutters like a butterfly trapped within a glass jar. I am sure that Sophia can see it flapping against my chest. I remembered Ishmael pleaded, begged with me before I murdered him to allow him to tell me why he changed my painting and about the two people who had an impact on his life – one of them who had to be Sophia.

Sophia fills my glass with water. "You are looking awful. Are you sure that you are well?"

I imagine that she is worried about whether I was fit enough to take care of Oñé. I cough into my napkin. "I think I might have a little food poisoning from the prawns I ate last night. It's nothing really. If you excuse me, I'll be back in a few minutes. Please continue eating."

I dash to the restrooms. Standing over the basin, I turn on the cold tap, splash my face and hold my head under the tap, gulping at the water. If only I had let Ishmael tell me what he wanted to tell me that night, it would have all made sense. Although it did not mean that I would not have killed him. Something took possession of me – a combination of anger, rage, pride and fear that I could not control once activated. What frightened me was the thought that it could happen again, maybe to Oñé. It was not impossible. I pat my face dry with a cotton hand towel, take a few deep breaths and return to the table. Sophia looks anxiously at me.

"Feeling better?"

"Yes, much better. Please go on. You were about to tell me about Ishmael's past."

Sophia sips her wine. "He developed Post-Traumatic

Stress Disorder from what he experienced in Syria. You will have seen the suffering of children especially on television. He was born and lived in Syria, in Damascus. The Civil War started in 2011 as a protest against the Assad government. Ishmael lived with his family in a residential part of the city. He was proud of its historic past. His life was a normal one before the war. He was a Lecturer in Fine Art at Damascus University. He enjoyed the fact that the courses he ran were both theoretical and practical. He liked to nurture students in developing their own unique artistic expression. He had a strong conviction that everyone had artistic talent. For him, art was an innate human skill."

She rubs her nose, circling the tip with one finger.

"Let me tell you what happened next. It is important for you to know how he came to Malmo. When the Civil War started in Syria in 2011, it was brutal but it was about to get worse. That first year it was not only adults but children who were executed and tortured in places such as Deraa, Homs and Latakia. Perhaps hundreds of thousands of children were killed. Can you imagine before they died, their sense of fear, abandonment and helplessness?

"Last year, after five years of war, they said in total more than a quarter-of-a-million people have died. You know about the attempts of families to escape the violence – over one million Syrians managed to get to Lebanon. Others were not so lucky. They tried to seek asylum in many countries and found themselves again on the receiving side of aggression."

I feel sweat rolling down the sides of my face. I begin to cough. Sophia passes me a glass of water.

"Would you like me to get some medicine for you? Do you want me to stop talking about it? You really don't look good."

I pull a handkerchief out of my pocket, wipe my face and sip the water. "Please go on. It is quite an emotional story that you are telling. I realise that I have not been sufficiently aware of the Syrian situation. What then happened to Ishmael?"

"You will have seen that he is a compassionate man. He went to Deraa where the children were being killed to see how he could help in the refugee camps. He found a camp run by the Red Cross. He worked with them distributing food to those who had fled the town and offering drawing and painting classes to help them express how they felt in this situation. He thought that this would help reduce and minimise the pain and fear held in their bodies. When he returned to Damascus in 2012, the war had escalated, and his parents' house had been struck by mortars. The family were all killed – his parents, two brothers, a sister, two uncles, three aunts and all their children. He was alone."

"What did he do?"

"He returned to Latakia and Homs, again found the Red Cross through his previous contacts in Deraa and

continued to help distribute food and teach the children
in the refugee camps to draw and paint. He tried to escape
from Syria but it was impossible to get a Visa. He tried to
get to Lebanon without success. When the refugee camp
he was working in suffered a mortar attack, hundreds of
people were killed and more injured. That was when he
met Gregoriano."

I jump to my feet, pressing my hands into my temples.
"What are you saying?"

"Did you not know? Gregoriano is a Doctor who
primarily works in war zones. In Syria he worked with
physicians for Human Rights and the Red Cross. When
he came to help the injured in the refugee camp outside
Homs, Ishmael helped him. Gregoriano learnt of his
situation and helped him to escape. He had a house in
Malmo which he had bought for Oñé and I. There was
a spare bedroom. I am a nurse with knowledge of Post-
Traumatic Stress Disorder. It was straightforward. I could
help him to recover. I knew what to say and what not to
say. It is easy to misinterpret the behaviour of someone
with Post-Traumatic Stress Disorder if you do not know
that they have it. They can feel alone, isolated, suicidal."

Oñé interrupts when he sees the opportunity with my
pause. He pulls at Sophia's sleeve. "Mamma can I have
the Butterkaka for dessert?"

Sophia laughs. "Ask the waiter to get you some. It's on
the sweet trolley."

She smiles at me. "You have to know that he has a

sweet tooth. Butterkaka is a cinnamon bun with almond and vanilla custard. Would you like some?"

I shake my head. "No thank you – but please do have some."

"I am quite the opposite to Oñé – I don´t like desserts. Let me continue, Ishmael arrived here with Gregoriano's help in December 2012. He returned to painting. However, this time I could tell that he wanted to exorcise demons from within. In the same way as he helped the children in the refugee camps to express their emotions through colour and form – he turned his attention to doing that himself. I was concerned about him because he didn't seem to be resolving the pain within but rather it was as if he was drowning in it. The pain became his identity. Yet in Syria he had been able to help the children to release the horror which had grown within every cell of their bodies."

"You mentioned that be became a gardener in Syria. I don't imagine that could have been easy growing flowers in desert conditions."

Sophia nods. "It wasn't easy, but he wanted the children in particular to have hope in new life. In some refugee camps, they were lucky to have a small oasis for water and irrigation. He was able to find families with knowledge of how to grow Damask roses, Hibiscus flowers which he called 'The Rose of Sharon', Orchids, Henna, Evergreen Blackberry and a range of medicinal plants.

"Where it was dryer but there was occasional surface water he simplified the gardens to include buckwheat bushes, rice grass, little leaf horse brush and black sage. He constructed a fire pit and the families would sit close to the gardens by a burning fire, tell stories and smell the scent of new life in the air. They would crush sage in their hands and hold it to their faces in the belief that it would scatter the evil spirits who wished them harm.

"I tried to encourage him to begin planting again here, in our small garden and to leave the painting until he felt that he could cope with it in a healthier way. I only managed to convince him to plant purple heather and he planted three small trees – a Rowan tree an Oak tree and an Orange tree.

"He couldn't seem to leave his paintings. They were obsessions for him and when he left here he was in a bad way. I worried what would happen to him. It was a relief when Gregoriano told me that he was in Mallorca with you. Gregoriano assured me that you were taking good care of him."

She pauses, pouring Oñé another glass of water and patted him on the head and asking, "You liked Ishmael, didn't you Oñé?"

Oñé pushes another spoonful of Butterkaka into his mouth, staring at the plate. He mutters through the cake, "Sometimes."

Sophia raises her eyes with a smile. "He's annoyed that he left us. It's understandable. He's too young to understand." She strokes Oñé's cheek and asks, "What was Ishmael like with you? I mentioned that people who suffer from Post-Traumatic Stress Disorder can be irritable – even aggressive. They struggle in extreme cases – Ishmael was an extreme case – to experience positive emotions such as happiness or loving feelings."

"No he wasn't like that at all. He seemed happy, with a wicked sense of humour, full of love and warmth for everyone he met. He was thoughtful. He didn't seem to think about himself."

Sophia beams a smile at me. "That's wonderful news. He wasn't like that when he arrived here in 2012. You must have treated him well. I am sure that he will return to work with you." She looks as if she is having second thoughts when she asks, "Did something happen to make him leave Mallorca?"

I shake my head. "No, quite the opposite. He seemed to be enjoying making sculptures and improving the garden."

Sophia looks me directly in the eyes. "That's odd. I don't understand it. There must have been something happening for him which he didn't feel he could share with you. You said that he never told you about his life in Syria. Perhaps keeping that a secret from you took a toll on him."

She looks at Oñé, who is sitting looking glum, elbows on the table and staring straight ahead with his head in his hands. "Maybe we should go for a walk now. I think Oñé is getting bored."

She kneels on the floor beside Oñé, buttoning up his quilted coat and placing a navy scarf with embroidered golden planets around his neck. As she puts on her own coat, I notice for the first time that her lips have a blue tinge. Her skin is white and transparent showing small blue veins around her neck. She looks fragile yet strong. After all, she is a survivor from what she had seen in Syria and Iraq. How did she avoid the emotional damage which had scarred Ishmael? Maybe she hadn't avoided it – it had instead emerged as cancer. I imagined that she did not mention her own suffering to Ishmael. That could not have been healthy, to sacrifice her own emotional needs to help Ishmael.

We walk together along the seafront in the direction of 'the strange place'. Sophia holds Oñé's hand. I watch carefully, attempting to learn how he is used to being treated, so that I can imitate what she does for him. He pulls her hand, trying to release his own. She speaks in a gentle voice to him, one which I know will be challenging for me to mimic.

"We're by the sea. It's dangerous. You have to hold my hand. When we get to the park, you can run around and chase the seagulls, but not here."

I think she's being overprotective. I would have let him run along the path. I couldn't see what harm could come to him. Oñé pulls again at Sophia's hand.

"Please, I promise not to run. I'll stay away from the sea."

Sophia releases his hand. "Don't go out of our sight."

When he can't hear us, Sophia explains: "It's not the sea that I am worried about. It's this place, Malmo. It's dangerous.

"Earlier this year, the police appealed to the public for help in solving a dozen murders and eighty attempted murders in the Rosengard district. It's an area where 80% of the inhabitants are migrants and less than 40% of the district's residents have a job. There was a terrible murder in January of a sixteen-year-old Iraqi boy called Ahmed Obaid who was shot dead. People were terrified when threats against his former schoolmates were posted under the photo of his dead body. This is a violent city of murders, beating, rapes, bombings, shootings and arson attacks. I am afraid about him being abducted – even on this path someone could take him if he is not close by to me. I fear that he could be forced away from me, even if I was holding his hand. I know that sounds crazy. Maybe I am paranoid but that is why I want you to take him to Mallorca.

"Of course, I have friends here but I would worry every day during my absence what might happen to him. He has Arab blood. You can see that, can't you?"

"Yes, I can. He has a handsome face – a straight nose, beautiful intense brown eyes, high cheekbones, an olive complexion – he will go unnoticed in Mallorca. It is a perfect place for him to stay for a while. It is peaceful. He will be in no danger. I can assure you of that." I laugh. "We have our Moorish past which is evident not only from the beauty of the olive terraces but is reflected in the faces of the men and women of Mallorca, our music, our sculptures and philosophy. It will be a pleasure to spend time with Oñé."

Sophia looks straight ahead and gasps. "What is he doing?"

As we are talking, Oñé has run ahead of us. He has reached the pier, separating the walkway by the sea from the cargo ships in the Port area. He now sprints along top of pier chasing a seagull which totters quickly ahead of him, taunting him.

Sophia and I race together towards the pier. As we approach the pier wall, cargo ships pull out from the harbour and sound deep warning horns. I scramble up a ramp of hard snow with Sophia behind me screaming at Oñé to come back.

My feet slip on the icy top of the pier. I watch Oñé reach into the air as the seagull launches itself into the sky. He slips. Everything is in slow motion. His feet seem to take a few seconds before they disappear from sight and the sound of the splash below appears too gentle to be that from waves which have opened their watery hearts to embrace him. Sophia shouts hysterically behind me, words which I cannot understand. I reach the end of the pier and frantically look into the water. Oñé bobs on the surface, his scarf floating away from him. For a brief moment I see his terrified eyes, wide open, before his head disappears under the waves. I jump.

The water is icy cold. In the silence beneath the waves, I open my eyes. At first, I can see nothing. I swim to the left, in the direction of the scarf. Then I see Oñé. His hands point upwards towards the surface which is only a short distance above us. He kicks frantically with his legs and flaps his arms but makes no progress moving towards the surface. I kick my feet desperately, simultaneously pushing water away from my sides with fast rhythmical precision. I catch him by the coat, placing my arms under his armpits and pointing us both towards the surface, moving my legs with extraordinary vigour and energy which comes from I know not where. We break through the surface and I hear Sophia screaming at us before throwing us a lifebelt which splashes on the choppy sea before drifting within reach. I manage to slide the ring over Oñé's head and then pull his hair to get him through the ring. I hold tight onto the lifebelt and push us towards the shingle beach where Sophia now stands quivering and silently gasping with her hands over her mouth.

We have only been in the water for one or two minutes but we're both shivering and trembling. Oñé lies horizontal on the tiny pebbles. I check his pulse. Fast, but he seems to be OK. I perform CPR in case water has entered his lungs. He moans a little, watching me with open eyes. His lungs are clear. Sophia removes her coat. I strip Oñé's from his shaking body, replacing it with Sophia's. She kneels beside him and wipes his face with her scarf. She turns around and looks at me.

"Are you alright? An ambulance is on its way."

I nod. "I'm OK. A blanket would be appreciated."

I'm aware of how understated that sounds. My heart races and my breathing is shallow, erratic as I rapidly suck in air. I begin to violently shudder when the siren from the ambulance gets louder and it screeches to a stop on top of the pier.

Oñé and I are kept overnight in Malmo Hospital for observation. We are together in a private room and Sophia spends the night in the room with us, on a lazyboy lounge chair recliner with a Nordic quilt over her, close to Oñé. She holds his hand as he sleeps. I find it difficult to relax at all but I lay on my back, with my eyes closed and pretend to be asleep.

The following day we head to a pizzeria on the Salongsgatan Street, near the Turning Torso. Oñé whimpers apologies to Sophia and thanks me. I wasn't sure if the words coming out of his mouth were sincere or whether he had been coached in what to say by Sophia. I judge by the look in his eyes that it was the latter. I eat my pizza with smoked salmon and rocket lettuce and have to admit that my life saving act of heroism hasn't brought with it a glimmer of fondness for Oñé.

I don't share that thought with Sophia. I feel obliged

by Gregoriano to take care of the boy in Mallorca. The fact that I didn't like him was evidence that Gregoriano was right in his assessment of my selfishness. I would learn something. The events for Sophia had removed any lingering doubts she may have had over my suitability to do so. If she knew what I really thought about him, I was convinced that she would not have let him leave Malmo to stay with me in Mallorca.

My mind compulsively returns to an unanswered, unspoken question which I have for Sophia but cannot bring myself to ask. Who was Oñé's father? Why could he not take care of Oñé for six months, if he was still alive? Why did Gregoriano choose me to be a temporary guardian of Oñé?

15

PABLO PICASSO

"It takes a long time to become young."

In the Park Inn I lay in bed pressing my head into the feather pillows which I dragged halfway down the bed. For the first time in a long time, I had a night of unbroken sleep. Sophia had asked me to book flights to return with Oñé to Mallorca on Wednesday 18th October. That would be three weeks since Ishmael's death. I imagined that for the rest of my life I would be counting the weeks and that guilt and remorse would never diminish. A conscience emerging within me was my own death sentence.

I understood that prisoners on Death Row in the United States must have a certain sense of relief if their conscience is triggered, and that they are guilty, that there is a planned end to the debilitating odious feeling of guilt with an execution date in place. Everything which Sophia had told me about Ishmael's past made sense. It also increased my sense of forsakenness and alienation. Nobody would ever love me if they knew what I had done. I was alone with the knowledge of who I had become.

I took some relief in imagining myself walking along a tiled corridor towards an execution room where a wooden chair sat in the middle, surrounded by chairs for those who would witness my death. I visualised myself sitting on the chair, my head shaven, a watery sponge placed on top of my head, with drops of water running down my face, onto my shoulders. There would be silence from those watching, an inward gasp as they saw a black hood placed over my head. My terrified eyes and trembling lips would not be seen as electricity raced through my body. I would shudder and then be forever still. The only person who would feel compassion for me would be my mother, Monica. She would hold her hands over her face even though there was nothing to be seen other than the last twitching moments of my life.

The mobile phone rang, wriggling its way across the top of bedside cabinet. I picked it up and saw that it was Gabriela. I squirmed into the middle of the bed, the mobile pressed against my ear, my breath short and rapid. "Hello. Is everything OK?"

I heard her voice trembling and shaky. "Where are you? I have been up to Can Animes to let you know that I saw Ishmael in the Plaza. I didn't talk to him. I think he saw me and then disappeared down the street beside the Farmacia. I reported him as missing to the Local Police after you left. Do you think I should go back and tell them I've seen him and to say that he is not a 'missing person' but for some reason doesn't want either you or me to know what he is doing? The Police told me that they wanted to talk to you when you return as you were the last person to have seen him. What should I do? I don't think that I am mistaken in that I saw him." She paused and repeated, "Where are you?"

I squirmed up the bed to gasp for air. My heartbeat changed to a slower pace. I thought it would stop completely. I couldn't breathe properly. I jumped out of bed still holding the mobile phone to my ear and opened the window. I drank in cold air, melting like ice cubes in my throat. I pressed the phone close to my ear so that I did not to miss anything.

"I'm in Sweden."

"What are you doing there?"

"It has to do with Ishmael. It's complicated. I know more about where he has come from and where home is for him. He is from Syria. I thought that he had returned there to help his people but if you have seen him in Soller maybe that is not true. I do not understand why he wouldn't want to talk to you. Pep Conejo told me that you and Ishmael were closer than I realised. Is it true that you had coffee with him every Saturday in the Plaza?"

I was pleased with deflecting the attention from what I was doing in Malmo to Sophia's activities in Soller. There was silence from Gabriela which I broke by asking, "Did you know about his life in Syria?"

There was again silence which ended this time by her hanging up.

I paced around the bedroom, punching at the walls, feeling that I was going crazy.

I was sure she would ring me back. I should have realised that she wouldn't, not at all. She had heard my lies. She saw the darkness in my soul. Why would she me ring back? She knew something I didn't know and which she didn't want to share with me. I could have rung her back, but I had not the strength to continue with my lies. They were exhausting me.

I went for a walk before meeting with Sophia and Oñé. Snow had fallen heavily overnight and the pathways had been cleared to make this place walkable, driveable and liveable in its frozenness. The sun appeared today, and it sparkled on the snow, glimmering and flickering on and off like miniature Christmas tree lights. Overnight someone had made a snowman which had already been covered with another fall of snow which made it barely recognisable. Beside the snowman, obediently there sat a snow dog with a twig in its mouth. I couldn't see its eyes and imagined them to be dark brown glass marbles.

I felt my lips cracking open with the cold temperature. I wiped them. There was blood on my hands. I was not prepared for life in this land.

I decided that today will be the day I ask Sophia who is Oñé's father. I dismissed the possibility from my mind that it was Ishmael. There was a certain relief in the knowledge that I had not murdered Oñé's father.

We lunched together in a shopping centre café. There were people sitting alone, looking at one another in the way I look at people these days. They frighten me because I do not know them. I do not know what they do when they return to their homes. How do they pass the minutes of every evening, with seconds ticking by incessantly towards the next moment?

I look closely as Sophia and Oñé pull out their chairs and begin to look at the menu. My eyes scan the café. What about the man beside me, to my right? He looked at me. He is drinking a mug of something, tea or coffee. I can see he is going to make it last for several hours. What else has he got to do, to trample the snow outside, where there are no longer in the darkness sparkling diamonds but ice? He will walk crisply on the familiar icy ground and find his home.

Sophia ran her finger down the menu and spotted something for Oñé. She picked a reindeer hamburger with chips. For herself she chose a selection of pickled herrings with mustard, vinegar and something slimy which was most likely another member of the herring family. I ordered a pizza which was called 'sweet and sour' with beetroot, goat's cheese, rocket salad and honey.

Oñé went to the toilet. I took my chance to ask Sophia: "If you don't mind me asking – as Oñé will be with me for six months – who is his father? Is he alive?"

She helped herself to a glass of water. "Yes. You know him. Gregoriano is the father of Oñé."

She seemed matter of fact about it, as if it was obvious. I felt encouraged to continue with my questions.

"Is it safe for Oñé to go to the toilet alone, after what you have said about the danger of Malmo?"

"Yes, it is safe. I can see the door and I know the

waiter well. You can see that the waiter is also an Arab and is aware of the dangers." She smiled at me. "I'm glad that you are taking your responsibilities seriously. It's a good sign."

I pulled at my pizza with my knife and fork. It was soggy but quite tasty. I kept my eyes on the toilet door to stop talking when Oñé emerged.

"Does Oñé know his father?"

She stabbed at her pickled herrings which had arrived. "Of course he knows who he is."

"Why is he not here with you and Oñé?"

Oñé opened the door from the toilet and walked slowly towards our table. Sophia whispered to me before he sat down. "That needs a little bit more explanation. I can't do it now. You will have to trust me. Oñé knows that his father is Gregoriano. He has never seen him in the flesh, although I have shown him a photograph of him when he was a baby. Gregoriano held him. It was my choice that Gregoriano and I did not marry. We met in Iraq before Saddam Hussein's hanging in 2006. Oñé was born in Baghdad the following year. I can't say anymore, he will hear us. I will tell you another time, when we have more privacy. I think Oñé is secretly hoping to meet Gregoriano in Mallorca. Don't raise his hopes. Make up a story that will seem plausible if he asks about him. He knows that he is a Doctor and works in war zones. He knows he travels."

16

PABLO PICASSO

"The chief enemy of creativity is 'good sense'."

Oné is here with me in Mallorca. The day we landed at Palma airport, he asked me if he could see his father. I told him that his father Gregoriano had taken a little break – he had gone 'Walkabout' like the native indigenous Australians. Then he would continue with the work that he was doing in Syria. I am so used to telling lies these days it almost feels exciting to come up with one that is better than the one before. I wondered if he believed in what I said.

He asked, "Why does he choose to know you and Ishmael more than me, his son? I have never talked to him or seen him face to face. I only have this."

He opened a wallet and showed me two photos, protected behind plastic held in the leather frame of his wallet – one was of Sophia, with dark hair cascading over her shoulders and her blue eyes shining with what seemed to be genuine happiness. The second was that of Gregoriano, staring intently into Oné's eyes. I could not see whether he looked happy or not. Oné looked at the photos.

"My mother tells me that he is a good man who risks his life for others. I would like to know him. Why would he not want to know me? He could help me."

I made him a cup of thick hot chocolate and found a sweet muffin in the cake tin. I didn't want to eat or drink anything. I gestured to him to sit on the sofa and pulled a small table beside him, setting the steaming chocolate and bun beside him. "What help would you need from your father?"

Oñé bit into his raspberry muffin. "He can't help me to be like Ishmael, who is a great painter. My father is not a painter. But if he is brave in the way my mother has explained that he is he could help me to be a hero. I would like to be brave – that would help my painting. I could be the bravest man who ever existed, save people's lives in the way that my father does and also be the best painter in the world."

I didn't know what to say to him. I thought it childish nonsense. One day he would grow up and know how naive he sounded. I searched for what I thought Sophia would say in response. That was hard as she had not told me really much about Gregoriano. I took a portion of his muffin. "May I? There are more muffins if you want them."

He nodded. "You can have it. I don't want any more." He sipped on his chocolate.

I placed the muffin in my mouth and talked, eating with my mouth full as I knew that Oñé liked to do.

"I can't help you to be brave as I am a coward. Maybe you can teach me how to be brave. I think you know how to be that better than me. I will help you to paint – although I can't guarantee to be a better painter than Ishmael."

He stopped drinking his chocolate and ate the last of his muffin. "Why does no-one want to stay with me? Ishmael has left. My father never wanted to be with me and you will leave me too when Sophia is better."

I replied, "No-one who loves you ever leaves you. They are always with you."

He shook his head. "Then I have never been loved."

I gave him a second muffin. "No, you don't understand what I am saying. Even if people who love you are away in a distant land or even if they are dead they can still be with you if you touch their souls with your mind. They can never be apart from you."

"But my father never touched my soul with his mind."

I shook my head. "I think he did. You both did when you looked into one another's eyes. I saw it in the photo. He will never leave you. He's gone to help people who really need his help. That's what he does. He will return."

Over the next few weeks, I didn't know what to do with Oñé. I found being in his company tedious, frightening and also intriguing. I know it's an odd mixture of responses, but it is what life has become for me. It is confusing. What am I meant to do with this little lump of life? He decided that he will start school after Christmas.

So until then, I have to occupy him. I bought him a plastic beach ball even though summer is long over. I walked along the beach with him and threw the ball into the air for him to catch. I felt as if I was treating him like a dog. I didn't know what else I could say to or do with him. He ignored the ball as it flew into the beautiful blue sky and thudded onto the muddy sand. It had been raining for several days. I mostly detested having him around me. I even made him sit on the bench around the sculpture. I shocked myself at my own depravity, making Oñé sit within arm's reach of Ishmael disintegrating body.

I knew that there was possibly no end to how Oñé and I may want to surprise and hurt one another – consciously or unconsciously, over the next six months. For example, he ignored the ball which I threw to him. When we were back in Can Animes, he ran towards the sculpture and tapped on it, looking at me.

"What message are you giving with this sculpture? It seems pretty boring to me. Are you really a great painter? I suppose it can only be an improvement upon this sculpture. I like the other sculptures you created with Ishmael. I imagine that it is his influence that made them so good." He tapped at the sculpture again. "I don't believe he had any involvement in this. There is nothing of his soul in it. Let me see your paintings."

I wanted to slap him around the head. I did not know why I agreed to having him here. Maybe I hoped that I could fulfil Gregoriano's wishes that he had written on the page burnt in the fire in the Castle and repeated in his letter sent to me after Ishmael's murder – 'learn to love someone deeply other than yourself'. Instead I found myself loathing this tiny, spotty faced ten-year-old. I wondered if that was what Ishmael felt about him. "Maybe that was why he had run away, to escape him," I heard myself say.

"I do mostly installations, not paintings." That was another lie, but I wanted to impress him. I thought that he wouldn't know the difference between a painting and an installation. I would sound even more impressive than Ishmael. What could a mere boy know of world class painting?

He interrupted the dreamlike rambling in my head. "Let me see your work then. I would like to compare them with Ishmael's paintings."

He ignored the fact that I called my work installations. Without saying a word, I walked towards the front door and Oñé followed me. We trampled past the fountain, the sculpture, the herb garden, following the path to skirt the labyrinth and walked along the pebbled path towards the Studio.

I opened the door and sidled past a number of boxes which had been prepared to be sent to my exhibition in Japan. In the Studio I had one of my installations waiting to be hung in the Joan March hospital near Soller. There were five large tables onto each of which was draped a flimsy material. I had five more pieces of material hanging like curtains on the wall. The tables now looked to me to be like experimental beds for animal operations in a pharmaceutical 'sleep lab'. I began to think of my art collectors as voyeurs who liked to see the beauty of the world tortured onto a canvas or a piece of gossamer and silk.

Oñé looked at one of tables and drew his head close to the silk. He appeared to be listening for a heartbeat. I wondered if he needed glasses as he lowered his head towards the fabric and then touched a blue hummingbird made from a raised silk. He raised his head and asked, "What does it mean?"

"Mean?" I repeated myself to give time for a response. "Mean?" I scrambled to uncover a painting I had done earlier, awaiting final touches and covered with silk cloth. "What does this mean to you?"

He looked at it. It showed a chalice which contained business cards from friends, a host of a sun hanging above the chalice, spilling life into the cup which floated within a background of the mountains and waterfalls. Oñé looked at it and looked at me. "I like the Devil."

He pointed to the left of the Chalice where I thought that I had painted an olive tree. I saw that he was right. I had created a Devil side by side with everything that was good within and outside the Chalice.

I was not going to be disturbed by his observation. I would not let him get the better of me. "Interesting," I commented and then walked towards my installations.

"With permission and before you talk I will tell you that these are about silence and healing. They will be hung in the Joan March hospital for the terminally ill. It is my gift to ease the suffering of the dying. The birds represent new life and the space around them is a space of stillness from which the healing may take place or the transition can be made to calmly depart the body into the deathless realms."

Oñé replied, "It looks like toilet paper. It would be better cut up and placed into small rolls in their bathrooms."

I decided not to respond to this offensive taunt. Instead I asked, "Why don't you paint? I would love to see what you can do."

Oñé smiled at me. "Find me a large canvas and oils. I will be glad to oblige. I will recreate one of Ishmael's paintings – the one which led to the 'incident' as my mother liked to call it."

"What incident?"

"Did she not tell you about his illness?"

I nodded, feeling my breathing speeding up. Had this anything to do with Ishmael's Post-Traumatic Stress Disorder? I tried not to look too interested in case he might not continue. I straightened the installation lying on the table and cut with tiny scissors a loose thread hanging from the beak of a miniature eagle.

"Yes, I know that he suffered from Post-Traumatic Stress Disorder based on his experiences in Syria. But I had limited time with your mother. She did not have time to tell me all of the details of how this illness manifested itself in the time he was with you. What happened?"

Oñé looked around the Studio as if not paying attention to what I had asked. I knew that he had been listening. It was as if he searched for the answer to my question not in his head, but in the Studio. He no longer sounded confident as he continued, instead more like how I would expect a ten-year-old to remember what happened four years earlier.

"He arrived at our house in December 2012. I was five years old. I remember every moment that he spent with us – including him leaving the house in a panic before Christmas Day 2013. He left before my sixth birthday on Christmas Eve. He had finished painting a magnificent painting. It was a terrifying triptych which for me had elements of the influence of Hieronymus Bosch. There were three scenes, one within each pane. Ishmael explained to me that they depicted a modern version of a Descent into Hell, Judgement and Transformation."

I looked at Oñé. How could a child of ten be talking like this, know these things? It couldn't be real what I was hearing. It was as if he were channelling Ishmael. A child wouldn't have the vocabulary to be able to speak like this.

Since the death of Ishmael, I was used to my head spinning with feelings of confusion and nausea. I knew that I had to steady myself; I needed to find out more about Ishmael, the triptych and what kind of 'incident' seemed to have forced him to flee from Malmo. I asked Oñé in as gentle a tone of voice as I could to disguise my hysterical mind.

"What happened? What was this 'incident'?"

A white line appeared above his upper lip. I noticed his nostrils shaking in an extraordinary way before pulling down towards that white line above his lips. I felt my heart quiver with him although another part of me did not want to know his pain. I didn't want to be a part of it. I forced myself stay with this fibrillating heart.

He asked, "You really want to know?"

No. I didn't. Truth be told, I wanted him to be back with Sophia, with me having discharged my duties and never to know anything more about him. I looked at him. He looked away as if he could not bear my presence. If he was here, I thought I might as well find out as much as I could from him about Ishmael.

"Tell me what happened. When he returns, it will allow us both to help him."

I touched the hand which was dismantling one of my Albatrosses on the first installation. He picked out a part of a long wing and threw it onto the floor. The whiteness above his lip had returned to a normal shade of beige. I thought that I detected a few hairs of a possible moustache appearing on his upper lip. I felt flooded with a momentary compassion for this body in front of me that had little control over how it was being transformed from a child into an adult. I felt a responsibility to help him. He didn't look at me as he continued.

"Ishmael never asked any questions about what I thought about his paintings. He had arranged to have the last one installed in the Reina Sophia Museum in Madrid. The night before it was to be shipped, he decided to sit with it. He wanted to be alone. I offered to stay with him, as did mother. He refused. We went to our bedrooms.

"We don't know exactly what happened but around four o'clock in the morning there was a blood curdling scream from the sitting room where he sat. Mother and I ran downstairs and met Ishmael in the hallway. He slammed the door of the sitting room closed and shouted that we should not enter the room. His face was tinged green and his eyes were heavily bloodshot. He could hardly speak. He gulped at the air. He then told us that the panel on the left – the one symbolising a Descent into Hell – had 'come alive'. He was horrified that he had the power to bring Hell alive. Even though the painting was being sent to the Reina Sophia in Madrid the following day and that he wouldn't have to look at it again, he told us that he had to go away for a while.

"He said that he wanted to escape from himself. He explained as best as he could, that the painting moved into life and he saw himself moving within the scenes. Yet he had not painted himself in there. I so much wanted to open the door to the sitting room and to see for myself if it continued to move with life as he described. I thought that would have been wonderful to see. Mother stood in front of the door, blocking my way into the room, as if she read my mind. She said that I could only look at the painting in the morning when it was light. I think she was worried about Ishmael's state of mind and that by finishing this painting, he had triggered a memory of the Hell he had lived through in Syria."

"What happened then?"

"Ishmael placed his hands over his ears and ran upstairs. I wasn't sure why he did that. It seemed to me as if the figures in the painting were continuing to talk to him. Mother followed him upstairs and as I watched, I saw her in Ishmael's bedroom, helping him pack a small rucksack with cotton shirts and light beige trousers. I could see that he wasn't planning to stay in the coldness of Sweden. Because it was a small rucksack, I thought that maybe he wouldn't be away very long. I was wrong. It's now four years since he left. I don't know if I will ever see him again.

"Mother called a taxi. It was six in the morning. I watched how they said goodbye to one another. Ishmael stared beyond mother as he embraced her. His eyes settled on mine. They were filled with fear. He looked quickly away. I wondered if he could see that I couldn't tolerate his level of cowardice. I noticed that he hadn't bothered to shave or to wash. Normally he spent an hour in the bathroom, emerging with his hair gelled away from his face and a waft of Chanel trailing behind him like a smoke screen. His embrace of Mother seemed unreal. It was an automatic act of farewell. There was no real connection between them. She pressed her hands into his upper arms. I couldn't tell if she was pushing him away or attempting to give him energy. He looked floppy; like a plant wilting from dehydration. Then she kissed him on both cheeks. I thought it was as if she was settling on each cheek like a butterfly. The lightness of touch didn't seem to match the seriousness of what was happening.

"The taxi tooted. Ishmael didn't kiss me or shake my hand. He opened the front door and ran into the snow. Snowflakes settled on his hair like dandruff before melting. I heard him shout to the taxi driver, 'Copenhagen airport'. He closed the door of the taxi gently. He never looked back at mother or me. I watched the dark outline of his head move towards the front of the taxi as if he were talking to the taxi driver but I knew that he was only looking ahead, longing for the long bridge which would take him from Malmo to Copenhagen airport and after that I did not know where he wanted to go and when I would next see him."

When Oñé stopped talking, he looked at me, waiting for a response. There was an eagerness in his eyes to make contact with me. I knew he thought that I had understood him. Maybe I had, but his questions raised more questions for me than he was capable of explaining. I wanted to know why Gregoriano did not visit his son. I wasn't sure if he wanted to or didn't want to but that made the situation more complicated. Why did Gregoriano seem more interested in what happened to me than he was with helping his own son?

Oñé waited for me to reply. I had to do something to acknowledge the trust he had shown in me by telling me what he knew of Ishmael's disappearance.

"So you think that you can recreate this triptych which triggered some kind of Post-Traumatic Stress response in Ishmael? You are ten years of age. Creating this triptych seriously disturbed Ishmael. You have been placed in my care by your mother. How do I know that painting this will not cause you to have an 'episode' like that experienced by Ishmael?"

I didn't wait for his answer; instead, I pulled the installation from the first table and threw it on the floor. I thought that he would be impressed by how little regard I had for my art. His face remained expressionless. I walked slowly to the back of the studio and found an easel with a large new canvas and dragged them both towards him.

"Do you like to paint sitting down or standing up?"

Oñé rubbed his hand through his hair exactly the way I had watched Ishmael do. He narrowed his eyes as he asked, "Have you ever had a painting come alive?"

I shook the installation which I had thrown on the floor into the air. "Do you not see the birds flying?"

He laughed. "I understand why Ishmael would have

enjoyed his stay with you." He pushed a pine chair to one side. "I paint standing on my feet. I don't run away, no matter what happens. I want to be rooted to the ground when I paint."

I searched for oil paints laying them on top of the table, rummaged in a cupboard for turpentine, placed an array of brushes into a vase like a bouquet of flowers and pulled a large wooden platter from the wall for him to mix his oils.

"Begin."

He looked around the room. "Can I have an apron and a cloth?"

I left him arranging his colours on the wooden platter and ran down the path towards the house. The sun was amazingly hot for November. My face tingled. My feet stumbled a little on the pebbles. I cursed that I had not put a paving path instead of a moving, crunching sea.

I hated the fact that I was running. I felt like a dog and Oñé was whipping me into submission. That thought made me change my mind. I searched for a white sheet. I cut a hole in the top of it for Oñé's head to fit through. I hid the apron in the bottom drawer beneath the frying pan. "I couldn't find the apron but this will protect you from splashes."

Oñé placed his head through the hole and looked like a ghost. I sniggered. How could I have such an ambivalent response towards him? One minute I had empathy for not knowing what his father thought about him and the next moment I didn't care. He ignored me or pretended not to hear me as he stretched his arms into the shape of a cross.

"Thank you. I would have preferred an apron but if you can't find it I will find it later. I begin."

He chose a large brush which I hadn't cleaned properly. He dipped it into turpentine to soften it, left it in the turpentine and then squeezed yellow, blue, white, black and red oils onto the bread board which I had brought him as a palette. He gave the appearance of knowing what he was about to do.

The mobile rang. I didn't recognise the number and it wasn't in my contacts list. I immediately thought that it had to be the Local Police. Gabriela had said that they wanted to talk to me about Ishmael's disappearance. I wondered why it had taken them so long to ring. I had been in Soller a few weeks since returning from Malmo. I had begun to think that they didn't suspect me of Ishmael's disappearance, or they would have met me at Palma airport and escorted me for questioning by the Guardia Civil.

It was the local Police from Soller.

"We would like to see you tomorrow. We need to talk about the disappearance of Ishmael Domini."

17

PABLO PICASSO

"To draw you must close your eyes and sing."

Wednesday 8th November 2017

The Local Police in the shape of Jose Miguel and Pep Serrano arrived at ten o'clock. I made sure that Oñé was painting in the Studio before they arrived. I knew that he could be unpredictable in what he might blurt out. I heard the Police motorbikes rumble up the driveway. I pulled back the lace curtain to see them dismount from what looked like bright coloured toys with flashing antenna lights. They exchanged a few words with one another and then looked directly at the window. They had seen me.

I let the curtain fall into place and cursed myself for being so careless. I peered at them like a pervert who had something to hide. Of course I had something to hide and it was right in front of them in the sculpture. They wore black uniforms with dashes of white lettering. I thought that symbolised perfectly the mind of anyone who wanted to join the Police – black and white thinkers with no use of colour, no understanding of grey or paradox. They would need to find a 'baddie' set against a society of 'goodies', for which they were the foot soldiers. I continued to watch them through the lace curtain, stepping back a little to ensure that they couldn't see me. They swaggered towards the front door, looking around them through large black sunglasses. The dwarf- sized one pointed at the sculpture and they approached it looking into the fountain and around the garden. The taller one pointed at the labyrinth before touching his pistol and knocking at the door. I opened it.

"Pep Serrano from the local Police."

I shook his hand. "Agustin Silvero. I've been expecting you. You want to know about the disappearance of Ishmael Domini. Please come in."

Pep Serrano looked at his colleague, who also extended a hand. "Jose Miguel."

I waved a hand inviting them inside. "Delighted to meet you both. How can I help?"

Jose Miguel looked like a film star from a 1950s black and white Hitchcock movie – *Dial M for Murder* or maybe *To Catch a Thief*. He had a Clark Gable look – a dark bushy moustache, oiled black hair, brush strokes of eyebrows. Even in that short glance with the raised lace curtain, I admired his deep brown eyes, black locks stretching a little too far down his cheeks and his lips moving almost independently from the rest of his face. Pep Serrano was how I imagined Sancho Panza might look, as described in my favourite novel 'Don Quijote'. He was a small, squat man with a bulging tummy pulled tight like a balloon twisted by the belt around his waist into a snake shape.

I watched myself rubbing my hands together, not knowing what to do next after the initial welcome. Sancho Panza spoke in a determined voice which surprised me. He hadn't given me the impression that he was the leading officer on the case.

"Let's cut to the chase. We are here, as you obviously understand, to talk about Ishmael Domini. About his disappearance. Your co-operation is appreciated."

I took a few steps backwards. "Of course. I am more than happy to do so. Would you like a coffee?"

Sancho Panza scratched at his stubbly chin whilst Clark Gable folded his arms over his chest and stared at me. Neither accepted my invitation to sit and ignored my offer of coffee.

"Where is the son?"

"Who?"

"The son?"

Sancho Panza sat on the sofa, joined by Clark Gable. He snorted. "I see this is going to take some time. You seem to need everything repeated twice. Yes, a coffee would be welcome. What about you José?"

Clark Gable nodded. "It's always helpful to waken up the brain cells."

As I moved towards the Nespresso machine I fumbled with the pods and decided to give them a decaffeinated coffee. In a loud voice from beside the coffee machine, I said, "I don't have a son."

The Nespresso machine grumbled and spat.

Sancho Panza accepted his 'cortado'. "We are not talking about your son – but somebody's son. A boy who is living with you, who entered Mallorca with you on the 18th October 2017. Maybe it will help your memory if we remind you that his mother is Sophia Andersson. I am sure that you have his passport with you for identification purposes and know that he is the son of Sophia Andersson and Gregoriano Balsano. His name is Oñé Balsano Andersson."

I rubbed my nails across the stubble on my chin, imitating Sancho Panza.

"Perhaps you know more about this child than I do. I have only responded to a compassionate request by both Gregoriano and Sophia to take care of their child for a six-month period, while she is undergoing treatment for cancer. I have to confess that I did not know whether or not they were married, although I knew that they were Oñé's parents."

Jose Miguel and Pep Serrano glanced at one another. Pep Serrano clarified. "We did not say that the parents were married. They are not married."

I found his tone quite aggressive but replied in a gentle voice which I knew was essential when working with either the local Police or the Guardia Civil.

"I can find Oñé's passport for you if you wish?"

Clark Gable took control. "Thank you. We have certain details on file but would want to see the original passport. Do you have a means of copying it here?"

"Yes, I have a photocopier and scanner if necessary."

I was becoming bored thinking of them as Clark Gable and Sancha Panza. I was also afraid that I might say those names out loud by mistake.

José Miguel continued: "We understand that Ishmael Domini knew Oñé. What was the nature of their relationship?"

I sipped on my double strength espresso.

"Ishmael Domini is my gardener who left my home on the morning of Thursday 5th October for unknown reasons. He worked here for two years. Prior to that he was a gardener in La Coruña, working for a good friend, José del Pardo. I believe that he was one of the unfortunate immigrants from the conflict in Syria and took refuge in the house of Sophia Andersson with her son Oñé before leaving for La Coruña to work for José del Pardo."

Sancho Panza asked, "Did you check when he arrived here, that he had the correct visa requirements to work in Spain as your gardener?"

I shook my head. "No. To be honest I made the assumption, which I now know to be inaccurate, that he was Spanish."

"Are you aware if he had been involved in any terrorist activities in Syria?"

"I am sure that he had not. He was a Lecturer in Fine Arts at Damascus University. When his family were all killed in a mortar attack, he helped refugees under the guidance of the International Red Cross."

"Yet you had no evidence of this background, when you employed him as your gardener."

"That is correct. I accepted the recommendations and references for his work from my good friend José del Pardo."

"How did he develop his reputation and skills of being a gardener if his formal education was as a Lecturer in Fine Arts?"

"I knew nothing about his previous career of being a Lecturer in Fine Arts in Damascus until I visited Malmo and met with Sophia on the 11th of October of this year. I discovered that he had learned how to grow plants, shrubs, trees and medicinal plants in the refugee camps with the help of specialist knowledge from the refugees. He had a gift for making anything grow, which was quickly recognised by others. He knew that if could make plant life and trees grow in desert conditions, he could do that anywhere. He was right. I can show you around the extraordinary garden he created here if it would be helpful. You won't find another garden like this in Spain. I have photographs of what it looked like before he began his work. You can also speak to my previous gardener, who has returned to work for me. You may know him

– Pep Conejo. He is well aware of Ishmael's gardening genius."

Sancho Panza nodded his head. "That would be helpful. Let us see Oñé's passport, photos of the original garden and it would be helpful to see the new garden and have a word with Oñé before we leave ... today."

I could see that they were planning to return. They must have received more information to cause them concern than what they had chosen to reveal to me. I explained: "The photos are on my mobile. Let me find them for you."

I scrolled down through my gallery to the photos Ishmael and I had taken together of the old garden layout the week after he arrived. There were a few photos taken by Gabriela of Ishmael and me together; my arm around his shoulder, looking at him, whilst he stared straight ahead, smiling at Gabriela. I handed the phone over to Sancha Panza making sure that the first photo he would see would be of Ishmael and me obviously happy in one another's company. "I'll find Oñé's passport."

I left them scrolling through the photos and heard them from upstairs making comments about them to one another. I couldn't hear exactly what they were saying, even though I hovered over the landing in the West Wing and tried desperately to at least hear what was implied by the tone of their muttering voices. They seemed suspicious of me. I was convinced that they had lowered their voices to ensure it would be impossible for me to hear them.

I removed Oñé's passport from the safe in my bedroom and descended the stairs.

José Miguel looked through each page of the passport. "I see Oñé was born in Baghdad in 2007. That is one year after Saddham Hussein was hanged. It continued to be a dangerous place to live for several years after that. Why did his mother Sophia not return to the safety of Sweden before 2011?"

I shook my head. "I don't have an answer to that question. I know that Gregoriano Balsano was a Doctor working with the Red Cross, who left Iraq to go to Syria in 2011. Sophia was working as a Nurse in Iraq with Gregoriano. That is where they met and where Oñé was conceived. I imagine that by 2011 when Oñé was four, she thought the time had come to return to Sweden – the country of her birth – and to take care of Oñé's education."

Pep Serrano nodded. "It is unimaginable to me that a mother would allow her child to grow up in such a war zone. Neither do I understand what Ishmael was doing living in the house of Sophia Andersson."

I nodded. "I understand your confusion. I also was surprised to find that Ishmael had lived for a year in Malmo with Sophia and Oñé. I believe that it was a compassionate decision made by both Sophia and Gregoriano that he should stay there. Sophia is a Nurse who has specialist knowledge in Post-Traumatic Stress Disorder. Gregoriano managed to get a Visa for Ishmael to enter Sweden and invited him to stay under Sophia's supervision until he felt well enough to leave."

José Miguel asked, "Did you observe any signs of Post-Traumatic Distress Disorder during the two years which Ishmael spent with you?"

I shook my head. "Absolutely not. He had, if anything, a healing presence. The only concern I had was his unwillingness to speak about his past.

"Now I understand that it could have been a sign of his PTSD. I have been told that it can lead to people to behave erratically and can lead them to commit suicide. I hope that has not happened to him. I suppose it is possible given the sudden way in which he left."

Pep Serrano picked his teeth with a toothpick even though he had eaten nothing. "So now we are looking for two missing persons not one. Gregoriano Balsano – the father of Oñé – and Ishmael Domini. What can you tell us about either of their whereabouts?"

I shook my head. "I don't know where they are."

Sancho Panza interrupted: "You are Ishmael's employer? Why would he leave without telling you where he was going and attempting to guarantee his job security?"

"I don't know enough about PSTD. That seems the most logical explanation for what triggered his leaving."

"Gabriela Gonzalez, your housekeeper, informed us

that you had a deep friendship with Ishmael. This would make it even more unlikely that he would leave without saying anything to you. As for Gregoriano Balsano, Gabriela has informed us that he had a sinister control over you. Although she never saw him – she based this on what you confided about him to her. She told us that you could not refuse his wishes. Is that not why you went to Malmo? It was not your choice. The decision was made for you by Gregoriano Balsano?"

I couldn't remember that I had said anything to Gabriela about Gregoriano. But then again, I couldn't be sure that I hadn't. I had told Ishmael about Gregoriano but not Gabriela. Had Ishmael betrayed my confidence, I wondered?

"I do not believe that Gabriela had ever seen Gregoriano. I am confused as to why she would share with you anything about my relationship with him and in particular to say that he had a 'sinister control' over me when she never saw him with me."

The two Policemen glanced at one another. I felt that I had won a point and that they were unsure of what to say next. Their eyes locked onto one another as if transferring shared data before speaking. I decided to speak first.

"It is my belief that Gabriela was infatuated by Ishmael. I observed them having intimate conversations on several occasions – although I do not have evidence that it went beyond the early stages of infatuation before

Ishmael left. It is quite possible that he left because of the oppressive nature of her clinging to him. Not being a psychiatrist myself, I would hazard a guess that it was she who was trying to manipulate him into a deeper relationship which he rejected. If we are to talk about control issues, I would say that she was attempting to control Ishmael and also me. I now know that Ishmael was a friend of Gregoriano. It is possible that Ishmael spoke with Gabriela about the nature of his friendship with Gregoriano. Ishmael may have felt controlled by Gregoriano and projected this onto me. You have to remember that Ishmael had a history of not staying long anywhere ever since his family was wiped out in a mortar attack in Damascus in 2012."

Pep Serrano glanced again at Jose Miguel. This time I thought that I had exactly anticipated what I needed to say to convince them of my innocence.

I threw myself on the sofa where I had sat so many evenings with Ishmael. "Well, if you are going to need more time for your questions I hope you don't mind if I sit down. This is tiring work."

Jose Miguel spoke first. "I think we are ready to see the garden and then Oñé. Before that, I would like to know how you would describe your relationship with Gregoriano Balsano?"

"He is an acquaintance I see from time to time. In my work as the Painter I have many acquaintances – not deep relationships. He is such an acquaintance."

Pep Serrano followed up as if they had written a script together. "So how do you explain that, having a superficial acquaintance, you follow his orders to travel to Malmo where you spend time with someone who turns out to have a relationship with Gregoriano and with whom he had a child? Do you not think that is a rather odd kind of relationship with someone you describe as an acquaintance?"

I threw my hands behind my head on the sofa. "He asked me in a letter to take care of Oñé and explained Sophia's need for support while she was having her cancer treatment. For once in my life I decided to do something for someone else. Perhaps we human beings are capable of being more altruistic if given an opportunity to be so."

As I uttered those words I knew that they were unconvincing.

Pep Serrano rattled the handcuffs attached to his belt. "Can we see that letter?"

I scrambled to my feet, almost slipping on the tiled floor. "I apologise but that will not be possible. As you can see my house is rather orderly. I have an obsession with having everything in its place and if no longer needed, I throw it out, give it away or burn it. On this occasion, I burnt Gregoriano's letter. I had no longer any use for it."

Pep Serrano yawned as he commented, "It's not sounding convincing considering the vast number of photos, letters and memorabilia in your house which we have seen relating to your 'friends' praise for your exhibitions. I would say you are rather a hoarder than someone who throws unusual items away or who burns them. However, as you are not prepared to be open with us, I suggest that we look at the garden."

Jose Miguel took out a notebook and jotted down a few words. "Before going to the garden, may we see where Ishmael slept?"

"Of course. I think I locked the room after he left."

I lifted a key from an olive branch attached to the wall. It held all of the keys for the house. My legs trembled as I climbed the four stairs that led into the West Wing. I heard sturdy boots clump behind me along the corridor. I reached Ishmael's room, placed the key in the lock to find that it was already open. I pushed the door. The bed was smooth with a scattering of purple cushions on top of a cream bed cover. The fire had been raked clean. I remembered removing the sheets from the bed, but I was sure that I had left unraked ashes in the fireplace. Who had tidied the bed and cleaned the fire?

Pep Serrano pulled back the bedspread. "So here we have freshly ironed, clean sheets. Is this in preparation for your next guest? Who are you expecting?"

José Miguel took out his notebook again and I was sure that he was going to ask if Gabriela had cleaned the room. Jose Miguel opened the wardrobe, rattled the empty hangers and opened the three drawers below.

"There are no signs that he will be staying anytime

soon. Was the room empty of his clothes when he left on the 5th October?"

I sat on the edge of the bed and rubbed my eyes. "Of course. He took everything with him. That's why I knew it was unlikely he would return. After my visit to Malmo, I realise that this is what he does. Having said that, I have not spoken to my friend José del Pardo. It seemed that he planned his departure from La Coruña in a more orderly fashion to accept the offer of being a gardener here in Can Animes. I was fond of him. His departure has been quite a shock."

Pep Serrano sat on the bed beside me, resting his hands on his black trousers. For a moment I thought that he was going to take my hand. I pulled my hands together in a desperate praying position on my lap to escape that possibility. Pep Serrano heaved himself a little forward on the bed to allow his feet to reach the floor. "He was a painter – like you?"

"I didn't know he was a painter until I went to Malmo. He was my gardener. It is true I should have thought about the ease with which he created sculptures with me. On reflection, I should have known that he had talent, but I was arrogant to think that it was my great teaching on how to make sculptures that made them so wonderful." I laughed and got to my feet. "How we are to be humbled in life."

José Miguel looked at his watch, tapped it, nodded at

Pep Serrano, and said, "Let's see the garden and then Oñé. It's getting late. Does the boy not need to be fed?"

We passed through the front door and I walked towards the fountain followed by the policemen. "This was created by Ishmael, together with the fourteen fountains and the other sculptures you will find scattered in the garden."

I pointed at the sculpture which held Ishmael's body and then pointed swiftly at the fountain.

José Miguel and Pep Serrano approached the sculpture. "Yes, Gabriela your Housekeeper mentioned she saw this on Thursday 5th October."

I tried not to hesitate but felt myself shivering. "What else did Gabriela tell you?"

Jose Miguel laughed. He threw back his head, his oiled hair resting on the shoulder of his jacket. "We ask the questions."

I rubbed my lips with my hand. Jose Miguel leaned towards me, stared into my eyes. I saw myself reflected in his pupils.

"Answer the question once again – when and where did you last see Ishmael Domini?"

"We had cena together cooked by Gabriela on Wednesday 4th October. She will have told you that no doubt. It was a pleasant evening which we finished with a nightcap and we went our separate ways to bed."

I emphasised 'separate ways to bed' with a slowed down pace and a deepening, meaning-filled voice.

Pep Serrano asked, "Where did he sleep?"

"Why are you asking that again? It is the room which I have already shown you in the West Wing."

Pep Serrano took his handkerchief out again and wiped the side of his face, breathing heavily asked, "So remind us again of when you realised that he had gone?"

"He didn't appear for breakfast on the morning of the 5th October. I had made pancakes with maple syrup – his favourite. As the pancakes were going cold, I checked his room to find that it was empty. He wasn't there. All of his possessions – few as they were and mostly clothes – were gone."

Pep Serrano ignored the path I was taking to the swimming pool and instead turned right, followed by José Miguel, towards the labyrinth. He staggered a little as we walked toward the two fountains which marked the entrance. I wondered if he had taken a drink before arriving or whether he had suffered a stroke. He was unsteady on his feet and one leg trailed behind the other in an ungainly way which I hadn't noticed before.

He asked, "What did you do then?"

I shook my head. "What could I do? He had no mobile phone. I had no way of contacting him. I could only wait to see what would happen next."

Jose Miguel ran his fingers through his hair as if he was looking at himself in a mirror. "Did you ask Gabriela on 5th October what she thought might have happened to him?"

I shook my head. "I wanted to protect his privacy. If he wanted to escape from her it was none of my business."

Pep Serrano tapped on his truncheon with what I observed were brittle fingernails. "I can see that you may have a problem distinguishing truth from fiction. Gabriela has shown us photos taken on her mobile which indicate that their relationship was one of a significant, deep friendship."

"Did Gabriela also tell you that she had subsequently seen Ishmael in the Plaza before I returned from Malmo? He tried to escape from her and ran down a side street."

Pep Serrano touched one of the fountains at the entrance to the labyrinth. "That is new information which we will check out. It all helps to sort out lies from the truth."

Meanwhile José Miguel was taking an unusual look at the labyrinth wall. "Cypress Leyandii and Red Robin Shrub – a great idea." He smiled at me. "I am a keen gardener myself. This works well to disguise the monotone nature which can come from using only a Leyandii hedging."

He reached his hands into the depths of the labyrinth wall. I looked away. I could not bear to witness what I knew was going to happen next. It was my worst nightmare. His arm disappeared into the depths of the hedge and retrieved the Cupid's arrow with its leaden tip which I thought I had expertly concealed.

"What is this?"

I looked at the entrance to the labyrinth, pretending for a few seconds that I had not seen what José Miguel was holding. Then I mustered a voice of surprise. I rushed towards him with arms outstretched.

"That is wonderful. I didn't know where it had gone. It is the other arrow belonging to Cupid. It had disappeared from the fountain. Gabriela asked about it. I noticed that it was gone myself but thought that Ishmael had taken it with him to make a sculpture. He never much liked it."

Pep Serrano said, "Obviously he didn't take it with him. He couldn't have, could he?"

I stuttered. "What do you mean?"

"Well, it's here in my hands, after being deliberately hidden in the labyrinth. Who hid it? Why did they hide it? From my experience it looks like a panic hiding. It's not particularly well hidden do you think, if I found it so easily? José Miguel, pass me the bag please for forensic testing."

José Miguel pulled the rucksack off his back, opened it and produced a large plastic bag with a zipper seal. He put on a pair of white gloves, took the arrow from Pep Serrano and inserted it with precision into the forensic bag.

José Miguel asked, "Can you give us your explanation as to why the arrow was hidden in the labyrinth?"

I nodded. "The most obvious explanation is that we have visitors to the garden. There is a competition for who can visit as many sculptures as possible within a given time. Children love to get involved in this. I imagine that one of the children visiting has hidden the arrow as a prank. They may even have been planning to return and steal it."

José Miguel raised his eyebrows in disbelief. "Let's see what the forensic team say. I think we will save a thorough investigation of the garden for another day. Now we will see Oñé."

I pointed at the Studio. "It's not far, follow me."

On the way to the Studio, I could not believe why I had not left the leaden headed arrow in the fountain. Gabriela had spotted the morning after the murder that it was missing. That was the second biggest mistake that I had made that evening.

We reached the door of the Studio. What was Oñé going to tell them? I opened the door and shouted: "Oñé, we have visitors to see you."

Pep Serrano and José Miguel spent fifteen minutes 'interviewing' Oñé. I listened insisting that as his temporary guardian, I needed to be present. Thankfully he repeated the story which he had told me about Ishmael leaving Malmo. He even looked quite cheerful as he squashed oils onto the palette. There was only one comment which he made which Pep Serrano captured in his notebook, writing feverishly.

"I get the feeling that Ishmael is around – not far away."

Pep Serrano asked him, "Have you seen him here?"

Oñé shook his head. "No. It's only a feeling that he is close by. He is watching over us. He will appear when the moment is right. He does that, he picks his moments for appearing and disappearing."

I knew they thought that he was a ten-year-old without a developed capacity for critical thinking. I was delighted that Oñé hadn't uttered anything to implicate me in Ishmael's murder. Of course how could he?

For now, I was safe – although it was disturbing watching them take Cupid's arrow out of the rucksack and ask him if he had seen it before. He shook his head. They nodded. He was a boy, confused by his mother's illness and his abandonment by his father. There were more pressing issues, like women being thrown off balconies by jealous husbands. They didn't ask me to go to the Town Hall and make a statement. That was a good sign.

Instead Pep Serrano asked Oñé: "Do you have an item of clothing – anything which would not have been washed which Ishmael would have worn prior to leaving you in December 2014?"

I could see that Oñé's eyes watered as he replied, "Yes. I have a hat."

Pep Serrano patted Oñé on the head. "Can we please take it with us for a few days? It might help us find Ishmael and make sure that he is well. I promise you that we will return it."

Oñé looked at me asking permission with his eyes. I

said, "Of course Oñé – please go and find it for our friends here."

When he left the studio José Miguel said, "It will be for routine DNA testing. We will send specialist officers around tomorrow to take samples. They will also test the arrow which we found in the labyrinth hedge."

I stayed calm. "Anything which can help trace Ishmael is much appreciated. I would love to see him again and have him return here to work."

José Miguel and Pep Serrano shook my hand. "Thank you for your co-operation."

Oñé returned within minutes holding the hat I had seen him wear several times when we were on the beach or climbing Barranc. It was unusual – a sports cap covered in what looked like sheep wool. Oñé proudly said, "Ishmael told me that it was a Swedish military cap. He placed it for me on my pillow, the night that he left us."

Pep Serrano placed it into a plastic bag. "It will be returned when the investigation is completed."

When they left, Oñé asked, "Did I say or do anything wrong?"

"Of course you didn't. You behaved perfectly."

I gave him a deep appreciative hug. We went to the kitchen and I made him a cup of thick hot chocolate.

When I went to bed that night I wondered what DNA evidence would they find. Was Ishmael's blood on the Cupid arrow? Could that be traced back to Ishmael by evidence which the forensic experts would collect tomorrow? That was a terrifying thought. Equally frightening was the thought of what my mother Monica would think of all of this. I put my fingers in my ears as if she was talking to me. I didn't want to hear her words in my head. I knew what they would be. It was worse that they would be loving words, filled with forgiveness. I wanted, needed, harsh words like those of the art critics who proclaimed to the world that I had lost my talent.

Thursday 9th November 2017

The forensic officers arrived at ten o´clock. There were four of them, wearing white jump suits with hoods pulled over their heads, gloves and white rubber boots.

Oñé asked if he could accompany them and they refused to allow him.

They stayed for six hours.

Thursday 16th November 2017

The police asked for samples of my blood and that of Gabriela for DNA purposes. I made arrangements for Gabriela to contact the Local Police. I took Oñé with me to the Police Station as samples of blood were extracted from my arm, swabs taken from my tongue and the roof of my mouth.

Oñé thought that it was exciting and asked if he could provide samples. To my surprise the officers said yes, and with my permission, extracted his DNA samples.

Thursday 23rd November 2017

I received a call from Pep Serrano saying that there was a match with my DNA on Cupid's arrow but not for either Gabriela or Oñé. There was evidence of a second sample of DNA. They did not have a match for it and would hold the evidence on file, pending further investigation.

There was no evidence to link Ishmael with the arrow. There was the unsolved issue of unidentified DNA from the blood on the tip of the arrow. Investigations were continuing.

18

PABLO PICASSO

"Everything is a miracle. It is a miracle that one does not dissolve in one's bath like a lump of sugar."

Wednesday 27th December 2017

I took my journal out from the usual place in the bedroom, out of Oñé's sight. He had once interrupted me and seen me place it in the drawer beside the bed. I told him that I was recording ideas for new paintings and exhibitions as they often escaped my mind if I didn't write them down.

I was in a more reflective mood. I wrote:

"I never had a child of my own. I wanted to work out what life was about before I would think of bringing a child into the world. And I never found a woman I loved enough. I would have wanted a woman with a sharp mind who criticised me and kept me in control.

"The women I met were more interested in my money and fame than helping me find the meaning of life. They took a lot from me, including trying to ruin my reputation. You know the way the world has become so politically correct. These women wanted my money and were happy to spend it. Yet they sold their version of stories to the press about how I had sexually tormented

them. I don't remember it that way. My memories were of the enjoyment of pure mutual lust – certainly not of a love for any one of them. How many of them were there? If I go back through my bank account statements I can tell you by the money I threw at them. I suppose it's no more than others spend on high class prostitutes. I kid myself that I have never slept with a prostitute. Of course I did. I called them girlfriends. Why did they leave me? In most cases it was because that they had found someone with more money.

"Oñé convinced me that it had been the right decision never to bring a child into the world. Our interchanges with one another do not make me feel better – rather, worse. What is strange is that it seems to me that he is now clamping onto me like a father figure. He even seems to like me. It is a sickening feeling to be liked. I am more comfortable with being hated."

Sophia is arriving this afternoon. I feel anxious about how I can handle the visit. I now know about 'the incident'. Should I tell her, or will that be a betrayal of Oñé? Although she did tell me that Oñé would help me understand what had happened with Ishmael. Maybe she would be disappointed if he hadn't revealed to me what happened with 'the incident'.

Oñé has been painting. I decided not to look at the painting until it is finished, although he kept tugging at my jumper and asking me to have a look. I shook my head. Now I have learned to do that with gentleness and a soft look in my eyes. There is half of me that is genuine about this gentle communication. The other half of me that wished that Oñé wasn't here and that his mother was not arriving to spend the New Year. She phoned me to say that her treatment was going well but that I shouldn't be shocked by how she looks. I can't imagine her looking anything other than beautiful. I don't know how many times she apologised to Oñé for not being able to arrive for his birthday on Christmas Eve. That day she had to receive chemotherapy. It made her quite sick and she didn't want Oñé to see her like that. I am aware that she could die at any time. That thought makes me aware of how precious and fragile life is. I know now how little sensitivity I must have to have been able to kill twice. I could blame those murders on being gifted as a Painter. Do I not need to be filled with passionate emotion to paint? Do I not need intense rage within me to murder?

While my mother Monica reads Butler's 'Lives of Saints' for inspiration about the highest unselfish motivations of humankind, I read about the lives of artists, writers and musicians who have sunk into levels of depravity worse than or as bad as mine.

My favourite was Caravaggio from the sixteenth century who lived two lives like me. In one he moved within a refined society, attending soirees and being a protégé of a cardinal. In the other, he mixed with what others called 'the low life' of Rome where he was ill-tempered and constantly in trouble – slandering his rivals, hitting waiters, carrying a sword with him in the hope of picking a fight. Eventually he did murder a man in a fight, forcing him to flee Rome. However, he continued to work and his painting of 'David with the Head of Goliath' shows, I think for me, remorse for his murder of an innocent man.

In the same century Benvenuto Cellini who was a goldsmith and a sculptor, painter and writer, killed repeatedly without any sense of apparent regret. He stabbed to death his brother's murderer with a long, twisted dagger which he drove down through the man's shoulder.

If I choose a writer, I might think of William S Burroughs who killed his wife Joan Vollmer in a drunken rage and who claimed that he would never have become a writer if he had not killed her. He proclaimed that he wrote as a form of sorcery to protect him from what he thought was possession by an evil entity.

Maybe there is hope for me. I do have remorse. I write this journal to exorcise my demons. I continue to paint but no matter how wonderfully my art is improving, I have already asked you to burn them – burn those paintings – that is the only way to end for ever the life of the exorcised soul. You may keep this journal. Let others read it as a cautionary tale of the nature of genius and the fall from greatness.

I am determined not to kill again. Yet I am not sure if I am strong enough. I understand that once I have the taste for killing – I have crossed a line. It is like losing your virginity. You can't go back to a state of innocence. I yearn for pleasure again. I know that sounds dreadful. I have decided to be honest in this journal. So I can tell you that I have also felt regret after illicit pleasure. I have learned that pleasure contains violence. Why was I created in that way? I don't know. Maybe we are all the same.

I can continue with my research. The nineteenth century painter, Richard Dadd, murdered his father. The composer Carlo Gesualdo ran a sword through his wife. Then there was the insanity of Francisco Goya evident in his paintings, Vincent Van Gogh, Paul Gauguin with his multiple suicide attempts, Edvard Munch with his inner demons evident in the 'Scream' and Agnes Martin with her psychotic breaks and schizophrenia who managed to 'recover' (if you could call it that) in the tranquillity of New Mexico with the help of a Zen Buddhist practice.

I've read that there are those – even my namesake Saint Augustine – who managed to go beyond desire and therefore beyond the world of infinite dissatisfaction. I cannot imagine achieving that state myself. I feel that I am learning to have patience with myself. I am learning to understand what I like and don't like and not to act out liking or not liking. With Oñé I am learning by observing him.

At times being with Oñé, I feel a power bursting through Oñé which frightens me. He seems too intelligent for his age. I keep searching for his imperfection. Every time he is good, I feel him pushing me beyond what I can endure. He is gentle at times in a way that I have not yet learned. He forgives me when I shout at him or even worse when I throw one of his paintings in the rubbish saying, "You can do better than this, you little freak of nature."

I search for his imperfection. I think that I have found it.

He likes to discover the weak points and vulnerabilities in others. Then he hurts them by touching them with his mind. He reminds me of a child I knew at school who liked to pull the wings of a fly and watch it struggle to become air born.

I wondered if Oñé had learnt to survive in Iraq by discovering the weaknesses in others. For example on Christmas Day, I knew that I should have bought him a present. In fact two presents. He told me that Ishmael had left him on his birthday which was Christmas Eve. I didn't buy either a birthday present or a present for Christmas Day. We didn't celebrate his birthday with a special dinner on Christmas Eve which is also the day when Mallorcan families share a special meal together. Instead, I made him a cup of hot chocolate and gave him a piece of 'ensaimada' – a lard based local delicacy, with options to have it filled with apricots or figs. I chose for him instead a cream-filled cake. He thanked me profusely as he drank his chocolate. He didn't mention anything about his birthday, even though I had heard him talk about it on the phone with Sophia.

I took him out for a walk up the Barranc on Christmas Day. As I pulled on my slashed jeans, struggling to button the waist, I realised that I was piling on more and more weight while taking care of this child. It led me to ruminate on how his presence had changed my world. When I say ruminate, I mean that these thoughts about him have become compulsive. He even appears in my dreams and I have a nervous, trembling feeling in my body when I look at his smiling face.

It's as though I'm waiting for something horrific which he is going to do to me and I don't know what that might be. Being an artist or a Painter as I like to call myself means I am familiar with the workings of my mind. They are the containers for my inspiration with all of its coarseness or finesse. I know about projection and denial. I enjoy seeing how I can turn another person into a version of my shadow self – my darkness – which I don't want to work on removing because I enjoy it. I know that I see myself in him.

As for the small irritations, for instance, since he arrived, I find myself eating more. I have to make him meals – three meals a day. Alone, I eat when I feel like it. That might be typically only a cheese and tomato sandwich in the evening. Now I have to think of his breakfast, his lunch his cena. Enough. I feel like a fattened pig. He is fattening me for some party at which I will be the pig roast.

Sophia is arriving today. A bed is ready for her in Ishmael's room. It is untouched since Pep Serrano and José Miguel saw it. I never found out who made the bed and raked the fire. It must have been me and I forgot that I did it. It must be the stress of murdering Ishmael.

Thinking of Sophia's arrival, I looked at the empty drawers. Would Sophia not think it strange that I had thrown out all of Ishmael's clothes? If he had left suddenly for a 'Walkabout' the house would still be filled with his presence – clothes, books, aftershave, and hair gel. I didn't know what to do. I was fairly sure that Sophia would not remember what she had packed in his small rucksack when he left Malmo. She hadn't seen him in three years. Nevertheless, she would expect some sign of his presence in the room, some evidence which insinuated that I anticipated his return. I had thrown them out the day after I had murdered him.

Today, I rushed down to the Calle de la Luna and bought a few shirts, two pairs of trousers, aftershave, and hair gel. I cut the labels off the clothes and crumpled them a little to make them look worn. Then I remembered that Ishmael would have left them perfectly ironed, and as Oñé continued with his painting, I ironed them all again. Although I thought that Sophia would say that Ishmael would never leave a crease in his shirt. I breathed a sigh of relief as I looked at the bedroom. I thought that I could smell Ishmael's presence but maybe that only came from the vase of dark red roses which I had placed beside Sophia's bed.

I opened the drawers to check that everything looked OK. My heart fluttered as I realised that I had thrown out all of Ishmael's underwear. It was too late to do anything about it. I threw myself onto the bed, looked at my watch. I had to leave for the airport in one hour.

Oñé walked into the bedroom. He coughed to encourage me to open my eyes. I was singing a Cat Stevens song – not out aloud but in my head – about a hard-headed woman. God knows why I started thinking of that song. I had never met a hard-headed woman. I dropped that thought and shouted at Oñé, "You need to get ready. We have to collect Sophia."

"I've finished the painting. Will you look at it now?"

I rolled onto my stomach without looking at him and breathed into the pillow. "We have to collect your mother."

I turned my head to see him standing with the sheet over his head. He had decided not to change it for the apron which he discovered in the drawer. He told me that he would use the sheet with is splashes of paint as an installation. I had to confess that made me laugh. The dots of cerise, dark blue and rose with the smudge marks of where he had wiped his hands indeed did look like one of my installations. It only needed a little outlining of form which I was sure Oñé was capable of skilfully doing.

I found his silent attentive stare irritating. He then spoke: "We have an hour. You have time to look at it. You promised me you would when I finished. It is now finished."

I pushed my head into the pillow. "How do you know that it's finished? I never know."

Oñé's voice penetrated my ears and caused a wave of nausea to move through me. "If you don't know when it is finished you can't be a real painter can you? Maybe you need to face up to that."

I knew he was saying painter with a small 'p'. He was implying that I was only capable of splashing paint onto a wall. I jumped out of bed with a raging anger moving through me. It was a wave of emotion that started in my stomach and moved to my head where it took on swirling intensity which confused me. I shouted at him: "Let's see your fuckin' painting then, you little smartass."

I couldn't believe that I had said that in such an angry tone of voice. I had tried so hard to control my anger with Oñé. I knew that it was my problem, not his. I had to work on it. Having Oñé in the house was a step too far for me at times – too much, too soon. I should have started with having a little dog that loved me unconditionally, licked my face and was always pleased to see me or a cat that jumped on my lap and allowed me to pet it.

I sat on the edge of the bed and looked at him, filled with genuine remorse at my anger outburst. He closed his eyes which surprised me. He took a few deep breaths.

"You are not like Ishmael. He loved to look at my paintings. Even though I was only seven, he encouraged me. It felt good to be around him. I learned from him. I haven't learnt anything from you, other than remembering not to be angry with my mother. Do you want to have a look or not? It's up to you."

I slid onto the edge of the bed and bent down pretending to tie my bootlaces in an attempt to regain composure. Without looking up, I whispered, "Of course I would like to see it. Are you pleased with it?"

Oñe spoke confidently back. "An artist can never comment on his own work. It speaks for itself."

I heard his tiny feet press softly onto the wood tiled bedroom floor as if he were wearing thick socks. I thumped on the floor behind him. He ran across the pebbled path. I wondered whether he was attempting to escape from me or whether he wanted to show me how much older I was and how much less fit. I took a few deep breaths to prepare me for what I would see in the Studio.

Inside Oñe removed the cover from his canvas. The cover was a piece of plastic which I had retrieved earlier from the garden. I didn't want to give him Egyptian cotton or silk with which I covered my paintings. That would have given him the idea that he was a painter like Vermeer, that he was someone who deserved to be noticed, masterly in his treatment of light. In thinking of Vermeer I shuddered at my own hypocrisy. Vermeer was a genius. I was not. Vermeer had eleven children. I had not even had one. Vermeer had made no money in his lifetime. I am a millionaire. I remembered what Catherine Bolnes – Vermeer's wife – had said about Vermeer, 'He lapsed into such decay and decadence … as if he had fallen into a frenzy, in a day and a half he went from being healthy to being dead'.

Why did I remember that? Because I had felt since the arrival of Ishmael that I had indeed fallen into some kind of a frenzy, which hadn't improved with Oñé's arrival.

I watched him fold the plastic cover into four and place it neatly on the ground.

He had originally insisted on a large canvas, which he had now divided into three. I was shocked by what I saw.

I was a key character in each of the three parts of the triptych. The first part – 'Descent into Hell' – had a black background. I was portrayed as standing on my head or falling into darkness. My arms were out-stretched as if diving. At my feet were three small flames. I looked more closely and could see that the background was not entirely black as I had first thought but filled with perhaps a hundred tiny faces each one with slightly different shades of emotion including fear, disgust, hatred, anger and horror. Their eyes strained to follow my descent.

My face twisted as I looked at the painting and felt that in the Studio, with Oñé looking at me, I was showing with my eyes and lips, the terror Oñé had exquisitely captured on canvas. I turned my gaze to the centre of the triptych which Oñé had told me was called 'Judgement'. It depicted a large fish with my face, swimming in a sea of knives, broken hearts, moving towards a tunnel which had a dark entrance and an exit with shooting stars like fireworks bursting into the sea and turning it into a vibrant turquoise.

I said nothing until I looked at the final part of the triptych which Oñé called 'Transformation'. I was there and my hands were pointing upwards, in the direction of a golden sky. I wore a white tunic with garlands of roses around my neck. I held my right hand in the air, showing three fingers as though I had counted something and wanted the observer to know that three things had been achieved. I was smiling, not a self-conscious false smile that I knew myself to be capable of producing, but a transcendent smile of knowing something which no-one else knew. Something which could only be known face-to-face not in words; only in a relationship between me in the painting and the person looking at me. I didn't know what to say. I blurted out, "I thought that you said that you were going to reproduce Ishmael's painting. He had never met me when he painted it, so how come you have painted this?"

Oñé stuttered. "Don't be angry with me. It is the truth. Ishmael painted you into his painting. I don't know why or how. Although when he said that the painting came alive, he thought that meant that he had painted himself into it. I knew when I met you in Malmo, that it was you.

You can see the original for yourself if you don't believe me. It is in the Reina Sophia, in Madrid."

I felt enraged by his lies and by what I imagined was some kind of psychological game he was playing with me to make me feel that I was going mad. I walked swiftly to the kitchen, opened a drawer, took out a meat carving knife, walked back to the painting and slashed at it. "Do you see how I have improved it?"

I didn't tell you how Oñé's hair had grown since Sophia handed him over to my care. It was quite beautiful in its natural state – allowed to grow rather than to be pruned. He grabbed the knife from my hand and began to chop at his hair. Clumps of hair fell onto the ground in a way which produced another panic attack in me. I breathed in deeply attempting to lengthen the short breaths. I clenched my fists into two tight balls and for what seemed an eternity, avoided eye contact with him.

When I plucked up the courage to look at him, he had taken the knife from the table where he had left it after his hair cutting episode. He walked briskly towards his painting and made three more slashes. He turned and looked at me.

"I think you're right. That was what was needed. A little bit more do you think?"

He held the knife in his hand and waved it at me. His voice shook. I saw that he had managed to slice not only the painting but also his left hand. A few drops of blood fell onto the ground making small Pollock purple dots on the Tuscan yellow tiled floor. His eyes were wide open like the day in Malmo when he fell into the sea, before he disappeared under the water. The thought crossed my mind that he would plunge the knife into my heart or maybe into his own. Instead, he threw it on the ground and moved towards me as if (I trembled at the thought) he might embrace me.

My voice croaked as I asked, "Show me your hand. Have you hurt yourself?"

He held his hand out in a fist. I pulled it open. There was a small gash. Nothing that I thought would need stitches and mean that we could be late in collecting Sophia. I looked at him, commanding, "Stay here, I'll find a plaster. Do not do any more damage to yourself or to the painting. Think about Sophia. She needs a calm and positive atmosphere for her stay here."

I stumbled down the pebbled path towards the house, into the bathroom, pulled out the first aid box that Ishmael had filled for me with cream for burns, a bottle of oxygenated water and plasters. Grabbing the water and plasters I ran back, slipping on the pebbles and fell, crunching my head against the small stones. I lay there for a minute, turning my head to one side and breathing deeply.

As I pulled myself into a kneeling position, there was a shadowy figure beyond the Studio looking at me. I don't know if I had bumped my head on the pebbles and had suffered a slight concussion, but I could have sworn that it was Ishmael. I shouted at him.

"Ishmael help me. I need your help. Don't leave me."

A fleeting fear filled my body that in some way he had come back from the dead. I knew that was nonsense. No-one had ever appeared to me from the dead. My mother Monica, who might deserve such a visit if it were possible, had shared with me that it had never happened to her except in dreams. I wondered if I was dreaming. I looked around me. The orangery was close by, with orange trees heavy with fruit. I struggled to my feet, touched my head and gazed at the deep red blood on my fingers. I felt tears welling up at the unfairness and uncontrollable nature of life. I walked slowly towards the nearest orange tree, pulled an orange from it and bit into the skin. I tasted its sweet bitterness. This was not a dream. I had never tasted anything real in a dream before. I licked at my hand. It tasted of iron. It was human blood. I looked carefully around. There was no sign of my dream manifestation of Ishmael.

After washing Oñé's small wound with the water and sticking a plaster over it, I dripped the oxygenated water onto my own head and asked him, "Have a look – is it a bad cut? Does it need stitches?"

I knelt on the tiled floor at his feet, bent my head forward. I felt his tiny fingers gently pull my hair apart and his eyes drilling into my scalp. "It doesn't look too bad." He laughed. "Do you think it will have knocked some sense into you?"

My body shook with laughter. I remembered that feeling because I rarely laughed those days. It was bubbliness like champagne rising all the way up from my knees pressed in a kind of prayer through my throat where I was making a sound like a donkey braying and then up further into my eyes which stung. I didn't know at that point whether I was laughing or crying. I wiped my eyes with the sleeve of my jumper as I leaned on a chair to get to my feet and mumbled, "What will your mother say about your hair?"

Oñé looked at me with a look of curiosity as if he didn't know who he was looking at. "She will say what she sees and thinks. How can I tell you what she will think? I am not her."

I walked to the drawer in the kitchen area and found a pair of scissors. "You sit down and I will sort this out"

The hairdressers were closed. I found a peg I had used to attach the installations onto a clothesline. I held it against each handful of hair to ensure that his hair was cut evenly all over. I lifted the mirror from the studio bathroom to show him how it looked from behind. He laughed in that familiar way which I maybe in the past had mistakenly interrupted as being aggressive.

"Mother will be delighted. Did you never think of a change of career?" Oñé brushed his hair from the floor. Without looking at me, he commented, "You haven't said

what you thought about my painting apart from the fact
that you didn't like to see yourself in it and didn't believe
that Ishmael had painted you into a painting which nearly
drove him crazy and forced him to abandon Sophia and
me."

I knew that I had to move this conversation onto
something less judgemental to allow the mood to be
a welcoming one for Sophia. "I think the texture and
colours are impressive – although I can't see anything
like this being accepted for the Reina Sophia. It's like
nothing I have seen before."

Oñé picked up a glass of water sitting on the table
and threw it at me which I didn't expect at all. I mean
the whole glass – water and glass. The cold water hit me
full in the face and the glass splintered on the tiled floor.
He shouted at me, "Don't be so patronising. I have seen
your 'works of art and installations'. Do you think for a
moment that they are better than those of Ishmael which
I reproduce?"

I was beginning to think that Oñé had serious
psychological problems which may have been caused,
as José Miguel and Pep Serrano had hinted, by his time
spent as a child in Iraq. Perhaps, I thought, they had
been exaggerated by abandonment issues. He had never
met his father and had been abandoned by Ishmael of
whom he was obviously fond.

I had no idea of how to respond. I felt guilty that I had

provoked this outburst. I walked towards Oñé, wiped my face to dry it on his installation apron.

He tore the sheet away from my face. "Wipe your tears on someone else's clothes, not mine."

I sat on the ground and began to talk in a way that was so disjointed that I couldn't even follow it myself. It had little to do with what Oñé had said.

"We must try to become wise – both of us. It will help our art. We don't want to turn into one those mad Painters. You can be a great painter and be sane."

Oñé curled up like a worm on the floor – a worm that moves slowly and is shiny on the outside. He shouted at me from a mouth stuffed into the sleeve of his jersey.

"Stop talking about wisdom. You know nothing about it. Ishmael was a great painter. I do not know if he was wise or what that means."

I knelt on the floor beside Oñé, edged close towards me. I held him in my arms.

"Yes you are right. Ishmael was a great painter. I see that in your art. You are a better painter than I am."

He shouted at me. "You don't listen. I am no longer talking about being a great painter. I am talking about being wise like no-one I know."

I felt an emotion which I had never experienced before. I can only describe it as something painful around my heart. I saw that the hole I had cut for him to wear the installation a little too small. He must have squeezed his head through to wear it because it seemed to choke him.

Or maybe there was another reason why his face turned cherry red. I lifted the installation and tugged it over his head. I folded it neatly as he had done with the plastic.

"It's time to collect your mother."

We climbed into the front seats of the BMW. I patted at Oñé's head the way you would pat at a horse. "Are you looking forward to seeing your mother? It has been a while. It can't be easy living with a stranger."

Oñé looked out of the car window to his right. "She thinks that I don't know, that I am a child and don't deserve to know. I know that she is dying."

I heard myself say, "She told me that you knew that she was having treatment for her cancer. We are all dying. It's only a matter of when. Your mother could outlive us both."

Oñe ignored me and tapped on the window as if sending a Morse code signal. "When will I meet my father?"

I reversed out of the driveway with more haste than normal, scraping the door against a lamp on the ground and hearing it shriek at me as it tore into the door. "Why do you want to meet him?"

Oñé dropped his voice to a level that I could scarcely hear. "Why wouldn't I want to meet him? He is my father. If you were me, would you not want to meet your father?"

I bumped against the pavement as I turned out of the driveway with my heart thumping again in its panic mode. My hands sweated on the steering wheel so much so that they were slipping and sliding. I gripped the wheel tightly, aware that drops of sweat were running down my face in a way that reminded me of my first sight of Ishmael walking up to the house. I tried to make my voice sound calm, "No, I have no desire to meet my father. Just as well. He is dead."

Oñé looked at me with that direct look he had already perfected with his few short years on earth. "What about your mother? Do you have any desire to see her? Is she alive?"

He was beginning to do my head in. "I see her when I can."

I pressed my foot on the accelerator and headed for Palma.

Sophia looked a little lost as she came through Gate C at Palma airport. She looked to the right and hadn't spotted Oñé and I standing with a bunch of half dead flowers which I had insisted buying in a nearby garage. She held her head very straight over her shoulders. She wore an African scarf wrapped around her head. She turned to look to the left and waved energetically when she spotted us.

I embraced her and kissed her, aware that I was doing everything gently, almost in slow motion. I smelt her perfume. It was not one that I recognised although I had kissed many women in my life. It was light and flowery with hints of lemon and lime. I pulled back as soon as I realised that I had kissed her first rather than allow her to embrace Oñé. Maybe I pulled back too abruptly as she looked startled and embarrassed.

Oñé stayed with his hands at his side, like a soldier being inspected by an army Major. He allowed himself to be kissed by Sophia but did not kiss her back.

Sophia rested her hands on his shoulders and turned to look at me. "I like the new 'look'." She smoothed her hand over his hair.

I breathed deeply and gave Oñé a meaningful look. Sophia looked again at Oñé and then at me. "I see that he has talked to you about his desire to see Gregoriano."

How could she have known that by looking at us both?

I replied, "No. He has not talked so much about Gregoriano. More about Ishmael."

19

PABLO PICASSO

"There are only two types of women – goddesses and doormats."

31st December 2017

We celebrated New Year's Eve in Can Pintxos. Sophia changed her African headwear for a white beret. She wore long black boots which came up over her knees, black hot pants and a cream lace blouse. Her legs were a little thinner than I had remembered but her face was radiant – glowing with happiness. I don't think Oñé had smiled at Sophia since she had arrived, yet he grinned at me from time to time.

There was a set menu in Can Pintxos starting with a glass of cava. Oñé sipped on an orange Fanta as Sophia and I clinked glasses.

"Happy New Year."

As I said that I was aware that she may not survive the year. She seemed to know what I was thinking.

"Let's hope so."

She ignored Oñé and began talking as if he weren't there. "You see Gregoriano asked me to take care of Ishmael – as he asked you."

I shook my head. "He never asked me to take care of Ishmael. I needed a gardener and my friend José recommended Ishmael."

Sophia sliced her small scallop into four pieces. "Sometimes that is the way that Gregoriano works. He works indirectly, enlisting third party help. The more that you know of him, the more you see that he is a mystery who becomes more and more intimate as time passes. Even if he is not with you, he somehow becomes tenderer. He slips through the cracks of our words and gestures and opens us up to a different level of being." Staring at the ceiling, she added, "With me he was both direct and indirect."

She stopped. "Is Oñé okay?"

She looked to her right where Oñé watched the black and white screen playing scenes from Charlie Chaplin and Laurel and Hardy on the wall of the restaurant. He sipped on his Fanta. Sophia winked at me; the first time she had done that since we had met.

She smiled answering her own question. "I think he is fine. He loves anything which makes him laugh. What he doesn't like is what he sees in me as an ineffective mother. He would like to have a man around as a father. Even for a short while Ishmael knew how to step into that comforting role. When I refused Gregoriano access to Oñé, it was to protect him from the harm of loving someone who had chosen to put themselves in high risk situations where they could die. I then believed the day to day risk that his father could be killed would be damaging. I did not appreciate the full significance of abandonment issues for a child, in spite of my training as a psychiatric nurse. I was too young. There are things to learn about love and life which need time. I was selfish enough to think that I, alone, could provide Oñé with enough love – that he didn't need a father whose death could destroy him."

She sipped the cava again. "Who am I to decide who will live and who will die, or what value the time we have on earth means? How insane was that thought that he needed a young father? Look at me? I could die at any time."

She didn't look as if she was looking for sympathy – more that she was being realistic. "Let me tell you what happened. I went to Baghdad as a nurse in 2005. The Iraqi War had been running for two years. I was a qualified psychiatric nurse, just 23 years of age. At first, I was needed more for my medical than psychiatric skills. I worked with the doctors to remove shrapnel from faces which would remain forever severely disfigured. We treated terribly wounded bodies with what little resources we could find.

"One day, in 2006 they wheeled a man into our make-shift hospital. He had chest wounds from multiple gun shots. He was 59 years of age – a lot older than me. I had to get him ready for theatre. He was conscious. We talked. He told me what had happened to him. Working as a doctor, he treated the wounded in a hospital in Baghdad. While he dressed the wounds of a young woman who had lost her arm, soldiers from the Assad army entered the hospital ward, spraying it with gunfire and he was hit. He said that one of them stood on top of his stomach, looked into his eyes and said, 'We will leave you to die the slow way. That's what you deserve'. Before stepping off his body, he fired another shot into his chest, saying, 'Let's make sure that it's not too easy for you'."

I played with the scallop on my plate, finding it a bit slimy and retching as I swallowed it. "What happened?"

Sophia watched the waiter who silently removed the starters and served a small lamb dish on a bed of mashed potato. The candlelight flickered on her face.

"That man was Gregoriano. He had a job to do – a special job. I knew that. He recovered. I knew that he would. It was easy to fall in love with him. For me, he radiated love itself. That was irresistible. How could I not love him? During the day we worked together attending to the wounded in the hospitals, schools and driving in Red Cross jeeps to refugee camps which were under attack. In those conditions, time seemed to expand. The moments we had together when not working were precious occasions. We would drink thick black coffee from a coffee pot bubbling on a fire pit and share whatever food was available with the refugees.

"I had never felt so connected to the soul of another human being. There was destruction all around us and yet we saw in other human beings and in ourselves resilience and learning not to give up in loving and helping others survive from one day to another. I know this will sound quite ridiculous, but I have never felt happier than those first two years working with Gregoriano in Iraq. I was young. I felt that he poured all his knowledge, hopefulness of spirit and faith in human nature into me. I gave all of myself back to him. I didn't even consider that it was an unequal giving and receiving. The age difference between us dissolved into a love which flowed from him, which I received. From an ageless being I didn't know, he allowed himself to empty incredible love from the depths of who he was. This made it easy for me to allow the unknown depths of who I was to flow into him. When there is a mutual movement of love like the love we shared between us, the atrocities of war became bearable.

"There were only rare opportunities to make physical love together. It didn't seem to matter – our exchange of being was at a deeper level than flesh. It was eternal. There were only three occasions when we lay together at a distance from the refugees in the camp, under the stars, embracing with only a blanket over us and our bodies bruised by hard stones and sand. On one of those occasions, I fell pregnant. I felt my age. I was twenty-five. Gregoriano was sixty. I was with child and for the first time and afraid. Not afraid for me but for the child we both were bringing into an insane world of violence."

I ordered a bottle of white wine. The same as the one she had ordered for me when we first met in the Turning Torso in Malmo and another Fanta for Oñé who seemed totally absorbed by Laurel and Hardy.

As the waiter filled our glasses, I shared, "But what you are describing is a relationship which should never have ended. It sounds beautiful, unique and worth all the risks in the world which you had already taken in being together!"

"I know that now but I had to think of Oñé more than myself. I have to do that even more so now that I may soon die. Gregoriano wanted to marry me. I refused. I thought that his life was too unstable. Even now he is not only working in Syria but in Yemen where another ghastly conflict is destroying the lives of millions of innocent people. It is his vocation to work in these war zones. For him everyone has an equal right to life and he has a commitment to making that happen. He has Oñé but the children he meets in every hospital or refugee camp are equally important to him. As a mother I found that hard to accept.

"I told him that I needed to take Oñé to a safer place. Not one where he would learn through violence how to survive but one where he would grow up knowing love, security and community. I deliberately denied him access to seeing Oñé – apart from the one occasion when he held him in his arms as a baby of four weeks. I took a photograph of them together which I thought would be important for both of them. How insane of me to think that I could guarantee outliving him and be a carer for Oñé for the most important years of his life."

I squeezed her hand. "Of course you will survive this cancer. You will still be here for Oñé. You will have him with you in only a few months when you are given the 'all clear' and know that your cancer is gone – like a cloud disappearing over L'Ofre."

She kissed the top of Oñé's head. She laughed and said, "Thinking back then I loved the way he accepted my mistakes. Not allowing him to see Oñé was probably one of them. He told me that imperfection is the organising principal of spiritual reality. He liked my imperfection."

She shook her head, rubbed a little of her lipstick away as she cleaned her lips. She asked, "Why do you think he brought us together?"

I didn't respond but made a grunting noise which could have been confused with laughter. The lamb tasted fatty in my mouth. I felt that I might be sick. I asked, "What have you learnt from your time with him?"

Sophia rubbed the top of her glass of cava and made it sing. She took her time before responding. "He nudges people to waken them up to do the right things, rather than apply force. You will have noticed that he doesn't pressurise you to do anything, but he knows what you need to do. He lets you know when the time is ripe. He doesn't rush things."

Oñé dropped his fork on the floor. A waiter rushed to

give him a clean fork. As he lifted it, he grabbed Sophia's hand. "He hasn't nudged me, telling me what to do. Yet he is my father. He mustn't want to help me."

"Of course he wants to help you. That is why you are here. He wants that for your good." She was sweating. "It's warm in here." She removed her white beret.

All of her beautiful hair was gone. She didn't care that everyone looked at her baldness. She touched Oñé lightly on the nose with her finger. "He will tell you when the time is right. I said he doesn't rush things. It's like letting a plant reveal its beauty in time and not before."

Oñé started to whimper. It was New Year's Eve. I was afraid that there was going to be a scene and I would not be able to return to Can Pintxos which was one of my favourite places to eat. "I want to see my father."

The waiter brought three plastic cups each containing twelve grapes for us to eat at midnight as a way of welcoming in the New Year. Sophia asked, "Can we go the Plaza to hear the Church bells at midnight?"

We moved through the crowds gathering at the Church steps. Young boys wore black suits, white shirts and black ties. They created a sense of stepping into a 1950s film set. The girls wore sparkling short dresses and sipped on free cava. I noticed for the first time that Oñé also wore a black suit, white shirt and black bow tie. How did he know the dress code for the Plaza? I was also a bit shocked that I hadn't looked at him for more than a few minutes during the entire evening.

I had one hand in my trouser pocket; the other held the plastic cup with the grapes. I had become entranced watching my breath form clouds in front of my face when Sophia slipped her arm through mine. Oñé sat on the ground and counted his grapes for the third time. The Church bells began to chime and the three of us pushed a gritty grape into our mouths. We all managed to finish the twelve by the last gong. That was meant to be good luck for the New Year 2018. A firework soared into the air and exploded above the Church.

Sophia kissed me on the lips. I felt my heart thumping wildly in my chest. I knew that she would notice that I was breathless. I did not want to kiss her back. Her lips were slug-like. I couldn't understand why my heart continued to beat so strangely when my head and heart told me to push her away. Luckily Oñé threw his arms around my legs not moving from the ground. I had a reason to release Sophia's embrace, bending down to throw my arms around him.

It was then that I saw a shadowy figure on Oñé's right. He was sitting on a bench as people began to dance to the band now playing in the doorway of the Town Hall. I dropped my empty plastic glass on the Plaza floor in shock. I thought that I had seen Ishmael.

Oñé pressed his head once again against my legs. I thought that I heard him sob. I reached down and whispered in his ear, "Oñé, I may be mistaken but I thought that I saw Ishmael sitting over there." I pointed at the bench. "No. He's gone. It must have been someone who looked like him."

It was cruel talking to Sophia and Oñé about the possibility of Ishmael being alive. I had to stop this craziness of seeing Ishmael in other people's faces. It was pure insanity.

Sophia caught my hand after I hugged Oñé and she looked at me with a gaze that seemed to be filled with awe and a frightening surrender.

"Will you marry me?"

What was she saying? Gregoriano was the father of her child. Why would she want to marry me after she had described her deep mystical love for him? She didn't know me. She wanted me to step into a role to take care of Oñé if she died and Gregoriano was killed in some foreign war zone. That wasn't in my mind a good enough reason for getting married to her – or maybe it was? I remembered her slippery lips and dreaded the thought of what more could be expected from me.

That kiss from Sophia with her question about marriage was like another form of death. I felt like a shark caught on a hook and desperately trying to find a way to wriggle free. I knew the fear of being pulled into a foreign world in which I would never survive. A world in which I wouldn't drown yet where I would live yearning for water which I knew would drown me.

I didn't answer Sophia. Instead, I sidetracked her

question in the way I had become proficient doing with my public speaking, asking, "Did you see him?"

"Who?"

"I thought I saw Ishmael but it couldn't have been him – could it have been?"

She held my hand. "It's possible. It depends what state he is in. He will get in contact with us when he feels ready. We don't need to rush him."

20

PABLO PICASSO

"Art is a lie that makes us realise the truth, at least the truth that is given to us to understand."

Tuesday 2nd January 2018

Oñé spent most of the time in his bedroom during Sophia's visit, only emerging to eat a morsel or two. I ordered a takeaway pizza thinking that there can't be a boy on planet earth who wouldn't want to eat a pizza margarita. He ate a small slice.

Sophia needed to rest a lot so I decided that I needed more help to cope with the practicalities of having two house guests.

I plucked up the courage to ring Gabriela. I said, "Happy New Year. How have you been?"

"It has been complicated."

"I'm sorry for not being in touch sooner. I promised to reimburse you for all of the money you would have received since last October."

"Thank you. You gave me enough to last until the end of the year."

"I'll give you a bonus for Christmas and the New Year."

"Thank you. It's not really necessary but as you have

money to throw around you might as well throw it in my direction."

She asked, "Have the police been in touch about Ishmael?"

A wave of anxiety moved through me. "Yes. They came because of what you said to them."

"Of course."

"What did you tell them?"

"What I knew."

"Which is precisely what?"

"That Ishmael seemed happy that last night I saw him with you. Something happened to make him leave so abruptly. He didn't say goodbye to me. That is not the Ishmael that I know. You know that they have completed their DNA tests?"

"Yes. There is nothing to report."

She laughed sarcastically. "That's not what I was told. We will see. It's not a closed enquiry. So you are saying that you want me to return to work?"

"Yes. That is what I am saying. I need help with Oñé. Sophia, his mother is in the process of receiving treatment for cancer. She returns to Malmo on the 4th January for more chemotherapy. As you can imagine I could do with some help. I'm not used to taking care of a young boy."

Gabriela said, "OK. I'll see you on the 7th January – after Reyes."

She signed off without saying thank you or Happy New Year.

Sophia spent quite a lot of time in bed. I didn't talk about her proposal of marriage. After the call with Gabriela, I told Sophia that my housekeeper was returning in a few days. She seemed pleased that Oñé would have a woman's touch around the house.

That night, we each went to our separate bedrooms after preparing a cup of hot milk and honey for Oñé. When I knew that they were likely to be asleep, I got out of bed and walked to the Studio. The moon was a slither of silver against a velvet blanket of darkness. The wind had picked up, howling around my ears and chilling my body. I had not put a coat on over my pyjamas. My slippers slid along the gravel as if I was skating. I gave permission for the wind move up my legs, buffeting at my pyjama trousers as if I were a boat at sea and the trousers were sails. I enjoyed the coldness of those creepy fingers which I imagined came from near the moon. Hadn't I read somewhere that the moon was a piece of the earth's mantel jettisoned into deep space? As I stared at that scythe in the darkness, I imagined that it was throwing itself back to me. I had to catch it. I had to undo the failure of Oñé refusing to catch the ball on the beach. I held my hands out and watched the light of the moon fall upon my empty hands. The wind fluttered up my pyjama trousers.

I opened the door into the Studio. It felt as though I was seeing it for the first time or maybe that I was aware of how many things I hadn't really seen before. The lock was of black iron, the olive wood on the door dry and wizened. The door fitted within an arch of grey stone. As it squeaked open, I worried that Sophia or Oñé would hear it. I only pushed it a little to allow me to squeeze through. I didn't close it behind me in case there would be more noise. I walked quickly towards Oñé's canvas which I had covered a few days ago in Egyptian cotton instead of plastic. I threw back the cover and looked.

Something had dramatically changed. The painting had been healed. The slashes repaired in some unknown way. It didn't surprise me. Somehow it was what I expected. I covered the painting, left the Studio and walked as silently as I could towards the house.

I heard persianas open from the bedroom in which I knew Sophia was sleeping. I looked up at her leaning out of the window.

Her head was like a full moon glistening in the darkness. Her whispers carried towards me like a small boat on a stormy sea, heading into the safety of the Port of Soller.

"What are you doing out here? I thought you had gone to bed."

I pulled the string on my pyjama bottoms tighter. I waved at her as if saying goodbye. "No. I thought I heard an animal in pain. I was looking for it. I think it was only the wind."

Sophia laughed. "I am beginning to think that your hearing isn't the best."

I knew that she was thinking of that proposal she had

made. I blushed and shivered in the darkness. I waved at her a second time. "Sorry to have wakened you. Sleep well."

I heard her bolt the persianas closed. I gazed once more towards the moon. That little slither of silver against the darkness reminded me that even if you can't see something fully it doesn't mean that it isn't there.

There was a scuffling sound to my right, towards the Studio. I turned my head quickly. Now I thought that Gregoriano was there. I was sure of it. It struck me that they looked quite similar in spite of their age differences. Maybe it was Gregoriano I had seen in the Plaza on New Year's Eve. Now, in the darkness I recognised an outline which could have been of his body. He strode confidently into the depths of the orange grove.

I ran in his direction. I reached the tree where I expected him to be waiting for me with another place to go, a message to be fulfilled. I thought I could hear him breathing in the way he breathed on the yacht during our trip to Deia. He had a deep out-breath, followed by a short gasping breath as if he had surprised himself that he was still alive.

He wasn't there. Instead I spotted a tiny white hedgehog, trapped amongst the orange trees and attempting to scuttle through dry leaves. Should the hedgehog not have been hibernating? It stopped to look at me. I swore it had the eyes of Gregoriano. They were green. When I heard myself thinking like that, I knew I needed to return to the house. I was losing my senses again. I imagined that when I looked at Oñé's painting the following day, I would see it slashed. It would not be healed or repaired.

I would not be able to show it to Sophia.

I lay in bed listening to the wind rattling the persianas, wishing that I had kept a journal much earlier in my life. It would be so much easier to remember facts. It would have been good to have started it after that first meeting with Gregoriano when I was ten. I could then have tracked my thoughts and allowed myself to erase everything that I had written that wasn't the truth. That would have helped me. Insane thoughts are now a part of who I am. I don't know which thoughts to delete. A journal would have helped a discernment faculty to evolve in me.

I wondered whether Oñé keeps a journal in which he records his experiences with me in Soller. I wanted to encourage him to do so and at the same time, I dreaded that thought – that my whole reputation as the Painter would be destroyed by the wild ramblings of a ten-year-old. What would be even worse would be if he told the truth – if he discovered the truth. He was capable of doing that. Yet, I wanted the world to know who I am. That is why I have started to keep a journal. I want the truth to be known at the right time and to be told by me.

21

PABLO PICASSO

"What might be taken for a precocious genius is the genius of childhood. When the child grows up, it disappears without a trace. It may happen that this boy will become a real painter. But then he will have to begin everything again, from zero."

Wednesday 3rd January 2018

In the morning, I caught the sun in my hands – the heat from nearly 6,000 degrees centigrade rushing towards me from deepest space. I held it. I wanted to drop it and dive again into the darkness of the night. There are people who like to see the sunrise. I like to see it the sun set and feel darkness smother the Earth. The darkness brings with it silence. It scares and comforts me. I live more with paradox these days. I can be scared and comforted at the same time.

When I lie in bed the darkness takes away my body. I feel that I am dispersed in the space within the room. Maybe that it what it is like when you die. You're everywhere watching. Whereas in this body, I watch my thoughts as I lie in clammy sheets. Thoughts are mostly images which jump out of the darkness like a breaching whale and disappear again. I have the feeling that is what my life is like; a brief emerging from nothing and then disappearing. If the Big Bang did take place over 14 billion years ago and if matter was then imbued with spirit, I have to ask myself the question 'why'? Especially when I listen to Sophia explaining to me what her life was like in Iraq, in Syria and now for Gregoriano moving between Syria and the Yemen. I hear about the suffering of the world against the background of my decadence and privilege.

In the darkness of the night questions easily flash into my mind. What am I meant to do with this little flicker of life appearing and disappearing in such a short time when you think of the evolution of the earth, formed 14 billion years ago? As I lie in my bed the mystery of it all envelops me. I find myself searching in the darkness for an Intelligence that created everything including me. It is frustrating because I know that it is here, hiding from me – like Gregoriano has hidden from me – appearing only occasionally since the age of ten. I am sure that it is no coincidence that he chose Oñé to stay with me. He wanted me to know something. Of course I need to remember what he wrote in that letter inviting me to Malmo. I imagine that there is more to it than that. I will find out if there is more. Everything is getting clearer. What remains unclear is why Gregoriano is interested in me when he has so many other people to think about in

Yemen and Syria? I will find out. I'm getting closer to the truth of it all.

Tomorrow Sophia has to return to Malmo to continue her treatment. I don't want her to go. She has not talked about her friends and how they support her during her treatment. The only people she has talked about are Oñé, Ishmael and Gregoriano. I am beginning to think that she is like me, that she has no friends.

Maybe we are destined to be together. She and Gregoriano know that better than I do.

I looked at the alarm. It was only six o´clock. Neither Sophia nor Oñé would be awake. I wanted to check Oñé's painting to see if it had been healed and was suitable to show Sophia today before her departure to Malmo the next day.

I threw a jumper on top of my pyjamas and tip toed downstairs. I opened the front door and walked past the fountain, past the sculpture of Ishmael and then ran towards the Studio. Once inside, I removed the cover from Oñé´s triptych.

I laughed out loud and then covered my mouth with my hand, even though I was far from the West Wing where Oñé and Sophia slept. The painting was perfect. How had Oñé done this? I touched it to see if there was 'scar' tissue around where we had made the slashes.

No. It was smooth. The confusion about how this had happened didn't affect me. I didn't care. I danced back to the front door and found my way to my bedroom in the West Wing. I crawled into bed and slept a dreamless sleep until the alarm went advising me to get up and prepare breakfast.

I pulled Oñé to one side after breakfast and whispered to him while Sophia packed her suitcase.

"We can show Sophia your painting. It's perfect. She will be so proud of you."

"In what way will she be proud of me?"

"You're ten years old – no, I mean eleven." I slapped my head. "Your painting is exceptional. How did you fix the slashes?"

He shook his head. "I didn't fix them. The only person who could do that is Ishmael. After all he painted it for real. I've only copied him."

I put my finger over my lips and whispered insistently, "No. No. No. It can't be Ishmael. It has to be you. Ishmael is not here."

"You said that you saw him in the Plaza on New Year's Eve."

"I only said that I saw someone I thought was him or Gregoriano. Of course it wasn't him or he would have joined us to celebrate the New Year. I made a mistake. Adults make mistakes. You have to forgive me. I made a mistake. It wasn't a lie." I looked at him. He looked sad. "I know that you must be upset that Sophia is leaving."

Oñé put out his hand. "Give me the key. I will check the painting before we show it to Sophia."

I handed over the key and followed close on his heels.

Once inside, he whisked the cover away with a flourish. "It is exactly as I painted it."

I struggled for words to reply. What I saw was Sophia flying upside down descending into Hell, holding Ishmael with her right hand and Gregoriano with her left hand. I had changed into the observer of a thousand faces in the blackness watching them.

I shouted at Oñé: "You little brute – you are trying to make me think that I am going mad."

He tucked his hands into his trouser pockets and placed a hand on the canvas. "That isn't going to be so very hard to do is it? Let's see what Sophia thinks of it."

I lifted the cover from the floor and threw it over the painting. "How can you be so cruel as to show her that she is descending into Hell ..." I hesitated, "knowing ... that ...?"

Oñé pulled the cover once again away from the painting. He turned abruptly, pointing his finger at me. "Knowing what? You are only looking at one part of the triptych. There are two more parts to it."

Sophia clicked her way towards us dressed in high heels with which she amazingly navigated with ease the pebbled path. She wore a soft, fitted emerald dress with her black stilettos. Her head was covered in what seemed to me to be an ivory silk band. As she approached the painting my legs wanted to run. Sophia whispered in a strong voice that seemed to make the air in the Studio quiver as if her voice was coming from a viola or cello.

"Well, what have we got here?"

"It's Oñé's work."

Oñé turned to look at me and wiped his hands on his jeans. "Do you want to see it mother? I don't think Augustin likes it."

Sophia approached the painting and slowly scanned it from left to right. She moved closer examining the layers of oil, thickly spread like icing on a cake, layered in gold, orange and emerald green like her dress. I noticed that in the painting she carried a large orange handbag flying upwards towards the Heavens as her head dived south. Around her head she wore an ivory silk headband.

"This is Ishmael's painting. I am sure of it. Why is the paint not quite dry?" She looked at me with a quizzical look. "You have taken it from the Reina Sophia as a surprise haven't you and adulterated it?"

I shook my head. "Of course not. Oñé painted it. Didn't you Oñé?"

Oñé placed a finger over his lips and looked bemused. "I don't quite remember. Everything goes quite blank when I paint. Did you not paint it Augustin? How could I paint Gregoriano's face when I have never seen him?"

"How do you know that it is Gregoriano? No-one has mentioned that it is him – only you. You said that you were painting what Ishmael painted the night that he left. If you have a photographic memory you don't need anything else than the gift of your photographic memory."

Oñé looked a Sophia with a pleading glance. "It's how

I imagine him. It's how you described him. Is it how you remember him? I imagine that I should have painted him as an older man. He is seventy now isn't he? Do you not think it strange that in this painting, he looks younger than Augustin?"

I ignored what he was saying and turned instead to Sophia. "I think we should contact the Reina Sophia and see if the painting is still there. If not we will find out how it got here and return it."

I pulled at Oñé's cheek again with my finger and thumb. "It's easy to dab a piece of oil on a finished painting to make it look as if you painted it."

Oñé started to cry and rub his cheek with his hand. I could see that it was going to be bruised. I felt embarrassed that Sophia could also see it. I turned to Oñé and pointed at the painting. "This is excellent. You have done an amazing job on it since the last time I saw it. I know this is going to sound as if I don't trust you, but let's ring the Reina Sophia and put our minds at ease."

"How could I steal Ishmael's painting from the Reina Sophia? I have been here all the time. You have my passport. I don't know anyone here yet. I only start school after Reyes on the 7th January." He pointed at me with a hand beneath the painting gown he wore for protection which made him look even more ghost-like.

Sophia kissed Oñé on his purpling cheek. She rummaged in her handbag for her mobile phone, pressing the buttons quickly without referring to her contacts list.

I heard her asking for someone by the name of Jordi. She waited for almost a minute as they searched for him.

Then I heard her say with a laugh, "Thank you Jordi. I am sorry to bother you but as Ishmael has not returned, I wanted to be sure that everything was OK. As you know I am a bit obsessive about his art. You are saying that it is hanging on the wall and creating quite an interest – in fact a storm of interest – Madrid. That is good news. I will speak to you shortly. Thank you for your clarification. Speak soon."

She finished her call without looking at me got on her knees in front of Oñé. "It is your choice. You can stay here for another few months or you can return with me. What would you like to do?"

Oñé picked up a paintbrush, dipped it into turpentine and then onto his palette of drying oils choosing orange paint, dapping a few dots onto the handbag on the painting. I saw that they were orange flowers on the bag she was carrying which he had overlooked.

"I'll stay here."

Sophia searched in her handbag again, this time for a paper handkerchief, and dabbed at her eyes. "Will you come to the airport with me?"

Oñé shook his head. "I'll stay here."

Sophia's voice quivered. "You are too young to stay alone."

"I'm not alone. I'm never alone."

I whispered although I would have preferred to have

shouted at him: "Lock the door and do not go out until I return. We will go to dinner at your favourite pizzeria when I return."

I made myself smile at him and ruffled his hair in feigned friendship. Sophia shook her head and texted someone. She waited for a reply and when it came back her lips curled up in a way I couldn't work out if she wanted to laugh or cry.

The drive to the airport was dreadful. She didn't say a word but texted someone every few minutes. I felt sure that she was meeting him (it had to be him) to travel back together on the plane. I thought it had to be Gregoriano. I helped her with her luggage to the check in. She was silent.

Then, as she moved towards the escalator for departures, she took my hand. "You don't know yet what it is like to live on the edge of life. That edge that takes you to death, where we are all going. It is too much for us to bear. Yet we all get through it. There isn't a single human being born who hasn't got through it. I am like everyone else – so are you."

I held her hand as I went with her up the escalator. She kissed me on the lips before going through security. Her lips were still slug-like and unpleasant.

I heard myself say, "I will."

As she placed her boarding pass to enter the security area, she turned and looked at me with what I would say was a lost look.

"You will what?"

"I will marry you."

She didn't turn back to embrace me but rather walked through the opened gate and then turned to look at me.

"So be it."

She walked past the bottles of Jack Daniels, refusing the samples of gin, past the shelves of Clinique and Mac and turned left towards her gate.

After leaving Sophia at the airport and before arriving home to take Oñé out for his promised meal, I drove to the Port of Soller where I knew that one of the few places to eat or have a drink at this time of the year would be open – the Albatross Bar. It was cold, so I went inside. It had been recently refurbished and felt quite warm and inviting. I ordered a beer and then tapped into the internet on my mobile. I searched Google for information on Ishmael Domini. This time there was a post. Previously when I had searched there was nothing. There was a post now from art critic Akoo Larsson from Sweden. I opened the link. His review had been posted on the 2nd January 2018.

"Reflections on the work of Ishmael Domini at the Reina Sophia, Madrid."

Ishmael Domini is a recluse. You will find nothing about his life on Wikipedia. You will not know where he is living or how he lives. As an art critic visiting the Reina Sophia, Madrid, I discovered a triptych by Ishmael with a notification identifying that he created this work in Malmo, Sweden. The triptych's title is **"You and Me"** *Being inspired by his stay in Sweden, his work had a particular interest for me.*

The first part of the triptych **"You and Me"** *is* **"Descent into Hell"**, *the second,* **"The Judgment"** *and the third,* **"Transformation"**. *I was first entranced by his use of colour – swirling turquoises, orange and faint touches of rose which contrast with the greyness of his native land. It is reminiscent of the works of Marc Chagall who saw his work as "not the dream of one person but of all humanity." Ishmael expresses this within* **"You and Me"**. *The observer drops into the triptych as a snowflake falls to the ground and melts into his world of colour which you know as the swirling of your mind, body and soul. Forms are not readily recognisable as if Ishmael is telling us that they are unimportant in definition and more a reflection of mystery and change which are a part not only of the eternal human condition but of the cosmos itself within which we are implanted.*

In **"Descent into Hell"** *there is the shape of an amphora from Greek and Roman times which is a large two handled storage jar for oil or wine. It has a narrow neck and two handles. It is turned upside down and hurtling towards Hell. Each of the handles is clutched at by shadowy shapes. The amphora is being emptied and emerging from the narrow neck appears to be a Eucharistic host. As you look closely at the host, you* *see yourself within it. I challenge each observer of this painting to see if this is not the case for them. I have asked others for their perspective and have had the same response. They either see themselves in the Eucharist or the faces of friends or enemies they love or hate. It symbolises creation in all its human form being emptied into Hell and two people hoping for their salvation by holding onto the empty amphora.*

Hell, as depicted by Ishmael, is not a fire but rather a sea of faces, unknown animal shapes and bizarre plants from which gush forth hot steam which reaches to the hands and arms of those who clutch at the amphora.

*The second part of the triptych – **"The Judgment"** – is even more enigmatic. Colours have almost disappeared. There is a blank white canvas onto which are strewn distorted shapes of buildings, twisted human faces, splashes of crimson blood and dots of blackness. It seems to be influenced by Jackson Pollock. It is the whiteness of the canvas which gives the sensation of the observer of the painting who is judging. Hints of appearances and disappearances on the canvas give an impression of missed opportunities in life which, within the whiteness of the canvas, are now known in their significance. There is calmness in this knowledge symbolised by a golden sun to the top right of the canvas which appears to be a loving magnet for all of the objects of judgment. They are moving towards it in the dynamic which Ishmael builds into his wave-like structure of form.*

*The third part of the triptych **"Transformation"** returns to the vibrancy of colour and imagery of "The Descent into Hell". We are swept into greater expansive waves of light and shifting perspectives – reflecting the power of an undulating sea or the swirling beauty of clouds with contrasting turquoise and orange. You see mysterious forms again – wondering if they are animals, flowers or human beings. You have fallen into a dream world for a few moments, feeling yourself a God within the canvas which you have created, absorbing the whole of creation within one loving embrace and knowing it will die to give new life.*

*There is a question mark hanging over the painting which art critics have been unable to resolve. Who are the characters portrayed in **"You and Me"**?*

*I think we may be witnessing the emergence of one of the greatest artistic talents in the Western world with **"You and Me"**. I am looking forward to seeing more from this artist.*

I breathed deeply. This description of the critic bore no resemblance to what I had seen Oñé paint and what Sophia confirmed what was hanging in the Reina Sophia. However, I realised that maybe it was the same painting – it is the observer who interprets what they see, not the painter. My mobile sang at me. There was a text from Oñé.

"Emergency. Come home."

What had happened? I had been away for less than two hours.

I threw euros on the counter to pay for the beer. The waiter looked at me with his surprise. I think he expected me to order a second beer or a whiskey as I normally did.

I jumped into the car, screeched around the roundabout and turned right.

I drove home in a crazy mood of mind, terrified about what Oñé could have done, or what might have happened to him. Although Soller is a small town, there are still drug dealers looking for opportunities to rob from wealthy house owners. They could take Oñé hostage and demand a ransom.

Then I had yet another of my crazy thoughts – what if Sophia had left Oñé with me with the intention of having him kidnapped and blackmailing me? I know nothing about her. Why should I believe her story about Ishmael and Gregoriano? Why would she want to marry me? It seemed too rushed, a proposal of marriage. I should be more cautious and give myself more time to see if I am the right person for both of them. Yet, I have told her that I will marry her. I feel controlled and manipulated by her. Should I not be the one proposing to her? She controlled Gregoriano by not allowing him access to his own son and now, because he is seventy years of age, she has made a decision that he continues not to be a suitable father for an eleven year old because he is too old, too courageous, and too unselfish.

Why didn't she think of that when she was sleeping with him under the stars in Syria? From what she has told me, Oñé could learn a lot more from Gregoriano than he can from me. Gregoriano saves lives, puts himself in danger to help children survive in desperate conditions. I have a lived a life of indulgence, privilege and pride. I am not a saver of lives but a taker of lives.

I had a terrible thought. Although Gregoriano is not permitted to see his son Oñé, I know that he communicates with Sophia. Had he told her about the fact that I had murdered my own father? The tidal shame of that reality hit me like a hammer blow and raised questions why she would want to marry me if she knew. More than anything, the shame felt like a premonition for what I would have to face when the truth emerged not only about the murder of my father, but about the murder of Ishmael.

I ran to the Studio along the pebbled path, swung open the wooden door which Oñé had not locked to find him sitting crossed legged on the floor. It seemed as if he had pulled one of my installations from its pegging and cut it into tiny pieces like a jigsaw.

He looked at me in disgust. "So you said 'yes'. I knew you would. She can make any man say 'yes'."

I tried to imagine how I would have felt aged eleven. It was difficult because it didn't seem so different from how I felt now aged fifty.

"I am not any man."

Oñé threw a piece of a fragment from my installation into a bin. "I know you're not."

"How do you know that Sophia wants to marry me and that I had said yes today?"

Oñé raised his eyes to the Heavens as if he couldn't believe that I was asking such a stupid question. "Ishmael told me. Have you not heard of mobile phones? She texted him and he came here to tell me."

I knelt on the floor beside him and began gathering together the pieces of my work of art which was scheduled to hang in a ward in a hospital within weeks. I blocked out what he had said and continued with another question.

"You said in your text that I had to come home because there was an emergency. What was it?"

I looked around and could not work out what could have happened. He seemed calm. "What was or is the emergency?" I repeated in a firm voice without looking at him and examined a few of the fragments wondering if they could be salvaged and glued to another fabric.

Silence.

I raised my eyes to look at him. His eyes were closed as if he were in deep meditation.

"Ishmael came here. He cut up the installation. I didn't." He pointed to the scissors on the table. "That's how he did it. That's when I texted you. He left through the front door. I ran after him. But you arrived too late. You missed him."

My head started to spin. I had a new sensation of a

shortness of breath in my chest with a sense of panic in my gut. I rushed to the toilet without excusing myself.

When I returned, Oñé had retrieved the fragment of the installation which he had thrown in the bin and placed it on top of the other pieces.

I undid the black tie which I had worn to take Sophia to the airport and opened the top button of my shirt. I took a few deep breaths.

"Is he coming back then?"

Oñé stared at me in disbelief. "Unless you change the locks I imagine he will return whenever he chooses to."

My head was churning. He was saying that Ishmael was alive. I reasoned that this boy was sicker in the head than I could ever have imagined.

I was prepared to play along with Oñé's story to see how far he would take it. Referring to the blood on the ground, I asked, "Did you fight?"

"I tried to stop him destroying your installations."

"Let me see you hand."

He opened his hand and I could see that the small wound from the knife slashing incident had opened and a few drops of blood trickled along his palm onto the floor.

"You had that wound the day Sophia arrived. It has opened again because you've probably picked at it."

"I didn't pick at it."

Oñé got to his feet and reached into his back pocket for his mobile phone.

"I took a photo of him as he was leaving. I didn't manage to get his face. You can make him out."

I snatched the phone from him and stared at the photo. There was only a blur of black which could have been a man exiting from the front door. I attempted to expand the image. It made it fuzzier. I rushed to the window to examine the wood stacked for the winter which I had covered with a black tarpaulin to keep the rain from soaking it. The tarpaulin was not on top of the wood as I suspected but was rolling along the path towards the house. Oñé had most likely pinned it to the door frame to create a silhouette which looked like a human being and deliberately shook the mobile phone as he took the photo. He is, after all, an artist.

For a few seconds I admired his ingenuity. I also felt a surge of relief and adrenalin. This boy was playing mind games with me that I knew I could win.

"Do you not think it's hard to identify him? There's obviously something there but I don't think I could say it was definitely Ishmael. Good job, though, thinking about using the mobile."

I looked at Oñé to see his reaction. He pressed his right hand against his left to stop the bleeding. He looked at me, shaking his head. "You don't believe me, do you?"

I didn't expect that response. I put my hands in my pockets and was aware that I was shifting from foot to foot. It was as if Oñé was putting me through a lie detector test of his own making. I coughed.

"I'm being honest. I don't recognise him. Why don't we catch him out? Let's not change the locks on the doors. Instead we place a camera outside the Studio and obtain clear images of what he is doing. What do you think about that as an idea?"

He didn't smile as he replied, "Why did he not come back openly and talk with you? Why is he hiding from you? Maybe he wants to hurt you. Do you not think it strange the way he is behaving?"

This was beginning to feel like a game of chess. I felt myself unable to move or to think. I heard myself say.

"What do you think of the camera idea? Maybe you have a better one? I imagine it must also be upsetting for you when you have spent quite a lot of time with him. He was an important part of your life. I don't like to think of you fighting with Ishmael. Sophia would be extremely upset."

My tone of voice was gentle. I was not accusing him of anything or defending myself. It sounded as if I was open to hear what he thought and felt. He gathered the remaining fragments from the installation into his hands and threw them into the air like confetti.

"It's a good idea to put a camera outside the Studio."

I sat on a chair, resting an elbow on the table on top of the lacy confetti, placed my hand on my chin and looked down at Oñé who had returned to sitting cross legged on the floor,

"Now let's change the subject. You're back at school

after Reyes on the 8th January aren't you? How are you looking forward to that?"

Being the feast of the Epiphany on the 6th January, Reyes signalled the end of Christmas period and was also the day when Spanish children receive their big presents. I was conscious that I had not bought him anything for Christmas and had to do something to win him over.

Oñé read my mind again. "I'm looking forward to Reyes. I imagine that school here is boring from the few people I have met. It was much better in Malmo. The teachers there were inspiring. Here I will know more than the teachers do. I will be teaching them. They will not know what good looks like when it comes to art. They will want photographs of reality. I've seen the paintings that they are selling in the shops and in the Can Prunera museum. Those are not art. Maybe the work of Picasso and Miró up by the railway station is better. But even they don't seem to know that colour doesn't really exist. We invent it. Nothing exists apart from what we create. The problem with teachers here will be that they will make up rubbish and I will be expected to imitate them. I will feel imprisoned as if I am in a mental health institution rather than in a Studio like here. I don't want to go to school. I want to stay here."

"How do you know that you won't like school when you haven't yet been to it, met any teachers or friends?"

Even as I finished my sentence, I wondered why I hadn't made an effort to introduce him to friends. He had been here for two months and the only person he had engaged with apart from Sophia's visit, was me. That couldn't be healthy for him, or for anyone. I imagined that was why he destroyed my installations. He was frustrated. I should be grateful that he didn't burn the Studio down. I imagined that he was capable of doing that.

Saturday 6th January 2018 – The Feast of Los Reyes

I bought Oñé a present for Reyes – a drone. That meant that I didn't have to put a camera outside the Studio because Oñé now had the responsibility of watching what was going on. He would have to provide me with a better photo of the alleged Ishmael rather than the shimmering floating black tarpaulin.

I had to decide between the DJI Phantom 4 which is a best seller and the DJI Mavic Pro which you can fold up into your bag and take on holiday. It was slightly more expensive than the DJI Phantom 4 but I didn't like the fact that the Mavic Pro was considered to be more 'jumpy' in flight than the Phantom and also had a narrower field of view. I didn't want Oñé to have any excuses for having more blurred images to show me. The marketing experts say that the DJI Phantom 4 captures 'silky footage' and holds its position even in moderate winds. It can also track moving objects and considered aesthetically to be a 'beautiful piece of sleek, white plastic'.

I wrapped the box in silver paper with golden stars

and even tied a golden ribbon around it. I placed it on Oñé's chair before he arrived downstairs for breakfast. I poured myself a coffee, made his hot chocolate and waited.

He delicately sat in his chair after setting the silver box aside and gave me a sideways look as if he mistrusted what would be inside. It seemed to take him an age to undo the bow and then to carefully remove the star spangled sellotape. His nails seemed to be too short to pick the sellotape away. I watched even though my deepest instinct was to rip the paper open for him.

When the drone was eventually unpacked, he jumped out of his seat and threw his arms around me. "This is the best present I have ever been bought in my life. You have read my soul."

I felt a little choked up that I had picked a present that he genuinely liked. He had already worked out how he could use it. He spent the whole weekend getting it into the air, flying it to Barranc and then over to the Port of Soller. It was true that the footage was superb – clear images, stable – like a mini-satellite hovering around the valley of Soller. On Sunday evening, as we were having pizza in the Port of Soller, he asked an obvious question which I had not considered.

"How will we ensure that the surveillance continues when I am at school?"

I sighed at my stupidity. I should have worked out that he would ask that. I certainly wasn't going to volunteer to play with operating the drone while I was getting a break with him being at school.

I gave in. "Well, let's get a backup security camera pointed at the Studio."

Sunday 7th January 2018

Gabriela arrived on her scooter which made its usual purring and crunching on the gravel before it stopped abruptly outside the door. I opened the door and invited her in. Oñé was still asleep.

I asked, "Would you like a coffee?"

Gabriela shook her head. "No thank you. I'll start cleaning." She looked around. "You have managed better than I thought you would on your own and with a child to take care of. It doesn't look too bad."

I pointed to the sofa. "Before you begin, let's talk."

She looked even more distraught than she had done the last time I had seen her. Her eyes were heavily made up with thick eye liner but there were black streaks down her face as if she had been crying.

I went over to find my wallet.

"Here is the money for another two months of work. My situation has changed. I am to be married on the 1st April to Sophia, Oñé's mother. She is currently in Malmo continuing treatment for cancer."

She rubbed her eyes. "Would you mind if I do have a coffee? How did you meet Sophia?"

I made us both a coffee. "You remember that I talked to you about an acquaintance called Gregoriano?"

"Yes. You told me that you first saw him when you were ten and he regularly appeared in your life since then."

"Yes. Gregoriano, I have discovered, is also a friend of Ishmael." I was pleased that I remembered to use the present tense. "I can explain. Ishmael is from Syria. His family were killed in the war there. He obtained a Visa, with the help of Gregoriano, to go to Sweden. Gregoriano is a Doctor who works in in the war zones of Syria, Iraq and Yemen. Sophia was a Nurse working in Syria. In Malmo she helped Ishmael deal with his Post-Traumatic Stress Disorder. He suffered some kind of PTSD episode, left Malmo, went to La Coruña and then came here. Obviously there is a lot more to understand about the situation. I thought it might explain why Ishmael left unexpectedly on the 5th October. What do you think about it all?"

I was aware that my leg was twitching – jumping up and down – and that my head was shaking slightly as I waited for her response.

She sighed. "That might explain why he doesn't want to talk to me. He is ill."

I nodded. My leg settled into stillness. I heard the sound of Oñé's feet on the stairs.

"This is Oñé. He likes hot chocolate and sweet buns."

He rushed into the room and threw himself into my

arms. I hugged him and, untangling him, said, "Here is a new friend – Gabriela. You will really like her. She makes even better hot chocolate than I do."

Gabriela embraced him.

"Lovely to meet you, Oñé. We have something in common. I knew Ishmael too. I know how you will be missing him. But he will return. He will have many adventures to tell us. I can't wait to hear them. Can you?"

Oñé looked at her. "I want to hear them, but mother wouldn't let him talk about his adventures. She said talking about them would make him ill. He got ill anyway. He got sick in Malmo and he got sick here. Maybe he is never going to be well again."

Gabriela looked at me. "Of course he will get well. And he will come back. Your mother is going to be well in a short while. She is going to be better than she ever was in her life. Ishmael will come back, and he will be strong and happy. I promise you."

Oñé held her hand. "How do you know?"

Gabriela laughed. "Women know things – the way your mother knows that she wants to marry Augustin and she knows that he will love you both."

Oñé sat at the table beside Gabriela who sipped her coffee beside him. He drank his hot chocolate and nibbled his raspberry and white chocolate muffin.

Oñé wiped his mouth with a napkin and looked at Gabriela. "I'm going to school tomorrow for the first time. Do you think I will like it?"

She paused before replying. "It might take a little bit of time to like it and it a little bit longer to love it. If you like learning, which I think that you do, you will see that you can learn from what you like and what you don't like."

I could see that Oñé enjoyed that way of talking. It must have been the way Sophia talked with him. I would have been harsher. I would have told him that he was lucky to have a school and to think about the children in Syria who had no food and whose faces were pressed up against wire fencing and would have loved to have sat in a classroom, learnt a new language and had the opportunity to paint. I was glad that I had not said any of that.

Oñé looked at me. "Could Gabriela take me to school tomorrow? I would like to go on a motorbike."

I looked at Gabriela. "Do you have an extra helmet?"

She laughed. "He can have mine. I will see if I can find another one. We will be okay one way or the other."

Monday 8th January 2018

Gabriela phoned me after she had cleaned the house on Sunday. I was getting Oñé ready for school which included making sure that he cleaned his teeth. She said that she had something urgent to tell me which she would like to do either before or after taking Oñé to school but didn't want him to be there. I said, "Why don't we talk after you have left him to school? We have more time."

She agreed.

When she returned after dropping him to school, I realised that I had made her a cup of hot chocolate instead of coffee. I apologised. "I'm sorry. I know you prefer coffee."

She pulled her woollen hat off and sat it on the table. She looked more relaxed than she had done the day before. I offered her a muffin which again I had forgotten she wouldn't like to eat.

She shook her head. I sat at the table beside her.

"Thank you for yesterday. You were so good with Oñé. You're a natural with children. How did he look when you left him today?"

She laughed. "I think he was a little nervous about not being able to speak much Mallorquin. But I was amazed how much he had learned in such a short time. He will pick it up very quickly. I could see one or two of the children approached him to say hello. I think he will be fine. It will be good for him not to be alone all the time."

I took a deep breath. "What did you want to tell me?"

She drank her hot chocolate hurriedly oblivious that it might be burning her throat.

"I want to clear the air and talk with you. You seem to be angry with me. I would like the atmosphere to be a happy one with Oñé here. I don't want there to be ill-feeling in the air."

I looked at the drinks cupboard and wanted to pour myself a large Jack Daniels.

"I didn't believe your story about Ishmael leaving unexpectedly." She wiped the chocolate away from her lips and pushed the cup away. "I was surprised that he was not here that day. He had told me that you were going to look for new roses and that when you were out, we could have a coffee together. He did not say anything about leaving." She looked at me directly. "I liked him. We simply discovered that when we met on Saturday in the Plaza and had a coffee together, we could talk about things that were different from the things we would talk about when you were around. He told me about Syria, his life as a lecturer in Fine Art, his family being killed, his work in the refugee camps helping the children paint and creating gardens for them."

"Why did he tell you that and not tell me?"

"Maybe because he felt safe with me, as Oñé feels safe. You don't realise that you can be scary at times. If it is not too much trouble, a coffee now would be good."

As the Nespresso machine bubbled, she walked from the kitchen towards the front door, which she pulled open and stared at the fountain.

I carried a coffee to her. "You'll like this better than the hot chocolate."

She sipped it, stepping outside into the January sunshine. She pointed at the fountain.

"I told the police that my motorbike stalled at the bottom of the road. I walked back to the house in the hope that you could give me a lift home. Before getting anywhere near the house I saw two men fighting with you. I hid inside the entrance to the labyrinth. I thought that I saw one person run away. I couldn't be sure. I ran to hide."

She looked at me. My body quivered. I knew that she was telling the truth about the fight and the murder – but were there two men involved in that fight with me? I didn't remember that. I only remembered one. I had to respond.

"There was a fight with Ishmael. It was upsetting but we had a dispute after you left. He ran away as you observed. I don't remember another person there. I had to get the anger out of my system. I went to the Studio where Ishmael and I had been working on a sculpture. I worked into the early hours of the morning – to get the horror of that argument out of my mind. That is the way I work. Have you not seen me like that before?"

She shook her head. "No. Never."

I reached towards her hand. She withdrew it. She looked at me in despair. "Don't tell me lies. Do you still want me to work for you?"

"Of course I do. This is a misunderstanding. I do not mind the police hearing what you saw and heard. I know what happened. Ishmael and I had an argument, a little bit of a tussle; but I wouldn't even call it a fight. He ran away. Of course, now that I understand his background, I know that what seemed to me like innocent banter, touched something deep in him, with his PTSD. I didn't know that then. He fled. He will come back, just as you promised Oñé yesterday. The question I have for you to help me understand that evening is that you said that there were two people engaging in physical contact with me. You know that one was Ishmael – what did the other person you think you might have seen look like?"

Gabriela walked to the fountain, placed her hands in the water. "This is where he died, isn't it? The person who you don't even remember murdering."

I took the coffee cup from her hands. "Why do you want to continue to work for me then, if you think I am a murderer?"

She laughed. "That is for me to know. Do you still want me to work for you?"

I reached a hand towards her. "Please. I need you."

She took a step towards the sculpture. "Did you murder Ishmael?"

I walked towards the house. "Don't be ridiculous. Why would I kill him? You know what kind of relationship we had. He simply had an 'episode' – maybe a psychotic breakdown about something I had said. I don't even remember what it could have been. I could have been wearing the wrong colour of clothes or made him feel rejected by not topping up his wine. God, I don't know the workings of his supersensitive mind."

Gabriela did not follow me into the house but sat on the edge of the fountain and stared at the sculpture. "I guess you're right. You don't have a supersensitive mind.

Let's talk straight. You don't have a sensitive mind, much less a supersensitive mind. Let's talk even straighter – forget about the mind, do you have a heart?"

She waved her hands around the garden. "I think that Ishmael is not dead. I have seen him. Who have you then killed? You don't know, do you?"

22

PABLO PICASSO

"The world today doesn't make any sense, so why should I paint pictures that do?"

Monday 22nd January 2018

Oñé has been at school for two weeks. He doesn't seem to be enjoying it. His nightmare has come true. In his Art class they have told him that he lacks basic skills in creating structure and form. That enraged me. He is only eleven years old. How can they say that to him? I think it is because they know he is living with me. The feedback is for me. I will show them what structure and form are all about.

Our lives have settled into what I would describe as an 'uncomfortable, and at times, a comfortable current of being'. The drone has at least made a difference. He is infatuated by it and plays with it constantly when he returns from school.

However, let me tell you what he did.

With the help from the packing company I always use, I packed five boxes for the installation which needed to go to Japan. I wasn't able to use the installation which Oñé had cut into pieces the day that Sophia returned to

Malmo. Toni and Miguel arrived to take measurements and make the coffins, as Oñé called them, for my installations nailing the edges of the boxes together.

That was two nights ago. They were to be collected today. When I went to the Studio one of the five boxes had been badly burnt, including the installation inside which was scorched rather than completely destroyed. I knew that Oñé must have done it. No-one else had a remote control for entering the property, apart from Gabriela and Pep Conejo who both kept a low profile. Who had a key to the Studio to allow precious little Oñé time to do his painting? There was no-one other than myself, Oñé, and Gabriela who cleaned the Studio once a month who entered the Studio unless it was a special day for guests visiting either to view the garden to my art in the Studio. Oñé and I watched the cctv together. There was no evidence of anyone entering the Studio other than Oñé.

My work for the Japanese exhibition was estimated at two million euros. That may be a price placed on my art but I know that it is priceless. It annoyed me that Picasso's painting 'Garcon A la Pipe' sold for over one hundred million dollars while my exhibition was only valued at two million euros. What infuriated me was that Oñé could torch what is priceless. Of course I am insured but the insurance premiums will soar for next year. The insurance inspectors reviewed the cctv footage and gave Oñé, who watched it with them, a quizzical look.

They asked me, "Has he a history of playing with fire?"

I assured them that he hadn't. I made up a story about there being a terrible storm (that part of it was true) on the evening that the installation had been destroyed. I suggested to them that the most likely explanation for the fire was that a fireball had entered the house, perhaps down the chimney of the unlit snug corner fire. I surmised that the fireball had rolled around the skirting board and connected with the boxed installations, setting one of them on fire.

They looked at one another. "Exactly how much of that explanation do you think it's worth capturing in the investigation summary and recommendation sheet?"

I was prepared for this. I opened a briefcase and handed them a brown paper envelope. They walked outside and counted it. I considered asking Oñé to switch on the cctv camera or record it with his drone, but I knew that it would adversely affect the claim.

They walked indoors smiling. One of them – I couldn't be bothered remembering his name – smirked as he asked, "It's odd that the fire didn't do more damage to the other four boxes of installations or the ceiling or the surrounding area. There is no sign of anywhere else being singed, including the skirting board, or of the fire spreading. How do you explain that?"

"The walls, skirting board and ceiling are all painted with a fire-repellent paint. The sprinklers did a good job in stopping extended damage, or the claim would have been higher."

I reached into my briefcase again and took out a second brown paper envelope. This one obviously bulged more than the first one and they didn't bother counting it.

The primary investigator, who asked most of the questions, touched his hat.

"I think we have everything we need. You have been most helpful. We are saddened by your loss. Although we will recommend that you receive full financial compensation, we understand you have lost something which can never be replaced. Would you mind if I took a photo of you?"

He reached for his mobile phone. I asked, "Is this for your investigation into the claim?"

"Absolutely not. It is purely to have a record of meeting one of Mallorca's greatest artists."

He turned to his friend. "Alfredo – can you take it?"

Alfredo stood to my left and the other inspector on my right. He said, "Why don't we do a 'selfie'?"

He clicked on his mobile. I forced a smile.

I slammed the door closed behind them after they left and watched them walk into the orangery like tourists, before nosily heading over to the entrance of the labyrinth and swimming pool, taking photos on their mobiles. I could imagine the story they would tell over an expensive lunch with friends, paid for with the contents of the brown paper bags.

For my sanity, I decided that I needed to take revenge on Oñé.

I spent a few days reflecting on what would have made him set fire to one of the 'coffins'. I had thought that our relationship had been improving. We were having conversations over meals and he gave the impression that he was enjoying walks in the mountains, watching the almond and apricot trees burst into white flowers signalling the arrival of spring.

However, in spite of my attempts to concentrate and focus on the positive improvements in our relationship, I knew that I had to do something with him to allow out the anger I felt about the destruction of my art.

I decided for a limited time I would give him tips not to improve his art but rather to destroy it. I encouraged him to paint over what he had already done with black oil and then to add splashes of white oil into which the observer could imagine himself observing the observer. It was totally nonsense, but it was successful in releasing my frustration with him. From time to time, I had to stuff a silk handkerchief into my mouth, to stop Oñé hearing me laugh. When he looked at me, I faked a few throaty coughs. Guilt kicked in after seeing him produce one painting. That was enough.

With my anger subsiding, I persuaded Oñé to work with me completing the installations for the Japanese exhibition. To my surprise he found a way of incorporating the charred remnants of the burnt installation with the chopped-up installation which he had vandalised and we created five installations which were an improvement on my original work. There were now mountainous reliefs, valleys, swirling dinosaurs with vibrant colours, against the charcoal background of the singed installation.

The new installations were dispatched to Tokyo with only two weeks delay, in perfect time for the opening of the exhibition.

Sunday 28th January 2018

Yesterday snow fell on the mountains above Soller. Oñé jumped on top of me in bed and said that he wanted to go up into the snow – it reminded him of home. I felt sad when he said that because I was beginning to think that living with me felt like home for him. I realised that there was still a lot to do before he would trust me. What I had noticed with him being here is that I can sleep. Sleep had become beautiful. I no longer rolled around the bed in a fever asking all sorts of questions to which there were no answers. I had learnt to find stillness within myself.

Sometimes it feels as if death is creeping over me. It must be how Socrates felt when he took the hemlock. It no longer frightens me. If death is like that it is peaceful. It might be better than this struggle I have turned life into day after day. I remembered thinking that when Socrates was sentenced to death, he asked "Who knows whether the place you are sending me to is better or worse than life?" He had an open mind about whether the people who were putting him there were doing him a favour or not.

I let Oñé bounce on top of me and pull at my ears which he had a habit to do now. I thought that he was trying to tell me to listen to him. Even though he was tall for his age, I carried him downstairs in my arms, sat him carefully on a chair at the kitchen table and toasted him a piece of baguette, spooning on copious amounts of home-made Mallorcan apricot jam which he loved.

Then we drove towards Lake Cuber. I knew that the snow would be heavy there. On the way up the winding mountain road, we passed cars descending with little snowmen on the bonnets. Oñé seemed distressed. He touched my arm and asked, "Is it not dangerous driving like that? They can't see where they are going."

I replied, "You're in Mallorca. It's good to learn how life can be different. People do things differently. Sweden is good. Mallorca is good. They're both good."

We stopped at Lake Cuber. There must have been a hundred people building snowmen. It was quite a production line. Oñé and I began making snowcats. We found pebbles under the snow for eyes and twigs for whiskers. I wanted something red for the mouth and peeled the skin of a purple plum which I had brought with us for a snack, shaped it into lips and added another circle of purple for the nose.

Walking very slowly, Oñé carried one of the snowcats to the car. He placed it gently on the bonnet and we drove home.

Before Oñé's arrival, a day could feel monotonous – boring. I increasingly felt excited to hear what he would say or do next. Sophia rang every day. I dreaded her phone calls. She talked about the wedding. At least she wanted to make it a small occasion, not to have a big fuss.

The last time we spoke on the phone I thought that I heard Gregoriano's voice in the background as if he were having a separate conversation on a mobile to someone. I struggled to ignore what Sophia was saying and to focus on the background dialogue. I heard someone say, "It will be the first of April. You must be there."

I nearly dropped the mobile onto the tiled floor. What did that mean? Who was he talking to? I thought the wedding was to be a small event with no strangers invited. I called to Oñé. "Your mother wants a word."

I passed the phone to him. He looked at me, shaking his head to let me know that he didn't want to talk to her. I insisted that he talked by passing the mobile to him, staying silent and looking at him in the eyes. "Hello Mother. What would you like to know?"

I wanted to grab the phone from him, appalled at how he could be so cruel knowing that she was still having her cancer treatment. I realised that for him, he wasn't being cruel, only honest. He also maybe wanted to continue to punish her for not letting him see Gregoriano.

After Sophia spoke with him about making the snowcats, Oñé passed the phone back to me. Sophia whispered as if she didn´t want Oñé to hear. "Have you heard or seen from Gregoriano? It's unlike him not to be in contact."

I replied, "I thought that he was visiting you in Malmo. Did I not hear his voice in the background?"

I imagined her shaking her head. "No. There is no-one here. I am alone. It has been months since I've heard from him. The last time was before you came to Malmo. He said that he was going to visit you. I've tried ringing his mobile but it keeps going through to voicemail."

I heard myself laugh in an unexpected way – it was more like a series of nervous grunts. "Don't worry. He's probably working in Syria. I know he will turn up for the wedding. He never misses a special occasion."

There was a silence at the end of the phone. "That's what I am worried about. That he will be killed in Syria, taken hostage and tortured. Oñé would be devastated. I don't want you to take this the wrong way but I would be really disappointed if he couldn't make the wedding. He wanted it to happen. He was right. I see what he saw in you."

I reassured her. "It is quite normal for him not to be seen for months – perfectly normal. Try not to be anxious."

Her voice steadied. "I was also wondering if you have heard any word from Ishmael? He needs to know about the wedding." She hesitated before asking me, "Do you still want to get married?"

There was a part of me that saw this question as a door I could find a way through to escape the turn of events in my life which would leave me handcuffed to Sophia and to Oñé forever. Yet another part felt that this was my destiny. It seemed the only way that I could become a sane and loving human being. For the first time in my life I had responsibilities. I had to live up to them.

"Of course I do. As you have said, it is not only what I want but it is what Gregoriano wanted. There is nothing wrong with an arranged marriage. That's what happens with on-line dating – except a computer chooses who you might marry rather than a human being. We both know that Gregoriano is wise. He knows what he is doing."

I listened to myself chuckle out loud. I think I sounded quite unhinged but Sophia also laughed. Perhaps my insanity was catching. She said, "It will be a marriage made in Heaven."

We ended the call promising to talk the next day. Oñé had gone to his bedroom. I had the urge to sit on his bed and tell him a story. It was something that had never happened to me before.

I climbed the stairs to Oñé's bedroom and knocked on the door before entering. He was lying asleep. Or was he pretending to be asleep so that I would go away?

I sat on the bed. I touched his forehead with the back of my hand. He looked as if he could be dead. His face felt cold. He was unmoving with scarcely a trace of breath obvious in the stillness of his body.

Suddenly, I was startled by a sound at the window. It was a tinkling sound like glass breaking. I got to my feet and strained to listen more intently. There were two more strikes at the window. I recognised the sound now. Someone was throwing pebbles at the window. I rushed over and scanned the garden which was in almost total darkness as there was no moon. A man ran into the labyrinth. I didn't recognise him but he had seen me. He must have wanted to contact Oñé.

I raced downstairs, opened the door and stared intently at the entrance to the labyrinth. I felt fear rising from my stomach into my throat. I couldn't bring myself to go into the labyrinth to find the stranger. Without Ishmael, I could lose myself within it. Even if I found the well at the centre with its dark and murky depths, which was like a magnet for everyone who entered the labyrinth, there was no guarantee that I would find my way out.

I closed and then locked the front door, pushing the memory of the stranger out of my mind. I slowly climbed the stairs to return to Oñé's bedroom. I gently knocked at his door before entering although it was now past midnight and I was sure that he would be asleep. The door squeaked as it opened. I peeped into the room.

His bed was empty.

I breathed deeply and quickly. Where could he have gone? I had been standing at the front door. So there was only one other possible exit he could have taken. It was through the door in the West Wing which led into the English country garden.

I dashed along the corridor in the West Wing, past Ishmael's bedroom and discovered, as I imagined, that the door into the country garden was unlocked. The keys were hanging in the lock. I removed them, cautiously slipped outside and locked the door behind me.

As I passed the purple bougainvillea, smelling a hint of jasmine in the air, I heard a flapping sound, like a seal playing, coming from the direction of the pool to my right. Laughter cut through the darkness. The laughter was from Oñé.

I trampled over spikey grass, my feet tingling as I realised that I had forgotten to put on my shoes. It was freezing. There was still snow on the mountains. As I approached the pool, a man heaved himself out of the water and ran towards the labyrinth. Oñé lay on his back floating in the pool. Was he dead? I didn't hesitate but dived in and thrashed through the water towards him.

He rolled over in the water and began to laugh. "This is such a funny game we play together. You feel that you have to rescue me."

I grabbed him around the neck and held his head under the water for a couple of seconds. I pulled him up and he spluttered. For the first time I saw fear in his eyes.

"Who was in the pool with you, you little brat?"

He pushed me away and swam to the edge. "There was no-one in the pool. I will tell Sophia what you are doing to me. That will be the end of your wedding plans."

If I could have ducked his head under the water once more I would have held it there for more than a few more seconds. As he pulled himself out of the pool he scraped his knees against the rough edge; in the darkness I saw blood trickling from his knees.

I yelled, "I know that there was someone there. Who was it?"

Oñé looked at me, wiping tears from his eyes. "There was no-one there. No-one threw stones at the window. You imagined it."

I shouted at him. "You pretended to be asleep. I didn't mention anyone throwing stones against the window. You heard them. You're too young to be a good liar. What's going on?"

He smeared blood from his knees across his cheeks. He hugged himself with his arms crossed over his shoulders and his body shaking. "I'm cold. I'm going to die here. What will you tell my mother then?"

He turned and ran towards the labyrinth. I followed him to the entrance. I couldn't go inside. I heard leaves rustling as he pushed forward. I sat on the ground outside, waiting. I looked at my watch. It was half-past midnight.

I called softly to him. "Oñé please don't do this. It's time for bed. I'm exhausted – you must be also."

I heard something growling from inside the labyrinth. It sounded like a large cat, a panther or a puma. Then I heard a couple of coughs. I didn't know if it was from Oñé or whatever animal was inside. I looked around for a long stick. There was one by the pool. Oñé must have been playing with it. I picked it up, returning to the entrance, prepared to enter as Oñé ran out.

He threw his arms around me. "I'm sorry."

I hugged him. "So am I. Forgive me."

I held him close to me for what seemed to be a long time. I buried my head into his wet hair. For the first time it felt as if he was truly my boy, my child. I had a warm feeling in my heart. I had a sense of being a part of Nature which wanted me to care for this boy as my own. I kissed the top of his wet head. I knew that he didn't want this moment to stop either. We both wanted it to go on and on and on.

I knelt on the ground, took his hands and asked, "I heard a noise from the labyrinth. Is there an animal in there with your friend?"

"I'll show you in the morning. I want to go to bed now."

I slept on the carpet on the floor in his bedroom, with a duvet to cover me. I listened to him sleep. He snored a little and turned around in the bed. I listened to his breathing. It calmed me. I fell into a deep sleep.

Monday 29th January 2018

Oñé reached under the duvet, searching for my hand. "I want to show you something. You are right. I have a special friend in there."

He pointed through the window in the direction of the labyrinth. I felt that familiar fear return to my stomach. He laughed. "Don't be afraid. Come and see him. You will be amazed."

Oñé led me to the labyrinth as if he were leading a blind man. I noticed that had cut ribbons of cloth which he tied to the bushes to avoid getting lost. He was breathing deeply, wanting to rush ahead, pulling my heavy weight behind him.

"He will be sleeping now. I need you to see him. He needs food or he will die. I can't help him on my own. You need to help me."

The labyrinth seemed to be a series of endless twists and turns but Oñé knew where he was going. He walked quickly ahead of me, glancing behind him, smiling at me. I listened to the wind shaking the tightly intertwined leaves. I looked upwards – the green walls were threatening to me, the height of two people standing on one another's shoulders. I remembered Ishmael telling me that the labyrinth was a mechanism for understanding the Universe.

I didn´t know then what he meant by that then but now I felt that he was whispering its truth to me in a curved path which seemed to circle back on itself. I felt the fear of my smallness within the immense infinity of the world. I had a desire to hide within the thick green walls and cover my eyes with my hands. I didn't want to understand the Universe. I felt that I would be stripped bare by it and then torn apart. The human mind wasn't designed to understand something so immense. It was designed for routine, for simplifying chaos, making life bearable, not understandable.

Oñé whispered to me as he began to run ahead of me. "We're nearly there."

We turned the last bend into the centre where I knew we would find the well but what else had Oñé discovered? My heart beat furiously in my chest. My breathing was rapid.

Oñé beckoned to me, placing a finger over his lips, telling me to be quiet. "Look, he's sleeping."

To the left of the well, I saw a duvet which Oñé must have taken from the house, folded into a circle. On top of the duck feathers, slept what I knew had to be a puma. It had a mixture of a yellow and tan coat, a round face, erect ears and a long tail curled around its body. It made a loud purring noise as it slept.

I grabbed Oñé's hand. "Don't waken him – don't you know that it can kill an animal several times its own weight?"

Oñé dropped my hand. "He is my friend. He wouldn't hurt me. He needs water."

He went to the well and threw the bucket into the blackness. I heard the chain spinning down until the bucket splashed onto the surface of what I knew was a dark yet pure source of water coming from a nearby spring. He pulled the filled bucket to the surface and lifted a large dish he must have brought earlier from the garden. He poured the water into the dish. I took a few steps back as he walked towards the puma. Oñé, placed the dish beside his head and began to stroke him.

The puma's eyes were open. He struggled sleepily to his feet and walked to where Oñé had placed the water. Kneeling beside him, he reached his hand out to stroke again the puma's head. The puma sat still, staring at Oñé and they maintained a deep contact of eyes for a few seconds. Then the puma reached out a thick paw and touched Oñe on the lips, before bending his head to lick Oñé's hand.

I couldn't speak. I was afraid that the puma would see me and his behaviour would change.

Oñé whispered to me as the puma licked at the water. "He needs food. He's surviving on mice, rats and other small animals that wander into the labyrinth. It's not enough for him. A few times I have seen that he has hidden a wild goat to eat later. I even saw him kill one. He stalked slowly behind him, jumped on his neck and bit him. He died within seconds. Christian then pulled him over there." Oñé pointed at a hollowed out part of the hedge. "That is his fridge." He laughed.

I took a few more steps backwards. "You call him Christian?"

Oñé continued to stroke the puma's back. "Yes. That's his name."

"Well, let's get out of here and we will find help for him. There are people trained to capture him and give him a good home in a zoo. That must be where he has escaped from."

Oñé's lower lip trembled. His eyes filled with tears. "I trusted you. You can't have him imprisoned in a zoo. He needs to be free. We need to feed him. He will die in a zoo. I can't betray him."

Christian turned and looked at me. I didn't know how to respond. I attempted to do what I had seen Oñé do – to look at him and not to move, although my body screamed at me to run. Then a strange thing happened, instead of running, I looked into his eyes. I felt myself falling into the stillness within them. It seemed as if Christian could remove fear from my body with only his gaze. We continued to look at one another for several seconds. Christian then turned to Oñé and licked his hand. Oñé slowly got to his feet and walked backwards with his eyes focused on Christian.

He then turned around when he reached me and said, "You will help me take care of him, won't you? You won't tell anyone about him. He will be safe here in the labyrinth, until he chooses to leave. You only need to make a sign to say that people should not enter the labyrinth as there are improvements being made and there are parts of it which may be dangerous. I don't think he will stay for too much longer. He wants to return to the mountains. There are lots of goats there. He will survive."

Sweat broke out on my forehead and chest. "But who was the man with you in the swimming pool?"

"He told me not to tell you."

"Tell me, if you want me to help Christian."

"It was Ishmael."

23

PABLO PICASSO

"Art is a lie that makes us realise truth, at least the truth that is given us to understand."

Tuesday 30th January 2018

Next morning with Oñé. I watched Christian curl up on the duvet in the labyrinth, resting his head on his paws.

"Let's go Oñé. Let's find food for him."

Oñé took my hand and we began our journey out of the labyrinth. He pointed to one of the white ribbons in the hedge. "There are seventy-seven of them if you ever want to enter alone. They are all numbered".

"What are you talking about?"

"The ribbons. I know that you are afraid of the labyrinth. So was I at first but it's under control."

He showed me a white ribbon where he had written with a felt tip pen the number thirty-two.

"This is halfway towards the exit which is numbered seventy-seven. The first number is zero at the well."

We walked quickly around the bends and convoluted curves. He took my hand and looked into my eyes. "Why are you not asking me about Ishmael? I said he was alive. I have talked to him. I have swum in the pool with him."

"Yes, you told me that you splashed together in the pool. I do not understand why you wanted to swim in a pool with temperatures barely above zero. What kind of person would encourage you to do that?"

Oñé looked at me. "I lived in Sweden. We used to enjoy swimming in the sea in the winter. We are used to swimming in cold water. It's never warm there even in summer."

I could understand that what he was saying could be true. I asked, "I know that there was someone there in the pool with you. How do I know that it was Ishmael?"

"Did you not recognise him?"

I shook my head. "I didn't."

Later that day Oñé and I brought food for Christian. With a certain relief, I watched him devour six skinned rabbits which we found in the market. Oñé filled his water dish and brought it inside the hollowed hedge. He looked at me as he stroked Christian.

He asked, "How do we make sure they don't see Christian from the air? They will be looking for him, if as you say he has escaped from the zoo."

We worked together, building a fence, with a roof made from an old olive door I had stored in the Studio, thinking that I could turn it into a sculpture one day. Oñé tempted Christian into his sanctuary by offering him two large steaks taken from the fridge, given that he had eaten all of the rabbits. The big cat followed, licking his hand. Christian sat calmly on his duvet and chewed on one of the steaks as we closed a fence around him and covered it with leaves.

As we walked away, we heard a noise in the labyrinth. Oñé placed his hand on my arm. "Listen. There is someone here. I don't think it is Ishmael. He told me he wouldn't be here today. Whoever it is are they watching us. Have they seen Christian?"

We were silent for a few minutes listening carefully. At first there was only the sound of birds cheeping overhead, a rustling of wind within the leaves of the labyrinth walls. Then there was a scuffling sound. It didn't sound like a small animal but something larger.

Oñé whispered, "Stay here. I will be back."

He ran first right, then left and was out of sight. I heard Christian whistle from his hideaway as if attempting to communicate with Oñé. I said 'Shuush' to him in a gentle voice before hearing a shout from Oñé, followed by a panting and a crunch of pebbles as he neared the centre of the labyrinth.

"I don't know who it was. I saw the back of a man as he ran from the labyrinth. It wasn't Ishmael. Whoever it was escaped. He seemed to know the labyrinth better than I do."

I lowered myself onto the ground sitting cross legged on the pebbles. "Let's forget about whoever that was for a minute. I don't think they had seen us, although they may have been trying to find us. Let's go back to Ishmael.

What did Ishmael say that he was doing? Why did he leave?"

I didn't feel good about asking that as I knew it to be a lie. But I had to find out who Oñé had been swimming with, who he was talking to and why he was pretending to me that it was Ishmael. "He said that he needed a little bit of space. He wanted to make sure that I was okay."

I asked, "Did he ask about me?"

Oñé nodded. "Yes. He said that he would see you when you felt ready to see him."

I gave up trying to find out the truth for now. It was exhausting.

I took his hand. "Christian has had his lunch. Why don't we do the same?"

We walked through the labyrinth, counting Oñé's ribbons.

I said, "That's a clever system you came up with."

We walked towards the front door, past the sculpture. Then there was the sound of the buzz of an airplane flying low over the garden. I put my arm around Oñé's shoulders.

"That is the police. You were right. They are probably looking for Christian. Don't worry, he is well hidden."

Oñé looked back at the labyrinth. I knew that he wanted to return and be with Christian.

I squeezed his arm and whispered, "Don't go into the labyrinth – it will attract attention. Let's go to the fountain and clean it. They will photograph us and the empty labyrinth. They will not see Christian." I smiled at him. "Look relaxed and as if you are enjoying yourself."

Oñé picked up the gardening tools lying beside the fountain and began to clean the moss from the inside edge of the fountain. I sat on a wooden garden chair watching him, before I found my gaze fixed on the sculpture. The plane circled overhead sweeping low above the labyrinth. As I turned to see where it was going next, I again caught sight of the sculpture and looked away quickly. I had been unable to bring myself to look at it for quite some time.

My eyes smarted. I rubbed them with the back of my hand. How would I ever be able to let go of this intense shame and guilt for what I had done? I pressed my hands into my eyes.

Oñé dropped the tools he was working with and approached me and stroked my arm the way I had seen him pet Christian. Oñé looked concerned.

"Are you OK?"

I buried my head into his shoulder and began to cry.

He asked, "What's happening?"

I knew that I was frightening him with this strange behaviour. "It's nothing. Sometimes adults feel sad. It passes."

I moved from the wooden chair and lay on the grass. Oñé stood over me, looking at me. His voice seemed far away when I heard him say, "Christian has escaped. Augustin – get up."

I kept my eyes closed. I didn't move on the grass. I felt

the roughness of a tongue like that of a kitchen scourer move across my hand. Christian then approached my face. I heard him breathe deeply and cough from time to time. I remembered that he communicated with his eyes. I opened my eyes. He patted me on the face with a heavy thick soft paw and climbed on top of my chest. He sat on top of me with his paws spread across my shoulders. I felt a little pressure from his nails slightly pressing into me – the way that a kitten kneads the belly of its mother as it sucks on a teat. His eyes were magnets drawing me in. His strength flooded through me. He moved a paw, patting me on the mouth.

I said to him, "You can go now. You're free."

As he slid from my body, I realised how heavy he had been. I took a few deep breaths as he circled around my body a few times. I lay still. I noticed Oñé standing to my right watching us. Christian licked my face and moved towards Oñé who threw his arms around his neck. He rubbed his head against Christian's head and with one last lick of Oñé's face, the puma turned to the right, running across the spiky grass with a sloping wave-like motion towards the mountains. He easily jumped the wire boundary fence of Can Animes to Boulder Hill and disappeared from sight without looking back.

24

PABLO PICASSO

"When I was a child my mother said to me, 'If you become a soldier, you will be a general. If you become a monk, you'll end up as the Pope'. Instead, I became a painter and wound up as Picasso."

Tuesday 30th January 2018

Pep Conejo hasn't done a great job.

The garden is overgrown. Suckers sprout from the roots of the olive trees. Oranges and lemons lie rotten on the ground. The once clear pebbled pathways are turning into grass walkways speckled with stones. The bougainvillea which Ishmael loved to shape into bushes is spreading out of control across the thickened hedge of the labyrinth. It looks pretty but it is not the way Ishmael would have wanted it to be. He liked clean edges and spaces with beauty erupting from within and around, rather than the mingling disorderly forms of Nature which he preferred to contain with the English country garden. Not this mingling of Nature, taking over the world which he shaped. Not that he was a control freak as a gardener – quite the contrary; he loved the spontaneous energy inherent in plants and stones but felt that Nature itself wanted to be shaped by him.

He told me that he thought everything had a consciousness – even stones – and his role as a gardener was to help this unstoppable energy express its beauty. It was important where he placed a stone and how he tamed a bush or pruned a tree to allow the light to enter and fruit to flourish.

I had not got the energy to talk about this difference in their approaches with Pep Conejo. He wouldn't understand. I let it be.

I prepared for my first studio exhibition since Ishmael's death. Before Ishmael died I regularly offered an 'artist in residence studio' – typically before an exhibition – where selected guests watched me work and reviewed my paintings. This often resulted in pre-exhibition sales. There would typically be extensive coverage in the local press, fuelled by interest in the celebrities who attended including royalty and an extensive network of actors and actresses who have holiday homes on the island.

I felt no joy in doing in preparing for this particular exhibition.

I imagine that every human being does things that they regret. I believe we all have a conscience built into us by Nature. You might call it God, but I prefer not to call it God. For me the word God is too coloured by images of an old man with a long white beard sitting in judgement and separating the sheep from the goats. What Nature does is it educates me. It calls to me from deep within my body. It allows me to feel the wisdom of shame and guilt. That's how I evolve.

Monday 5th February 2018

The Monday of the exhibition I wakened at five o'clock with a sense of apprehension. I sat by the fountain on my favourite chair, sipping coffee. Bats circled around in the sky like moving dark stars. I didn't move until the sun shone in an azure blue sky. Birds cheeped within the shade of olive trees.

I didn't ask Gabriela to cater today. I couldn't face her presence with the guests demanding my full attention. She has continued to have an accusing look about her when she looks at me. Of course that could be me, being paranoid again.

I chose instead to use the German catering company – with Chris and Doris – who I had used before when Ishmael was alive. They assembled the tables, and covered them with white table cloths, cutlery and polished glasses. A dozen vases filled with red roses were scattered around the tables, randomly splashed on the white cotton tablecloths like a Pollock painting.

Chris and Doris cooked in the kitchen. I heard them hitting the Le Crueset pots which then sang like a meditation bowl. I watched them for a few minutes chopping carrots and peppers into small diced shapes which they then threw into a wok with oriental spices, fresh garlic, chilli and ginger. Delicious spice clouds from Arabia filled the kitchen and drifted outside. Chris emerged outside to prepare a fire to cook the suckling pigs which were already skewered onto a long rotating roasting spit. The buffet tables outside where being filled with dishes with a Moroccan theme, including, couscous, chickpeas and aubergines cooked in tagines.

Oñé hid in his bedroom. I asked him if he would join us for lunch but since Christian's disappearance, he had become melancholic. He sat in the hollowed space of the labyrinth where we hid Christian from the surveillance plane and stares at the well. I think he was hoping Christian would return. Why is he not happy that he achieved what he wanted, that Christian is free? What am I going to do with this boy who has endless desires which he hides from me? How can I fulfil them if he doesn't tell me what they are? I managed to persuade him to come downstairs and join us by asking him if he would show the King and Queen of Spain around the labyrinth.

Felipe the King of Spain arrived with his wife Letizia. Felipe wore a silk Italian charcoal suit, with a white Egyptian cotton shirt and cerise tie. Letizia wore white roses in her hair and as she walked her chiffon dress swirled in the gentle breeze which appeared to move the leaves on the olive and orange trees into life. They wandered around the garden, smiling and waving at the catering staff, before entering the labyrinth with Oñé for a private viewing before the other guests arrived. When they emerged, I walked with them around the garden highlighting the orangery, with its rose garden, the fig tree garden, olive grove and herb garden. I shared with them Ishmael's thoughts that the garden was meant to give the impression of stepping into one of my paintings. I explained that there were surprises in my new art work. Felipe stopped at the sculpture, holding Letizia's hand. He looked at her.

"What do you think of this?"

My heart thumped rapidly.

Letizia looked at Felipe. They smiled at one another without saying anything. Felipe broke the silence. "I think it is perhaps your best sculpture. Congratulations. I see it in the gardens of the palace of Marivent."

I smiled at them both, disguising the anxiety building in my stomach. "Thank you. Of course it is yours. You only have to name your price. When would you like it to be delivered?"

"If possible before the summer season when guests arrive."

I nodded.

There was a round of applause from the newly arrived guests as if I had staged my comment for approval. I didn't even know that they had either arrived or were listening. We sipped champagne, picked at tapas of gambas and lobster while a quartet played Sibelius in the background. It was a dreamy rendering, with violins like sirens tempting the listeners to look at the violinists rather than to engage in the food. Oñé emerged from the labyrinth, after his success with the King and Queen of Spain and seemed animated as he walked around the tables helping serve champagne.

Felipe and Letizia excused themselves as they had another lunch engagement. Letizia squeezed my hand, kissed me on the cheek and whispered, "Remember the sculpture is for Marivent. Don't allow anyone else to tempt you to sell it to them."

I bowed and said, "It was created with you in mind."

As I raised my head to look into Letizia's eyes there was a loud scream, a woman's chilling cry. Everyone looked towards the studio. Oñé dropped the bottle of champagne he was serving and the quartet fell silent.

It was Gabriela. She ran along the pebbled path. Her hair streamed behind her like an advertising banner from a small light aircraft. She wasn't wearing shoes. She ran towards me, pushing Letizia and Felipe to one side. I felt her hands turn into fists thumping into my chest with the rhythm of a heartbeat.

She screamed at the guests: "You need to know. He killed him. He killed Ishmael. Who will be next?"

It was a member of the Royal family's entourage who was first to use her mobile and call for an ambulance.

"This woman needs help. She appears dangerous. Keep away from her. She may have a knife on her."

I bowed to my guests. "I apologise to you all." I turned to Gabriela. "You are upset. You know that you are not well. Let us help you."

Leaving the broken bottle of Veuve Clicquot which had slipped from his hands onto the ground, Oñé ran towards Gabriela taking her hand. "Why are you saying that he killed Ishmael? It can't be true. You have seen Ishmael and so have I. We both know that he is alive."

I looked at him with mixed feelings wishing that he would stop talking about Ishmael and drawing attention to his absence. Yet another part of me was grateful for his attempt at defending me from the madness of Gabriela. Felipe and Letizia looked at one another as a black Mercedes rolled up the pathway, followed by an ambulance sounding a blaring siren.

Without haste, the King and Queen sidled into the Mercedes, waving at the guests as the car reversed and disappeared in the direction of Soller.

Gabriela dropped Oñé's hand and ran in the direction of Boulder Hill. There was a huge rock which had fallen from the top of the hill, which rumbled towards her as she attempted to scramble over the fence. The rock stopped without breaking its way through the fence. Gabriela fell back on the grass where she was gently helped to her feet by the ambulance crew and then led into the ambulance. The siren stopped as it made the slow journey down the pathway, before turning right to follow the King and Queen's Mercedes

I tapped a spoon against a glass to gain the attention of the guests.

"Thank you for your patience in dealing with this

rather awkward incident. I am sure that Gabriela will be taken good care of and I hope that she will soon be back helping me as she has masterly done for several years. Life brings us challenges in different ways. Let the next challenge today to be only your choice of dessert – a raspberry Pavlova and a favourite on the island, flan Catalan. Please can I invite you to offer a round of applause for our wonderful cooks and waitressing staff."

I clapped my hands triggering a lacklustre wave of acknowledgement around the table.

After lunch had been served, the guests' children ran around the garden as Oñé watched them from a chair. I had hoped that he would join in and play with them. To my horror, I realised that what was entertaining and amusing everyone was that they had decided to use the sculpture as a climbing frame. One red haired, freckled boy climbed up the arms and stood with a foot on either shoulder. Three others followed him. I panicked.

I jumped to my feet and shouted, "Get off the sculpture. It has been commissioned by the King and Queen of Spain and must not be damaged."

Parents jumped to their feet and gathered children into their arms, excusing themselves, piling children into cars which rolled down the driveway. I was alone again with Oñe. The catering company cleared the tables in silence and removed dishes and glasses. I wished that they would talk to one another. I so much wanted to hear laughter, jokes being exchanged and an explosive bubbliness of happiness in the air, a joy of being alive – manifesting itself in Can Animes. Chris and Doris were letting me down.

I sat on a wooden swing bench waiting for Oñé join me. He sat on the bench, pushing it with his feet to move swiftly backwards and forwards. He asked, "Why do you think Gabriela said what she said?"

I pushed the swing also with my feet to go even faster before answering. "I don't know why she said what she did. I didn't murder Ishmael did I? How could I have – you swam with him in the pool."

Oñé stopped the bench swinging by scraping his feet on the ground. "I know that you didn't kill Ishmael."

I rested my head in my hands and swung the bench slowly. "You said that Ishmael would appear when I said that I was ready to see him. The next time that you see him, tell him then that I am ready and would be pleased to see him."

Oñé nodded. "I will do that."

He then changed the subject, asking me a question. "Do I look like Gregoriano?"

I didn't want to tell him that he looked like his father – even if he did look very like him. It was also hard to tell him the truth that Gregoriano is a wiser and better man than I am, knowing that I am soon to be his 'father'. It didn't matter what DNA he had inherited. I would act like his father. I had to be a father. It was the only way to redeem my life. I had to take care of him and Sophia. It was destiny.

Yet Ishmael's death would haunt me. That terrible deed would stay with me and potentially destroy every relationship, including that with Oñé and Sophia. Was I capable of living such a lie? What damage could it do to both Oñé and Sophia?

I remembered one night with Ishmael when he sat on a chair in the sitting room. Logs burnt in the open fire. We looked for music on Deezer and he told me that he liked Cat Stevens. We found *Tea for the Tillerman* and listened to *Hard-Headed Woman*. He told me that he knew a hard-headed woman whom had saved his life. I knelt at his feet and listened to him talk about her. I didn't know then that he was almost certainly talking about Sophia.

Whoever this woman was, I felt that she could never come between me and Ishmael. We were friends without boundaries separating us. We merged into the chair, within the room, within the labyrinth, within the sky and its slither of moon, within the flow of the sea in the Port of Soller. We were the kind of friends that could never be parted – even death could not separate a friendship like the one that I had with Ishmael.

Answering the question which Oñé asked me about whether he looked like Gregoriano, I replied, "You do. You also look like Sophia."

25

PABLO PICASSO

"To finish a work? To finish a picture? What nonsense! To finish it means to be through with it, to kill it, to rid of its soul, to give it its final blow, the 'coup de grace' for the painter as well as for the picture."

Thursday 8th February 2018

I wakened to lights flashing in the bedroom and in my head. For a moment I thought that I was having an epileptic fit. What was strange was that it didn't worry me. I was interested in what was happening within my brain. What were these flickers of light and darkness? Ulysses the cat jumped on me asking to be taken outside. I ran downstairs as he followed me. The flickering continued. As I opened the door, the dark sky flickered in the distance, shifting rapidly between light and darkness.

As the storm rumbled towards us, the house shook with each roar of thunder. Lightning illuminated the sky through the window – a frame for a painting. At times it was as if the world was blotted out. On occasion there was only whiteness. It made me think that was what death would be like – a world of light and nothingness. At other moments lightening hid behind Boulder Hill, flashing and made a dragon shaped contour which stood out every few seconds, when the darkness was interrupted by lightning. I heard the sound of pebbles against Oñé's window next door. I knew what that meant. Whoever had swum with him in the pool had returned to talk with him.

I heard Oñé run downstairs, open the door. I walked to the top of the stairs, peered down as Oñé embraced a man and then walked hand in hand with him in the direction of the labyrinth.

I followed them into the labyrinth using Oñé's ribbons. I easily reached the centre and sat on the edge of the well as rain pelted me with tiny bullets.

There was no-one there. I searched but couldn't find them. I slowly made my way out of the labyrinth. It took quite some time, even with Oñé's help of the numbered ribbons. The storm flashed and shook the hedges around me. I staggered against them as if in a stupor. I clutched at thorny edges as if I was drowning. I held onto trembling branches before I ran into blackness broken by a silver light that erased my vision.

I reached the house, carefully taking hold of the handrail as I climbed the stairs. I felt that at any moment I might fall.

Oñé's door was closed. I opened it. Lightning continued to gently flicker on and off as the storm moved away. I saw Oñé's head pressed deep into the pillow. He sighed as if relieving himself from some dreadful burden. I took my shoes off to avoid making a noise which might waken him and padded towards the bed. I listened. He gurgled in the way a baby might blow bubbles at you. I slipped into the bed beside him and placed an arm close enough to allow him if he wanted to; to know that I was near but not wanting to waken him.

I closed my eyes. My body filled with an intensity of peace. This heaviness of peace within me felt as if I had been placed in a cleft in a rock and the hand of God was pushing me deep into this protected opening of earth. I was squeezed into a place of safety. I opened my eyes and saw Oñé's back. I had an urge to roll him over and look at his face but I knew that I couldn't. I closed my eyes, allowing the peace to begin to dissolve, to lose its solidity, I felt it flow effortlessly within me.

I placed a hand on Oñé. He did not move. His breath turned into a snuffling sound. I tapped him three times on the shoulder. I don't know why I did that before my hand dropped onto the sheet beside him. I fell asleep.

In the early morning, I awakened. Oñé was still asleep. I slipped from the bed.

I prepared a special breakfast – French toast dipped in egg and covered in icing sugar. Oñé ate two pieces of toast and drank two cups of hot chocolate before I picked up the courage to ask, "Did you sleep well last night?"

"You've forgotten haven't you?"

I poured him another cup of hot chocolate and sat facing him. "Forgotten what?"

He sipped on his chocolate. "You said that today we would go out on a yacht."

He was right. I had forgotten. "That's not a problem, we can still go. I will ring the owner of the yacht in Porto Cristo."

Oñé pushed his empty cup of chocolate to one side. "Let's do it then."

We drove to Porto Cristo. I was reminded of how magical the island of Mallorca is with its rugged mountains, flat valleys, vineyards and coves. Storm clouds were again building filling the sky with orange fire, surrounded by a blackness waiting to descend over the island. I was no longer sure about the sailing trip. We arrived at Porto Cristo to find the boat Mambia moored at the side of the wharf and two Germans who Carlos told me were to join us on board.

This time, I did not have a panic attack as I did when I was with Gregoriano on the yacht making our way to Deia. We easily crossed the gangway to where Carlos waited inside. He welcomed the four of us, reading a list of instructions about where life jackets were stored and told us that we needed to shower after swimming and not allow saltwater to enter the boat. A thirty-metre mast reached to the storm clouds. Carlos' assistant Kike from Columbia unmoored the yacht and then went to the back to raise the sails. Oñé sat and looked at our German companions.

Gunter was a man of my age. His hair shaved at the

sides leaving a long crop of hair on top which he caught into a small knot. His partner introduced herself as Friederike. She wore a white bikini which matched her whitened teeth. Each had the same colour of spray tan over toned bodies. They smiled a lot, took selfies and Friederike passed the camera frequently to Gunter who snapped photographs of her standing by the mast.

Carlos looked at the sky and told us that we would have rain by four o'clock in the afternoon. We needed to start sailing before the winds became too strong for it to be safe.

Our first stop was a small cove with sandy coloured limestone eaten away by the wind and rain and riddled with small caves used by smugglers and pirates to bring contraband onto the island. We were given snorkel masks to help us navigate in the deep waters and the narrow ceiling of the first cave. Carlos dropped the anchor and Oñé, Friederike, Gunter and I plunged from the yacht into the turquoise water. I found it difficult once we entered the cave to breathe properly but Oñé and the others splashed happily ahead of me.

I found it claustrophobic that the ceiling of the cave was no more than centimetres above my head. We had to swim into a second cave, clamber out from the water, and jump five metres into the sea again below. As I scrambled up the jagged rocks away from the water, I lost track of the others, including Oñé. I looked around in a panic removing my snorkel and taking deep breaths of salty air. I thought that I saw a man watching me from the depths of the cave.

I rubbed my eyes as it was hard to see into the darkness. Perhaps it was only a sculpture from rock which looked like a man but then I smelt cigar smoke. It drifted towards me from the dark shape and I saw the orange glow from a cigar intensify in the darkness. I know that there are many people who smoke cigars but that particular smell was reminiscent of the cigars which Ishmael loved.

How did he get here, whoever he was? It would be too far to swim from Porto Cristo and too dangerous to scramble up the cliff face outside. I nearly dropped my goggles into the sea as I squinted to see who it was.

My concentration was broken by hearing a cry from Oñé outside the cave. I scrambled quickly up the jagged rocks. There was no obvious path. Rocks cut into my feet. I emerged into the light and looked around me. There was no sign of Oñé. I heard him cry out again for help. I realised that he was in the sea.

I felt dizzy as I tossed the snorkel into the water. Holding my nose with my fingers I plunged into the roughening sea. Ignoring the snorkel to my right, I splashed towards Oñé who disappeared under the water, surfaced and disappeared again. He screamed for help. As I swam towards him, the sun appeared briefly and I could see that I was swimming through a shoal of small blue fish that scattered to either side of the wake I created. They had two small circles like eyes on the sides of their flesh. I was shocked that I could be so distracted in my efforts to help Oñé by these small coloured fish. I gasped as I thrashed through the choppy water. Oñé had disappeared from view. I dived through the fish and saw his body drifting motionless towards the sea floor. I pushed strongly towards him, caught him by his hair and dragged him to the surface. His face was white and he did not seem to be breathing.

Carlos and I managed to drag Oñé on board the yacht. I noticed a red whip-like bruise with slight bleeding on Oñé's lower right leg. I knew from the bruising that he had probably been stung by a Portuguese man-of-war. Oñé whimpered on deck, rolling from side to side in pain. He then stared in silence at the cumulous clouds which continued to build overhead. I knelt on the ground beside him and stroked his forehead. I asked Carlos for the special first aid kit which I knew would be on board and poured salty water over the wound, and then soaked it with ammonia before squirting shaving foam onto it and beginning to shave the wound.

I whispered to him, "This is going to be painful but it will remove any remaining venom."

I cleaned the razor carefully in salted water after each stroke across the wound. Oñé bit his lower lip but didn't cry.

I wrapped him in a blanket and as he slept, I thought about who it may have been who smoked that cigar in the cave. These caves were used by smugglers. Someone could drop a smuggler off in a boat and come back to collect him. Perhaps he was waiting for a small launch boat to take him back. Depending upon his level of courage he could have walked along the cliff path jumped into the sea and accessed the cave in that way. To return back by the same route he would need to be able to do deep water soloing – diving into dark and dangerous places. He would have to free climb up the cliff face with only the sea to protect him from injury if he fell. Deep water soloing is a popular sport in Mallorca and so someone interested in extreme sports might find it an exciting challenge.

Lightning ripped over the mountains to the left as the Mambia slowly moved towards its mooring place and Kike dropped anchor. Carlos carried Oñé down the gangway where a doctor was waiting.

When we arrived home, after putting Oñé to bed I phoned Sophia to explain what had happened. She seemed to be calm and had trust in the care that Oñçe was receiving.

I said, "I have been thinking, Sophia, that my life before meeting you was not something that I was proud of. I need to tell about it so that we can have total honesty in our relationship before we go ahead with our wedding. You deserve to know the truth."

There was a silence on the end of the phone which I had become used to in our conversations.

She laughed. "It doesn't matter, does it; to know the truth? There is only today. That's what matters. How we respond to this moment. Whatever you have done – it's not going to be anything worse than I have already seen in Iraq or Syria."

She changed the subject and began to talk about my paintings and the art exhibitions. She praised me for my paintings. All of her kind words seemed empty to me. My paintings were not good. My sculptures were of even poorer quality.

It had to be a joke that the King and Queen of Spain thought that the sculpture which held the corpse of Ishmael was my best work of art. Apart from the fact that I made it in a few hours – whereas I had painstakingly spent months working on my installations – I had to think about how I would respond to their request to send it to the palace of Marivent. I couldn't risk Ishmael's body being discovered and so I would have to attempt to make a duplicate which wouldn't be easy. I had never managed to recreate any work of art before. I know that there are those who are master imitators of great artists but that is not a talent I have.

I let those thoughts drop as I opened the door into Oñé's bedroom. He lay curled on his side in the bed, with only a sheet over him. I walked to the other side of the room to see his face. He was very still and looked peaceful – a peace of nothingness I thought, a peace of death beating within him with every heartbeat. I walked slowly back to the door, descending to the sitting room and sat on the sofa with my head in my hands.

Would I ever escape this nightmare of constantly being obsessed about Ishmael? I remembered him saying in the weeks before he died: "Your life isn't over yet. You have many things you can do to redeem your past. Shame and guilt will not go completely away. They will remain with you like healed wounds. Letting those wounds be seen will help you realise that you are loved. Someone will be sent to you to give you strength to complete the rest of your life using your talents to the full."

I remembered trembling, not wanting to look into his eyes. "Who will it be who will be sent to me?"

He laughed. "How would I know? I'm sure you will be sent someone."

I was sure Ishmael had been sent to save me.

As Oñé coughed upstairs, I was brought back to the present and was aware of a hollowness within me which I recognised for the first time as loneliness. I had so many ways of escaping that feeling of being alone – my painting, parties, travels to exhibitions and being the centre of attention when I entertained others. With Ishmael gone, I had been stripped bare. There was no Painter within – only a void, a darkness as deep as that within the well in the labyrinth.

The next day I awakened at five o'clock. From the bed I looked through the open windows at Boulder Hill. The black night sky was lightening but not enough for stars to disappear. The mountains were covered in candyfloss clouds changing from grey to cream. There wasn't a sound. Monica, my mother, told me that silence was the voice of God. I find silence a fearful experience. Perhaps it is the contrast between the noise in my head and listening to this blanket of silence emanating from Nature which frightens me. Silence is an echo of something I don't know, something which resides within me in the space around my expansive internal chatter. It's there at the edges. My obsessive thinking cannot completely wipe it out, any more than the stars and planets are capable of filling quantum fields and dark energy.

Although I am the Painter and create silence in the white spaces around splashes of colour, I do not look at the whiteness within my work. In that glowing whiteness, I see only darkness.

I was pleased by the distraction of Ulysses who had been sleeping at the bottom of the bed. He walked towards me with a wave-like movement and patted me gently on the nose. He wanted to be let out. We humans should be so grateful for animals. They never judge us. They forgive us and give us drops of water in a burning Hell.

I threw the sheet from me and opened the door into Oñé's room before going downstairs. He surprised me by being seated upright in the bed, also looking out of his window towards Boulder Hill. I walked towards his bed, followed by Ulysses.

"Are you in pain?"

Oñé pulled a sheet around him as he turned to look at me. "No. The sting is no longer painful. It looks red and lumpy. I think I will have an impressive scar. That will be something to talk about at school. The conversations there are normally boring."

I took his hand. "Why aren't you sleeping? It's too early to get up."

"I remembered the drone you bought me for my birthday present. I haven't really used it as I know that the stranger who visited the house was Ishmael – even if you don't believe me. Although I know I could try to find out the identity of the other man in the labyrinth who I didn't recognise the day we fed Christian. But he doesn't interest me. I want to use the drone to find Christian. I want to know that he is well."

He stroked Ulysses on the back and tickled him under the chin. Ulysses began to purr and rolled over onto his back. "Can I get up now and fly the drone? I imagine that Christian will be like Ulysses and be nocturnal. He might be prowling around looking for something to eat. If I wait until later, he may be asleep. Although, he liked to play with me during the day, he was mostly sleepy."

"What about school? You know I promised your mother that you wouldn't miss any classes."

Oñé pulled up the leg of his pyjamas. "Take a photo and send it to the teacher. I have a good excuse for at least two days off. She will understand."

I laughed at the way his mind worked. "Okay. I will speak with the school. You can have two days off school but not a day more. I'll get breakfast and you go find the drone. I think you left it in the Studio."

I made Oñé a banana and raspberry smoothie and placed his favourite granola cereal on the table. I heard the drone gently circling over the labyrinth and then around the house. There wasn't anyone to be disturbed as our nearest neighbours were a few kilometres away. It didn't make much noise even when it flew directly overhead. As I made coffee for myself, I noticed that I couldn't hear it at all. Oñé must have sent it further afield. I drank my coffee before Oñé burst into the kitchen, ignoring breakfast.

"You must look. I have found something I think you will recognise. Have a look."

We watched the drone video together. The drone had flown towards the Barranc. After taking a turn to the right, the drone now hovered motionless.

"Don't you know that house?"

I peered at a small castle with three turrets and tiles shaped like giant leaves on the roof. It was where I had met Gregoriano when I was ten. I had searched for it many times over forty years and could not find it.

Oñé drank his smoothie, looking at me expectantly. "Will we go there now and find him?"

I felt dizzy. I sat down and ate a piece of Oñé's toast which I cut into four. I found it difficult to eat anything but I knew that I had to eat something or I might faint. I talked with a mouth full of toast. "Find who?"

Oñé continued to eat his toast. "That's Gregoriano's house isn't it? Isn't that where you told me that you had met him when you were young? You can help me find my father."

"Yes, that is the house but we have no guarantee that he still lives there. That was a long time ago. We know that he travels with work, but we can go there if that is important to you."

Oñé's jumped to his feet. "Let's go."

I replayed the video before getting into the car. I could see exactly where I needed to park the car and the small path which we would have to take to find the castle. Oñé brought a pair of binoculars and his drone, placing them in his rucksack.

It was seven o'clock. The clouds over the mountains were tinged tangerine. There were no cars on the road. I was breathless. Oñé sat upright in the seat beside me scanning to the left and right with the binoculars in the hope that he might see Gregoriano walking along the road. We reached Biniaraix. I swung the car into a parking spot beside a stone bath where in the past, women would have washed clothes. As I jumped out, I heard the gentle trickling of water flowing along a grey stone pipe which filled the bath. Two turtle doves were sipping an early morning drink.

Oñé pulled at my shirt. "Which way?"

I turned left and scrambled up a stony cobbled path on the right. I heard Oñé following behind. The path looked familiar; overgrown, rocky, with no views of the town below or the mountains above, hidden by the pomegranate and wild blackberry bushes. We turned a corner. I laughed out loud. The castle was there. I really didn't believe that I would find it after all these years. Oñé shrieked.

"We've found it. We've found it."

I didn't feel like a man of fifty years of age but more like Oñé's brother as we ran towards the front door. I hammered it with my fist without even thinking that it was too early to disturb anyone. There was no reply. The persianas downstairs were closed. I couldn't see inside. I looked towards the roof. The green leaves which I remembered curling over the edge of the roof were there and as I lowered my gaze I saw that the upstairs persianas were open with the windows closed.

Oñé whispered, "There is someone watching us."

I took his hand. "Let's find out who."

He said, "Does he not want to talk to me?"

A shape appeared at the window. It was dark inside and it wasn't easy to see who it could be. We listened. There was the sound of feet descending the stairway. We heard four bolts being drawn back on the solid olive door and the sound of a heavy chain falling against the wood. The door opened.

It was Gabriela.

She wore a green silk dress which was unusual for early morning. It was as if she was dressed for a wedding. Her legs were tanned and she had diamante flat sandals. Her hair, which she would typically scraped off her face or let hang unkempt on her shoulders, was curled into long waves which glistened and shone in the early morning light which now flooded the doorway. She wore crimson lipstick, makeup and false eyelashes.

"What are you doing here?" I asked.

"I live here. The question is what are you both doing here at this hour of the morning?"

I stepped towards the door. "Are you not going to invite us in for a coffee?"

She shook her finger at me. "No. No. No. I think that would be inappropriate do you not? As you can imagine I have plans for today."

I looked over her shoulder to see if there was anyone else inside. There was a long dark coat hanging over a bannister with a leather hat sitting on top of it.

I asked Gabriela. "Are you alone?"

She smiled. "What do you think? Am I the kind of woman who would be alone?" She then giggled. I had never heard her laugh like that before – like a little girl. She continued. "I would recommend it to anyone."

"What?"

"Being with someone who tells the truth and who is capable of loving."

Before I could stop him, Oñé pushed past Gabriela

and ran inside the house shouting. "Gregoriano are you here? Please talk to me."

Gabriela ran after him, grabbed him by the arms, and pulled him towards the front door. "Oñé, you know that I like you but this is unacceptable behaviour."

I followed Gabriela into the house and saw the fireplace with the same chairs which Gregoriano and I had sat in all those years ago. Gabriela looked at me with a hint of fear twitching around her lips. "Please take him home. You have no right to be here."

I squeezed Oñé's hand. "You know that she is right. We have to leave here now."

I gave him a hug and Gabriela looked at the stairway as if afraid he might run upstairs. He insisted. "I want to see my father."

I felt my eyes stinging as I said, "You will see him. I promise you. He will turn up. He always does."

I struggled to my feet and gathered Oñé into my arms, letting his arms fall around my neck. I turned to say goodbye to Gabriela.

"I want to apologise. I made a mistake. I'm sorry for embarrassing you at your party," Gabriela said.

Oñé wriggled in my arms and I let him down. He was too big to be treating him like a two-year-old.

"What made you change your mind?"

"This isn't a conversation to have in front of Oñé."

I turned to Oñé and asked, "Would you like to sit for a few minutes in that special chair which I told you about?

It's a magic chair and you can tell me what you learn from being in it or you can play with your drone. Gabriela and I have a few words to share in private."

Oñé walked back into the house. "I'll sit in the chair."

I checked that he had climbed onto the chair rather than go upstairs. Gabriela linked me in a friendly way by the arm as we walked outside. I asked, "Why are you changing your mind? One minute you tell me that Ishmael is alive. Then you tell as many people as you can that Ishmael has been murdered by me. Now you say that Ishmael is alive again. That incident at the party when you ran towards Boulder Hill was quite insane. You almost got yourself killed. You know that Boulder Hill is dangerous. What's going on?"

We walked towards a small Zen Garden accessed through a gate, filled with chopped pine logs for seats, a pebbled path and a fountain. She opened the gate. She indicated for me to sit on a log seat and sat facing me on another one. "Please sit down. I will attempt to keep this as brief as possible.

"I told you before that I was there that night. I didn't tell you everything. It is true that my motorbike had run out of petrol before I got to the main road. I walked up the pathway to the house to see if you would drive me to the garage. The lights were on in the garden. You hadn't heard the gate open. I saw you fight. As I watched, I thought I saw you attempt to murder someone. I told you that I initially thought that you were struggling with two men but I couldn't really be sure. After a few minutes, I recognised Ishmael who was frantically pushing you away. I was totally confused. I thought that you cared for him.

"I hid in the labyrinth because I thought that if you saw me, you might want to kill me to avoid being discovered. I knew that I was being a coward, that I should have intervened. Instead, I hid near the well and listened.

"When I could no longer hear any noise, I slowly made my way back towards the entrance of the labyrinth and nearly ran into you as you hid the lead-tipped arrow in the hedge. I saw what I thought was the body of a man lying on the ground but I couldn't see anyone else. I walked slowly back into the centre of the labyrinth, in case you heard the sound of my feet on the path and hid once more near the well.

"The next day, when I visited the house, you were calm. I began to doubt what I had seen. When I thought that I saw Ishmael in the Plaza, I began to feel that perhaps I really was going crazy. I had flashbacks of images of Ishmael pushing you away from him. I didn't know whether they were real memories or fantasies. When I went to the party and caused a scene, I had convinced myself that those memories were real. I had seen you murder Ishmael. I decided that there never was a second person – that was my invention – a blurred vision of people jumping around that you get from strobe lighting. If there was a dead body it had to be that of Ishmael.

"So I came to a conclusion on the day of the party that you had killed him and that I could no longer continue with my cowardly ways. I had to speak up for Ishmael. What better way to do it than to accuse you in front of the King and Queen of Spain? For me justice would have been done for Ishmael. However, I was wrong. You didn't kill him."

I crossed my hands as if in prayer and asked, "So how have you come to this conclusion, that he is not dead?"

She bent down and picked at a small rosemary bush, lifted it to her nose and smelt it. "How do you know that this is rosemary? You smell it and eat it." She pushed it into my face. Not in an aggressive way but laughing at me. "Smell it. Eat it."

I smelt and then ate a little of the rough acrid herb. "So it is rosemary. What has that to do with Ishmael?"

She pulled more rosemary from the ground and rubbed it into my face. "Smell it. Smell the truth. After that day at the party with the King and Queen of Spain you sent me away in an ambulance. When I returned from the psychiatric hospital, I found Ishmael in this house. You know this house. It is the house of Gregoriano. I have lived here ever since he paid me to observe you and to be your Housekeeper. You will know that was many years ago. I have fulfilled my duties admirably even though I have never met him. He transferred money to my bank account for what he called 'Housekeeping for the Painter'. He transferred the house into my name. He paid the taxes for that to ensure that I would incur no financial burden from doing this work for him."

"Why would he want you to do that, to spy on me and to report back to him?"

She laughed again in what seemed to me to be in a rather insane way and I wondered if she needed another visit to the psychiatric hospital. She ignored my question. She was off on her own little monologue. I struggled to understand where it was going.

"You thought when I left your house that I drove to the Port of Soller where I lived. That shows how little you cared for me. You didn't even know where I lived. You never asked me where I lived. Every evening I drove towards the Port of Soller and, at the first roundabout, I turned around and headed towards the Barranc. In the time I have known you I have always lived here – in the house of Gregoriano. It was my secret." She repeated herself. "Gregoriano allowed me to stay here because he wanted me to tell him everything about you. I had to report to him weekly on what you were doing. The state of your mind. The state of your soul."

I looked around at the almond blossoms waving in the wind. I knew that they had been taken care of by Ishmael. They had the smell of Ishmael. My head was spinning with what she was telling me and with the questions I needed to ask.

"So you are telling me that Ishmael is living in this house with you?"

She curled her hair around her finger. "Yes. He has been a lodger here since the incident at the party. Before that he slept in the labyrinth. He didn't know what else to do. He should have told me what had happened to him the day I first saw him in the Plaza. He could have stayed here from the night you attempted to murder him. After all, we were both working for Gregoriano.

"You think that Ishmael was recommended to you by José del Pardo. It was never that way. Ishmael was sent to you as a gardener by Gregoriano. José del Pardo co-operated with Gregoriano as he is also involved helping Gregoriano with Red Cross work in Syria."

I felt a deep sense of frustration with the way Gabriela was handling this conversation. She was in control, talking about my life. I felt a fool, as if I was wandering around a labyrinth that Ishmael, Gabriela and Gregoriano had created in my head. I didn't know what to say next.

Without thinking, I spluttered out, "Well, can I meet Ishmael?"

Gabriela shook her head. "No. He's not here. He regularly sees Oñé in the labyrinth. He goes either early morning or late evening. Sometimes he sleeps there. He was in the labyrinth early this morning.

"However, if you are ready to meet with him, I know that he is willing to come to Can Animes. He would like Sophia and Oñé to be there. I was meant to go to see you today and ask you if you will see him with Sophia and Oñé next Thursday."

I nodded. "Of course I can do that but can you tell me why Gregoriano has been involved in my life since the age of ten? I don't understand it."

Gabriela got to her feet and brushed a few leaves from her dress.

"I do not believe that I am the right person to tell you. You need to speak with your mother Monica. She will tell you. Do you remember what Gregoriano wrote for you on that paper which he then burnt in the fire?"

I stood up and walked with her back to the house.

"Yes. I remember. Ishmael asked me to tell him. I pretended that I didn't remember but I never have forgotten those three statements. 'Know yourself. Love someone more deeply than yourself. Be prepared to give your life for another'."

She nodded. "Yes. They are statements which he has given to Ishmael and to me. Perhaps he gives them to everyone. That is why I was so shocked that I was not prepared to save Ishmael's life. I failed to live up to what I knew to be true." Before we entered the house, she stopped. "Well, you are close to solving the mystery of Gregoriano. Speak to your mother and find out what is missing. You will understand why he cared so much about you that he was prepared to go to enormous personal cost to fulfil a promise."

26

PABLO PICASSO

*"It took me four years to paint like Raphael, but a
lifetime to paint like a child."*

Friday 9th February 2018

I brought Oñé back to Can Animes. He was in exuberant
form. He held my hand as we walked around the olive
grove.

He asked, "Do you think we are getting closer to
finding him?"

I didn't want to answer him with a lie. I bought time
with a nonsense question. "Finding who?"

He dropped my hand. "You know who I am talking
about – my father. Are we closer to finding him? He is
a hero. I want to learn to be like him. I no longer care
about being a painter. I want to be like my father, to
care for people, to put my life at risk for others and to
keep my work hidden from the world. I don't want to be
famous. Who knows my father? I do not understand why
my mother did not stay with him. What is the point in me
living in a safe place, when my father's life is constantly
at risk? I want to be with him."

"Of course we will find your father. Yes, we have to be getting closer to know where he is."

We walked towards the English country garden which Ishmael had created on the boundary of the finca. Oñé pointed at Boulder Hill.

"Look! More rocks are falling."

He was right. As we watched, a rock perched on a cliff edge tumbled down the mountain towards the house. It stopped more than fifty metres short of hitting the reinforced fence which I had installed to protect the house. As the dust settled, I remembered that when I bought the house twenty years earlier, the surveyors had warned that the risk of danger from rock falls was high.

I ignored them. I enjoyed the seclusion of this place so close to the town of Soller. I was alone here and safe. There were no paparazzi. No-one cared that I lived here. I thought from time to time that no one cared that I lived, but that didn't matter. There was one person who I could depend upon to love me – my mother.

Even before the arrival of Ishmael, I learned to love plants, olive trees in the shape of human sculptures, fig trees bursting in the late August rains, spilling seeds onto the ground, a feast for birds to eat, orange trees with oranges plopping and tumbling like Christmas presents under a tree. I loved Boulder Hill. I was inspired by its instability and solidity. Its threatening nature kept me alert, made me feel alive, like a bird scanning its environment as it pecks at a worm digging into the earth.

Oñé continued to play with his drone, searching, so he said, for Christian. I had my suspicions that he was also searching for Gregoriano but how would he recognise his father? He only had one photograph of him taken eleven years earlier.

As he played and flew the drone, I sat on the bench around the sculpture. Since the talk with Gabriela, a dreadful thought had entered my head. Gabriela was unsure if there were two men in the garden that night. If Ishmael was alive, could it be possible that the second man – if he existed – was Gregoriano? I had seen him before near the house in the olive grove, the fig tree garden, the Orangery and the patio. I know that he talked to Ishmael the day before the fight. Could it be that Ishmael had escaped and that I had murdered Gregoriano? Was it Gregoriano's body hidden in the sculpture? I decided that I would smash the sculpture to see who, if anyone, was inside, but I didn't want to do it with Oñé around.

To save what little was left of my sanity, I had to find out from my mother the missing piece of the jigsaw about Gregoriano. She will be able to tell me why he is obsessed by me. I had arranged to visit her today for lunch, leaving Gabriela to take Oñé to the Japanese restaurant in Soller.

I haven't mentioned my mother much in this Journal. It might make it sound as if I never see her, but that isn't the case. Even when Ishmael stayed with me, I met with mother every week. We have one of those relationships where we didn't need to say much to one another. She lives in a house in La Huerta in Soller, only a five-minute walk from the Church.

She has lived a simple life, rarely leaving a five-kilometre diameter around the Church. She occasionally catches the tram to Soller or in the other direction to the Port of Soller.

When I visit her, we typically sit in the garden where she takes care of lemon, orange, pomegranate and walnut trees. She had an apricot tree but it died a year ago. That surprised me. I thought somehow that trees lived forever, but they don't. They are like humans, they die when their time comes. The apricot tree died quickly. Within a week it shed its leaves and dropped the remaining fruit onto the tilled land. She never replaced it, saying, "Know when the time has come and accept death – the death of anyone or anything."

In the winter months, we sat inside around a wood burning stove, as she baked bread and made paella with prawns and cod.

That Friday we talked. But mostly I understood her in our silences together. I knew what she thought of who I had become. I also knew that she loved me in spite of this.

She made paella. We sat together at the table. Since my father 'died', she didn't invite people to the house. It was as if she was afraid that the truth about the way he died – or how I had murdered him – would be revealed by the presence of others. She went to Mass at a different church each day of the week because there weren't enough priests to have daily Mass in the Church of La Huerta. I know she sought advice from Father as to what she could do to save my soul. I think that she gave up on that as a possibility as she seemed to let me do whatever I wanted to do without any judgement.

We scooped comforting warm mouthfuls of paella from the same dish. Imagining Gregoriano's body possibly disintegrating within the sculpture, I writhed uncomfortably as I asked, "I saw you talk with a man who I know as Gregoriano a while ago in the small chapel. How do you know him? What were you talking about?"

She looked at me directly. I realised that I didn't normally look at her eyes. I must have unconsciously kept my eyes on the ground during previous visits. I enjoyed this meeting of her eyes with mine. They were brown. I had never noticed that they were not chestnut coloured as a superficial glance revealed, but instead amber, fossilised from evergreen trees. In spite of her age, her hair was glossy black. It wasn't dyed. Rather a remarkably natural black without even a hint of grey at the temples. She twisted it into a plait which rested onto the shoulder of a long woollen green dress with a corded belt. The bottom of the dress was embroidered with cream daisies. She held onto the cream shawl thrown over her shoulders as she smiled at me.

"I wondered when I would hear about him from you."

I scraped my favourite part of the paella, the rice

caramelised and stuck to the bottom of the dish. I averted my gaze as I commented. "I know that he is a good man – a doctor – who works in dangerous war zones. What I want to know is how do you know him and what his interest in me is?"

Mother helped herself to a small spoonful of paella. "It is a bit of a long story."

I squeezed half a lemon over the paella and bit on a piece of crunchy green pepper.

"I should have asked you earlier about him. I know that I have caused you incredible suffering but even in my worst moments of selfishness, I have never wanted to hurt you. I didn't see the point in giving you something else to worry about – a man I thought may have been stalking me, who perhaps wished me ill, although there was no evidence of that.

"I admit that I have been a secretive person. I had to be to disguise my lies in my pursuit of pleasure. I learned not to tell anyone what happened in my life. Not that there was something bad to be hidden about Gregoriano. Quite to the contrary. He was a good man."

I stopped. Why had I said that 'he was a good man'? He was still alive wasn't he? Mother looked at me as if reading my mind. She said nothing. I continued. I found that the easiest way to dispel unpleasant thoughts was to continue talking, thinking or doing anything – even eating this paella. I struggled to be as honest as I could be. I knew that Mother would see through my familiar deceptions.

"What I mean is that he didn't need to say anything to me – only by being with him, I felt guilty. I didn't know what about. It was as if his eyes gnawed at my soul. Tell me more."

"I said that it is a bit of a long story. It is also a beautiful story. You have heard me talk about your great grandfather Josep who served in the First World War?"

I nodded. "Yes, he died as a member of the French Foreign Legion, in a battle in Turkey in 1915."

"That's right. What you don't know is that he gave his life to save Gregoriano's grandfather Pablo. It was an act of total self-sacrifice. Your great grandfather Josep, threw himself on top of Pablo and took the full impact of gunfire directed at the 3rd Battalion of the 1st Marching Regiment of Africa. Pablo survived. When he returned home, he wrote a letter to his family asking that forever the family of Josep would be watched over and taken care of. They would be guided in whatever way was needed. Gregoriano accepted that request from his grandfather, passed down to him from his father.

"As I only had one child – you, my dear Augustin – Gregoriano accepted responsibility to take care of what he would call your 'evolution' and your 'protection'."

I did not feel upset by my mother not telling me this earlier. Perhaps because I knew viscerally what she had suffered at my hands. I did feel angry that Gregoriano had not told me about this. Did he deliberately want to confuse me or was he playing some game with me?

"Why could he not have told me that? I would have understood. I would have been grateful to him."

"Pablo insisted in his letter to the family that the support and watchfulness of Josep's family must be discreet. Advice could be provided, but it had always to be minimal. There had to be what Pablo called a 'kenosis' – an emptying of self, a letting go in the helper. There had to be no attempt to control the other person. It was his wish that the helper would only ever guide and support. Pablo thought that this was how true love worked – to let the other be the other and to hold the intention of loving them whatever they chose to do.

"Gregoriano felt that if he told you what I am now telling you that you, you might feel that he was behaving like a controlling parent. He didn't want to be that. He wanted you to be free to live your life as you chose to live it but with a nudge from time to time to steer you in the direction he thought would bring out the best in you.

"I agreed that he could take you to the castle when you were ten. Do you think for a moment, that I did not approve of the guidance he wanted to give you? Of course I did. I thought that you might be more influenced by someone I thought you would see as 'a magical man'. I knew that you did not respect your father. I felt weak in my inability to respond to you in a way that was capable of helping you to waken up to reality. I decided that the appropriate response from me was to do nothing other than to accept you for who you were ..." She hesitated. "... and are."

She poured me a glass of red wine from the Macia Batle vineyard.

I took a large sip, before asking, "Do you have Gregoriano's contact details? I would like to invite him to a party at my home next week. I want to thank him for his presence in my life. He has introduced me to Ishmael, Oñé and Sophia, all of whom have enriched my life."

Mother shook her head. "No. I am sorry. He is not responding to my calls. I have not heard from him since early October of last year. That is not like him. He rang me every week on a Sunday at six o'clock in the evening. No matter what assignment he had chosen to work on, he never failed to ring me. I am worried that he has returned to Syria and perhaps something has happened to him." She sighed. "Perhaps he is dead. I feel that he is no longer with us." She wiped a tear away from her eye. "I mean in the same way. He's not with us in the same way. Whatever the spirit of Gregoriano was, I know for sure that it will never die."

I leaned forward and placed my hand on top of my mother's. I was aware how temporal that experience was – of touching her. One day, she would not be there for me, for others, with her wisdom and love. I felt a pressing knowledge in this moment of the uniqueness of her being, the specialness of the moment, its impermanence and the beauty of its passing. For a fleeting moment, even death was a part of everything. I did not mean that I could be spared from the consequences of killing another being – maybe Gregoriano. No, it wasn't that I was blasé about killing or about death, but rather I understood the preciousness of death being intimately linked with life.

The horror of deliberately and intentionally killing another human being, I now saw as an extension of what I did with harsh words, with deceit and lies when I killed the truth I killed the life that could have followed. I blew my nose into the paper napkin to disguise my tears.

I asked, "Would you like to go into the garden?"

"Yes. Thank you."

I held her by the hand in a way I had not done since the age of ten. We looked at the mountains where clouds of green swept into the valley as fine pollen dust flowed from male cones in search of the female cones. I turned to Mother.

"Ishmael told me that pine pollen is the most potent plant source of testosterone known."

She laughed. "So I will have a beard by tomorrow then?"

I gripped her hand firmly in a way I had never done before in my life. I felt a warmth flow through me which I did not recognise. Perhaps it was love.

"Not at all, breathe it in. Ishmael tells me that it boosts the immune system and is a tonic for the kidney, liver, heart and spleen. Take a deep, deep breath."

I pointed to the grass which bathed in sunshine and was covered with a creeping white flower and then to the purple and white daises bursting out of pots placed along the pathway.

"You have taken great care of the garden."

I returned to the theme of the mythical qualities of the pine tree.

"Did you know that along the Mediterranean Coast and in North Africa where they cut the pine trees in factories and throw the unused wood into the water, that female fish turn into male fish?"

"Why are you telling me to take a deep breath then? I will become a man with strong a heart, liver, kidney and spleen."

She bent over laughing dropping my hand. I knew the beauty which I had never known before in my life about how it is possible to turn a tear into a smile and then a laugh.

"Let's go back. There is wine to finish." Inside, she topped up my glass. "Gregoriano. Dear God, of course we cannot judge for good or bad, the soul of another human being." She laughed as she sipped on her wine. "But then again why not? The Church has been doing it for centuries – creating Saints. Do you know the Church has never said that a single person has gone to Hell? Do you not see what that means?"

She looked at me with a penetrating stare. I asked, "No, you tell me."

She wiped tears away from her eyes, but they were not tears of sorrow as earlier but tears of joy. "You're not going to Hell, Augustin when you die. Nobody goes there. You're in Hell now. You've created it and you can get out of it, if you want to. You can do it right now. It's only now. It's now that everything exists. There is nothing else. Do you see it?"

I pulled a piece of bread apart. I asked, "So there is no Heaven … No Hell. Only this? Is that not depressing? A piece of bread, an olive, a spoonful of paella, a glass of wine, the table, you and me and nothing else?"

She shook her head. "You don't see it. This … this … this if you allow yourself to truly experience it is everything beyond Heaven and Hell. It's magical. Gregoriano knew what that meant. That was why he was prepared to die in Iraq, Syria and Yemen. He saw it. I can't do any more for you than he did. You have to see it for yourself."

I searched in my rucksack for my notebook and a pen.

"Well, let's start with finding Gregoriano, someone must know where he is. He works for the Red Cross. They will know if he left the island to work for them somewhere in the world."

As Mother rummaged in a small notebook to give me two telephone numbers – one for Gregoriano's mobile and the other for the number which Gregoriano had given her for his work in Syria and Yemen. As I wrote the numbers down, I could only think of his body being in that sculpture. What would mother think of me then if that was a reality? Would I ever be able to hold her hand again and for us to laugh at the angst and beauty of life? That would be for me a living death. I had to find Gregoriano alive. My mind was over imagining things. Gabriela was not sure that there were two men involved in the fight that evening. Even if there were two men and Ishmael had escaped, there was no evidence that the second man was Gregoriano or that I had killed him.

Mother made me an espresso. "I have tried ringing both those numbers. The Red Cross told me that he is not in Syria but said that they were having problems in tracking if he had entered Yemen. They said that they would get back to me as soon as possible."

She served me with the coffee, and a slice of apricot tart, made from the last apricots which had fallen from her tree. She parcelled up portions for Gabriela and Oñé.

As we said goodbye, I asked, "Will you come to lunch Thursday of next week? You will meet Sophia, Oñé, Pep Conejo. I have been told that Ishmael will be there."

Mother cut three more portions of the tart. "This is for Ishmael then, Pep Conejo and his wife. I have heard great things about Ishmael from Gregoriano. Yes, of course I will be there."

Wednesday 14th February 2018

At mid-day Gabriela rang in a state of panic. She said that the local police Pep Serrano and José Miguel had called at the house that morning to see if someone by the name of Gregoriano Balsano lived there.

Oñé was at school. I was making plans for the arrival of Sophia later that day and for the party the next day. I flipped into a meltdown. "What are you saying? The police know about Gregoriano owning the house?"

She shouted at me. "He doesn't own the house. I told you that it is transferred to me. They want to know where he is living. His identity details show that although he legally transferred the house to me, he continued to be registered as living here. He never changed his place of residence in the Town Hall in Soller.

"Where is he living?"

She snorted in despair. "You are not listening. I have never met him. How do I know where he is living? We communicate by phone or email."

I steadied my voice. "Why are the police looking for him? What has he done?"

"Are you insane? He has done nothing. He has been lying in a coma in a hospital in Palma for four months. Apparently, he was found lying on the road to Soller in October of last year with a serious head injury. He wasn't even on the pavement. He was lying in the road. Do you hear me? The police think that maybe he was placed there so that a car would run over him and make his death look like an accident or that maybe he took a stroke and fell trying to cross the road. They were suspicious and began to investigate the possibility that someone had tried to murder him. He appeared to have been attacked and had a puncture wound in his back. They said that indicated that someone may have stabbed him. They ran a DNA test on him and there was a match with the Cupid arrow which they had taken for forensic tests."

My brain was spinning. In my confusion, I felt an incredible sense of relief.

"If they are looking for where he lives, then he is alive?"

I could almost hear Gabriela stamping her foot on the ground. "Yes – as far as I know – unless he has died since discharging himself from the hospital."

I asked, "Why did it take them so long to match the DNA? You know that they tested you, Oñé and I and we had the results back quickly. I would have thought that they would have turned up at your door months ago."

"It seems to be a case of human error. The hospital staff in Palma called the police when he was admitted in a coma state in October. They expressed concerns that there was foul play at work and showed evidence of the stabbing wound to his back. DNA samples were taken. Gregoriano remained in a coma state until yesterday. The DNA samples were misplaced before being recorded digitally and were only found this morning.

"The police interviewed him before he discharged himself and he denied that he had been attacked. He said that he didn't remember exactly what happened that evening but he had not felt very well – he had felt dizzy,

I think he told them. After the police left, Gregoriano discharged himself from the hospital against the Doctor's advice."

"The police would have taken a full report and asked him for his address. Did he not tell them where he was living?"

Gabriela sighed. "He gave this address."

My mind raced. I had no time for Gabriela's tears. "Why did the police not come here if there is the DNA link to the arrow?"

"I think they wanted to question Gregoriano further before approaching you. I don't know. If I were you, I would expect to see the police at any minute."

I couldn't believe what I said next. "What does Ishmael think?"

There was a pause. It seemed a long pause before she replied. "He's glad that Gregoriano is alive. He says that he will be in touch. He reminded me that you don't get shot in Iraq, tortured in Syria and Yemen and not manage to survive coming out of a coma in Mallorca. He asked me to check if you are still going ahead with the party tomorrow."

I knew that I had to continue with the party. What else could I do? Why would I cancel it? Sophia was arriving at six o'clock this afternoon. Oñé, for the first time seemed to be excited about seeing her. Mother would be there. Gabriela and Ishmael would be there. Pep Conejo and his wife, Francisca, would also be there. I began to feel as if I really had a family – real people – not people who wanted to hang out with me because of my fame and money.

I was so looking forward to seeing Ishmael. That was an understatement. I hadn't words to say how intensely happy I was to know that he was still alive. It's hard to describe how I felt. Maybe the best way to say it is to imagine the reaction of the parents of Lazarus in the Bible story when he came back from the dead – imagine how they felt. I felt even better. It was also excellent news that Gregoriano was alive. The world was falling into a place of beauty that I had not known for a long time. Of course I would party. I hadn't had a better excuse to do that in a long time.

I said to Gabriela, "Yes, the party is organised. We will go ahead with it. Tell Ishmael it will be great to see him – to see you both."

I had decided that we would pull the sculpture apart at the party. I wasn't sure if I could tell people why I wanted to do that. I would leave that until the moment but I wanted every new moment to be a moment of honesty and truth. That would be good enough for me for the rest of my life.

I had also decided that before we destroyed the sculpture, I would take a photo so that Ishmael and I could recreate it together for the King and Queen of Spain. I was convinced now that Ishmael was alive. I had to have been dreaming that night, having a nightmare.

Thinking of Felipe and Letizia, neither would know

that it was not the one which they had seen. It was still an original. To give the sculpture a final farewell, we would make a party game out of it – a piñata – where a Mexican paper donkey filled with sweets is hit with a stick by children to release its treasure. That would be a fitting end to the sculpture which symbolised and would always remind me even if in the palace gardens of Marivent, of my descent into Hell.

After breaking the sculpture into small pieces, we would together burn it in a fire pit which I will ask the caterers to create. The symbolic burning of the art of my insanity will draw a line under the last six months and my whole life until today – St Valentine's Day, the 14th February 2018.

My life was only just beginning.

27

PABLO PICASSO

"Who sees the human face correctly: the photographer, the mirror, or The Painter?"

Thursday 15th February 2018

Yesterday Sophia's flight arrived on time. Oñé had painted a small icon for her in which a woman held a bouquet of roses, her lips sparkled with diamonds and her eyes were two fishbowls with goldfish swimming in them. The fish reminded me of Mother's eyes which transformed from amber to something within this icon, once again fluid, moving within a liquid, no longer the resin of amber but seeing from a liquid holding moving life.

Sophia looked intently at it for quite a few minutes before she commented. "I love the mystery of it. You don't look at an icon. You enter it. It sees you. I see myself swimming within your eyes." Oñé smiled at her. An adult smile – one of knowing something which maybe I had to learn. They embraced and kissed one another. She turned to me. "What a difference."

I blushed. "What do you mean?"

"You both look different."

"Is that a good different or a bad different?"

"It's definitely a good different. Has something happened I should know about? Is there something that you haven't told me?"

"There's a lot to tell you. But first of all – would you do me the honour?"

I handed her a small box. I hadn't wrapped it in paper. She looked at me. "You didn't need to do this."

"I know but I wanted to."

She opened it. There was a ring inside. I had it especially made by Carlos, the jeweller, in la Calle de la Luna. He created an amber heart surrounded by twelve small diamonds. I wanted Sophia's engagement ring to hold the love of my mother's eyes always within the touch of Sophia's hand.

Oñé and I watched in silence as she placed it on her engagement ring finger. It fitted perfectly. I knew that it would. I had tied a string around her finger on New Year's Eve. I handed it to Carlos who I knew would not make exactly what I envisaged but make something even better.

I took Oñé's hand and that of Sophia and instead of kissing Sophia, we looked at one another within a small circle of life.

Oñé started to jump up and down in excitement. He dropped my hand. I embraced Sophia, kissing her deeply on the lips. With my eyes closed, my lips softly exploring hers. I disappeared into a flow of love between us. I scarcely knew her and yet I deeply knew her. It was right. What was happening was right. She was sounding herself through me with her lips. I would never again be alone. I would always be able to give to her and Oñé the immensity of which I now knew that existed between us as love.

Love. What an overused and misunderstood word. What it meant for me now was a peace, an acceptance of everything and everyone. I felt as if I should invite the whole Soller community to the party. Everyone. I loved them all, including the 'lepers' of Soller. After all, I was one of them. I can show you the stumps of my arms which cannot embrace Sophia in the way I would like to and the ulcerated wounds on my soul which I know are healing.

Lunch was to be ready at two o'clock. Chris and Doris had prepared a banquet. There was once again suckling pig roasting on a spit. The buffet table creaked with food and buckets of ice to chill champagne and white wine.

Pep Conejo and his wife Francisca were first to arrive.

Michael Lucarelli a classical Spanish guitarist played 'Malaquera' with a fast-paced bubbliness as I guided Pep Conejo and Francisca to their seats.

"Francisca – welcome. What can I offer you to drink?"

She looked at Pep and then at me. "Should I not wait for others to arrive?"

"Of course not. Please let me help you to …"

I looked around at the buffet table and tried to spot the most expensive drink which I knew Francisca would never buy or have tried for herself.

"What about a glass of bubbly?"

"What?" Francisca wiped sweat from her upper lip.

I explained. "Krug ... champagne?"

"Can you put a bit of brandy in it?"

"Of course. A champagne cocktail – what could be better. Pep, what about you?"

"A small beer." He opened his shirt and pointed at the scar from his heart operation. "You can't overdo it." He shot Francisca a reprimanding glance.

Mother arrived next. She moved quickly towards Sophia and Oñé. She tripped on the edge of a rug which had been scattered on the ground to give a Moroccan feel to the décor, landing face down with her arms outstretched. I ran to help her. She laughed at me as she struggled to her knees.

"It's only a sign of respect you know."

Sophia and Oñé laughed and they sat at the table beside Pep Conejo and Francisca.

I heard the sound of a motorbike on the driveway. It had to be Ishmael and Gabriela.

It was. I ran towards them as they dismounted from the bike. Ishmael stood unmoving for a few moments as Gabriela placed their helmets on the seat of the bike. He looked at me. I breathed in deeply. He was really alive. I had not murdered him. His lips moved into a smile. He raised his hands into the air as if to say, 'So here we are' – and then he took three long steps towards me, threw his arms around me and squashed me into his chest.

He whispered into my ear, "I am so glad to see you. It couldn't be better could it?"

He waved at Sophia and Oñé without letting go of me with his left arm.

I held him even tighter to my chest. I didn't want him to move. I felt him to be a pulsating stone in my arms. He was the Earth and Heaven combined in one body.

I brought my lips to his ear. "I'm sorry."

He rubbed my hair in the way that he used to do when we sat by the fire.

"There is nothing to be sorry about. What happened was only a tussle of love – nothing else."

He took Gabriela by the hand. She blew a kiss at me as they sat facing Sophia and Oñé. Michael Lucareli, the guitarist, played a fast-paced tune called *Tears of the Sun* which sounded to me as if Ulysses the cat was playfully running across a set of guitar strings.

I moved to the table to take my seat beside Sophia. The waitresses, in their pink lacy dresses which they wore at the inauguration of Ishmael's garden, poured everyone a glass of Krug. Gabriela held Ishmael's hand. She was wearing a shimmering blue dress with white silk embroidered stars and a blue silk belt. Her hair again curled and rolled onto her shoulders. Her lips were glossy red. She had sparkling dust, glittering on her cheeks. She looked like a Goddess at the table.

During the first course I talked with Ishmael. I didn't

need to say much. I explained that I thought that I had murdered him and placed his body in the sculpture.

He laughed. "Only you could think like that. I survived Syria. Do you not think I would have stopped you from killing me? It wasn't necessary. You were drunk and confused. That made it easy to escape from you. My biggest concern was that I would not see you again. I am grateful for this invitation."

It felt appropriate to be able to ask him a few unanswered questions. I looked to make sure that Oñé was not listening and saw that he was rather engrossed in a conversation with Sophia.

"Did you paint the triptych? The one in the studio which Oñé said he had painted?"

He looked puzzled. He shook his head. "No. I haven't touched a painting since I ran away from here in October. I can learn you know from my mistakes." He laughed. "Don't tell me that Oñé has a magical touch too."

I took his hand. "What about the box with the installations? Did you burn one of them?"

He placed a hand over his mouth in shock, removed it and laughed again. "Of course not. I would never do that to your work. I don't think Oñé would do that either – would he?"

I raised my shoulders. "I don't know. Maybe not. It must have really been a fireball from the storm. It doesn't matter."

Before the main course was served, I gave everyone,

including Chris and Doris, and waitressing staff, a hammer. We moved from the patio to the sculpture outside the front door.

For a brief moment, I hesitated as I thought perhaps that perhaps there could be the body of someone unknown hidden inside the sculpture. I dropped that thought. It had to be insane to think it.

I tapped a glass and said in a loud voice to the guests , "It's time for the piñata. Open it up. Let's see what is inside."

Everyone, including Pep Conejo and Francisca, laughed as they attacked the sculpture. It fell surprisingly quickly to the ground. Oñé jumped on it. I thought that perhaps it was getting a little too frenzied. I raised a hand.

"The deed is done. Stop. Let's see what is inside."

I peeled back the damaged ceramic skin from the sculpture. It revealed inside the twisted body of branches from an olive tree. I pulled them free and laid them on the ground beside the fire pit which glowed red. I felt a reverence for that ancient olive wood which had twisted itself into a human shape over centuries. I wanted to cover it in a shroud to give it dignity.

Oñé seemed to know what I was thinking and ran to the Studio to bring me his folded painting gown. I dressed the olive tree in his gown of cotton. Oñé helped me place the enclosed olive wood with the sculpture casing on the fire. There was a cheer from the guests. As the cheer expanded throughout the garden, everyone turned to see the figure of Gregoriano walk up the driveway. Oñé left the fire pit and ran to Sophia.

"Is it him?"

She nodded.

Oñé ran to his father, who scooped him into his arms. They stood motionless. Oñé's blonde hair falling over Gregoriano's shoulders. Everyone remained silent watching Gregoriano's eyes close. His lips moved as if saying a prayer but no words were heard. Then he and Oñé, talked to one another for a few minutes in low voices. No-one could hear what they were saying to one another. There was another embrace before they approached the table where the guests were seated in silence. There was a round of applause as Gregoriano asked, "Would there be space for one more?"

The catering staff busied themselves creating a place for Gregoriano beside Monica. Michael the guitarist played a gentle song as everyone looked at one another – no-one really knew what to say as the silence was broken with laughter and then friendly chatter.

I slowly stood up and raised a glass of champagne. "Thank you all for being here. I will say little … "

There was a whistle from Oñé who jumped to his feet. "It's Christian. Look Augustin – Christian has returned. He knew that I wanted him to be here."

He raced from the patio towards Boulder Hill.

Christian easily cleared the fence and bounded towards Oñé.

Francisca cried out in terror: "He will kill him. Someone save the boy."

She ran inside the house. The other guests walked towards Oñé and Christian and we stood in a circle. Oñé knelt on the ground. Christian licked his face and rolled his head against Oñé's chest. Although at first startled, the guitarist continued playing.

Suddenly there was a distant rumble. It was hidden at first by the sound of the guitar, until it became a steady roar, growing in volume. I looked to my right where an avalanche of rocks, rolled down Boulder Hill, accelerated towards the house. The guests returning to their seats for the first course were oblivious at first to the danger. I sat on the ground watching Oñé stroke Christian. I looked at the table. Sophia talked to mother and Gregoriano. I then recognised the sound of the roaring coming from Boulder Hill. As the rocks gained momentum, I could see that they were heading directly towards Oñé and Christian. There was no time to think.

As they smashed through the fence, I pushed Oñé with Christian to my right. The sound of the avalanche of rocks was now drowned by screams from the table. I felt a piercing pain in my lower legs. Oñé ran towards me and Christian bounded into the labyrinth. I could see blood oozing from my head on the ground. There was the sound of a police siren. Everything went black.

When I opened my eyes, Gregoriano was touching my legs. I heard something creak and move into place. He had already put a bandage around my head. My legs felt excruciatingly painful.

Pep Serrano and José Miguel stood to my left looking at me and then at one another. Pep Serrano started to talk, stopped and José Miguel continued, "I am sorry to say this under these conditions, but we have no option – we are here to arrest you for the attempted murder of Gregoriano Balsano on Wednesday 4th October 2017."

The silence was broken by Gregoriano. "There is no need. You may go home. I am Gregoriano Balsano. There was no attempted murder. This man is my friend. Why else do you think I received an invitation to this party? As you can see, we are a family of friends, we know how to party. It includes a few small scrapes and falls which happened as we celebrated together in October. I hadn't realised that I had fallen and was slightly concussed before walking home. I fell a second time on the road to Soller. The small injury on my back came from a silly game which Ishmael and I were playing with the two Cupid arrows. I staggered into Ishmael who was holding the lead arrow as we debated the differences between the meaning of the arrow tipped with gold and the arrow tipped with lead. It was a most unfortunate accident. I am sorry to have distressed so many people by being out of contact for a few months due to my hospital stay.

"We need to get Ishmael to hospital now as a priority

and perhaps someone can find Francisca in the house. She has a little bit of a 'nervous' disposition and the avalanche of rocks has more than likely induced in her a state of shock."

Sophia knelt beside me and wiped my forehead with her napkin. "Please, can someone call an ambulance?" She looked at the police. "Did you not see what he did? He was prepared to give his life to save Oñé. How could a man who is prepared to sacrifice his own life be capable of murdering another?"

There was a cheer from the table, for a few minutes the guitarist fell silent and Francisca emerged from the house holding a glass filled with brandy. Oñé grabbed a suckling pig from the table and rushed into the labyrinth as a cloud of apricot and almond flower petals swirled onto the ground.

Gregoriano took my hand as I heard the ambulance approach. "You did it. You were prepared to give your life for another. You have fulfilled the meaning of your life. Now you can live the rest of it and you will be surprised what magic it will hold for you. I can go now. I will continue my work."

I squeezed his hand. "Don't go. Think about Oñé. Stay."

He shook his head. "I will see Oñé often – but you are his father. A father is a person who acts like a father. Be a good father, a loving husband and a friend to the world – starting with everyone here."

Pep Serrano glanced at Boulder Hill. "Okay. It looks like we are done here."

"It was a surprise to have discovered Ishmael Domini living in the house of Augustin Silvero. Why did I not suspect that to be true? Ishmael's art reaches to the heart of every human being's soul. He paints our pain and captures our capacity to be free – not in a physical sense but free in the sense of a freedom of spirit.

The triptychs painted by Oñé, Augustin and Ishmael, hang side by side in the Reina Sofia museum in Madrid. As these three triptychs are exhibited, police continue their reopened investigation into the death of Augustin's father. We must not let this investigation taint the beauty of his art, which is unsurpassed.

I am an art critic and can only comment on the genius which I see in the works of Oñé, Ishmael and Augustin. I do not judge a person – only their art which for me is their being."

(Art Critic, Collector and Philosopher – Miguel del Salmorejo – Palma de Mallorca – 2018)

ACKNOWLEDGEMENTS

Thanks to Rachel Connor for her support, coaching and guidance.

Matthew Smith, a dream maker from Urbane Publications who gives life to a writer, and Kieran McNicholl, a generous friend.

I was the first person in the UK to survive a heart operation during which the surgeon never touched my heart. It was in Belfast in 1957. My mother was seven months pregnant when she became the second person in the UK to be operated on to repair a faulty mitral valve. Two months later I shot unaided into the world. On reflection I have always had a sense of being born alone, giving me insight into the ultimate aloneness of all human beings. We are mysteriously alone with others.

Living through the war in Northern Ireland gave me an interest in how human beings evolve, driven by the world of emotions. I began to see how we are all pushed and pulled within an emotional world of like or dislike, love or hate.

My writer's mind was from a mix of being both a reflective introvert and an expressive extrovert. It was a perfect combination for writing. I have loved brushing up against new people I meet in my job as a Leadership Consultant

– working in over 35 countries in the world and with over 60 organisations. Meeting these people has deepened my fascination with human beings. I wonder about them all – what makes the people I see sitting around a table on a workshop.

I like pushing the boundaries of being alive to their extremes. I studied for a Masters in Consciousness Studies and Transpersonal Psychology. I have been on silent retreats in Arizona, California and Canada and I have "sweated" several times in 'sweat lodges' with Native Americans from the Sioux tradition.

I have always been a "seeker" of the meaning of life. 16 years ago, I persuaded my husband that we should give everything away – sell our house in Oxford, give away all our possessions and move to Mallorca with two suitcases and our cat Ziggy. There was no planned future. That was both exciting and mad at the same time. I knew that I was pushing life to its limits.

Shortly after arriving in Mallorca I began to paint, studying with Argentinian painter Carlos. I began to write. I started with **Eden Burning**, and then followed, **The Secret Wound**. Now I have written **The Painter**. I love the world of writing because it allows me to go to the edges of life – to my own edge in being alone with others.

DEIRDRE QUIERY

THE

SECRET

W♥UND

'She carries a dark and deadly secret...'

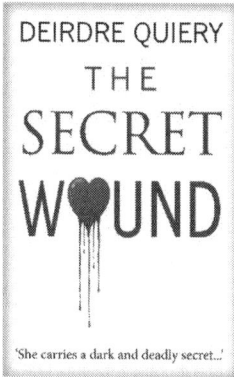

'This is an atmospheric and beautifully charged story, which
moves between time frames and locations to ratchet up the
building tension. The author evokes the Mallorcan landscape
beautifully throughout. Digging deep into mysticism, *The
Secret Wound* explores notions of connections, intimacy and
power and asks questions about the nature of home. Highly
recommended. A great summer read!' Rachel O'Connor

Deirdre Quiery's follow up to the critical success of *Eden
Burning*, *The Secret Wound* draws the reader into a complex
web of relationships within the ex-pat community in Mallorca,
discovering their dangerous secrets...and a potential murderer
in their midst. One of their number carries a dark and deadly
secret from their past, and has murderous plans for a fellow
ex-pat. Can any of the close- knit community discover the
brutal plans before they are all put in mortal danger?

Deirdre Quiery's gripping thriller is not just an addictive
page-turner but provides a compelling exploration of human
emotion and desires, and the terrible costs of jealousy and
ambition. Perfect for fans of Jane Corry and Amanda Brooke.

Deirdre Quiery

'Catapulting us into 1970s Belfast in the heart of the Troubles, *Eden Burning* pulses with conflict and introduces us to a cast of characters we profoundly care about, even when they are warring with each other. Above all, though, it is a novel with a true spiritual and emotional heart.'
Rachel Connor, bestselling author of *Sisterwives*

Northern Ireland, 1972. On the Crumlin Road, Belfast, the violent sectarian Troubles have forced Tom Martin to take drastic measures to protect his family. Across the divide William McManus pursues his own particular bloody code, murdering for a cause. Yet both men have underestimated the power of love and an individual's belief in right and wrong, a belief that will shake the lives of both families with a greater impact than any bomb blast. This is a compelling, challenging story of conflict between and within families driven by religion, belief, loyalty and love. In a world deeply riven by division, a world of murders, bomb blasts and assassinations, how can any individual transcend the seemingly inevitable violence of their very existence?

Urbane
PUBLICATIONS

Urbane Publications is dedicated to
publishing books that challenge, thrill and fascinate.

From page-turning thrillers to literary debuts,
our goal is to publish what
YOU want to read.

Find out more at
urbanepublications.com